'Fabulous mystery; really enjoyable read; couldn't put it down. Be prepared for some late nights once you start!' Jenny Brown.

'I didn't expect to relate to the characters and settings as strongly as I did, after having other books from this era over-analysed at school. It was a delightful experience to meet Sarah and her family and friends and also to understand more about the social pressures of the time. Having an intriguing mystery to solve was a real bonus, especially as the resolution was unexpected and very satisfying! I hope I'll have an opportunity to follow more of Sarah's adventures.' Marg.

'I don't normally read regency literature, but I am now a convert! The writing style takes one right back to that era in a way that one can almost feel the ambience. I also now understand that era's class system and the constraints it put upon people. I highly recommend it.' Trish Griffin.

I enjoy a well-researched background to a story, and this fits the bill well. The story reflects the life in the Regency period in England. It is an interesting mystery with a twist at the end. Sarah is an independent woman before her time. I look forward to any sequels.' Gloria Jeffrey

Ken has been writing professionally since he left school, and full-time for the past forty-five years. Most of his more than one hundred published books have been educational texts for schools and colleges, especially in the field of English as a Second Language. However, he has also had six novels published by major commercial publishers, written extensively for radio and television, and contributed to many magazines and newspapers. He now concentrates on researching and writing about all aspects of life in Regency Britain, and reviews new books, both fiction and non-fiction, for *The Historical Fiction Review* and other specialist publications.

Ken was born and educated in the UK but lived in Asia for many years before migrating to Australia where he now lives with his ceramic-artist wife, Sheila.

The Missing Baronet

Ken Methold

AIA PUBLISHING

The Missing Baronet

AIA Publishing, Australia

ABN: 32736122056

www.aiapublishing.com

Second Edition 2018

© Copyright 2018 Ken Methold

www.regencymatters.com

Ebook ISBN: 978-0-9876272-7-8

Paperback: ISBN: 978-0-9876272-8-5

Cover design: Velvet Wings Media.

Please note: This book is edited to Australian conventions.

Note: Although it is acknowledged that the wife of baronet is formally addressed or referred to as Lady with her surname, to avoid confusion with different members of the Browning family, in this novel the Dowager Lady Browning is sometimes referred to as Lady Augusta.

One

When Matthew Kedron arrived at the Sans Pareil Theatre in Covent Garden, the stage doorman greeted him warmly.

'Good day, Mr Kedron. I trust you're well, sir. It is some time since you last visited us.'

'I try not to bother my daughter, Jack. But today I need to talk to her urgently.'

'Miss Sarah is rehearsing one of the scenes for this evening's performance, sir. It was not well-received last night. Indeed, we feared a riot. Mr Scott had to bring down the curtain and make a speech appealing to the audience to be forgiving.'

'What was the problem?' Matthew asked, although he had a good idea what it had been.

'The audience were expecting a fine performance, sir, but unfortunately, our supporting actor was ... well, sir, I'm sure I don't have to provide further details.'

'Will he be sober this evening?'

'Who can say? One thing's for sure. If he doesn't moderate his drinking, it'll kill him.'

Matthew nodded and walked into the darkness of the theatre. A few guttering candles half lit the stage. After his eyes adjusted to the dim light, he made out his daughter sitting in the third row of the stalls, her head-bowed over her notebook as she studied her notes. As usual her lustrous, thick black hair sat in an untidy pile on top of her head.

As Matthew stood watching her for a few moments, he felt, as he so often did, waves of pride in his only daughter, now in her late twenties. Every movement of her head, every gesture, reminded him of his wife, along with her tall, slender, athletic figure.

Miss Jane Scott, Sarah's friend and mentor, employed her as an assistant manager, actress and playwright. Jane, now in her middle age, jointly managed and owned the Sans Pareil Theatre with her father, John. Sarah's ambition was to emulate her friend's success as a prolific and successful playwright.

As a fine horsewoman, Sarah Kedron enjoyed nothing more than a hard ride across country. Her dark gypsy eyes, inherited from her long-dead mother, looked at the world with an almost intense curiosity. She knew that her soft voice made her unsuitable for any of the larger dramatic roles and that success as a playwright was a more achievable ambition in the theatre.

The cast of the current production of Jane Scott's *Camilla the Amazon* stood about on the stage, gossiping as actors will. The rehearsal had paused for Sarah to give them her notes on their performances in the most troublesome scene. After the previous night's disastrous performance, the supporting actor had stepped aside. Although the experienced and talented actor George Davidge willingly stepped into the role, he had had little time to learn his lines, so thoroughly confused the cast with his erratic moves and garbled speeches.

Matthew approached Sarah and sat down beside her. 'I need to talk to you, my dear,' he said. 'I've just come from the Home Office. There has been an interesting development.'

Sarah looked at her father, alarm showing on her face. 'You're not in trouble, Father! Not again.'

She spoke with anxiety in her voice, knowing that certain people regarded her father's publications, especially *The Weekly Informer*, as dangerous. On several occasions, he had been threatened with prosecution for criminal libel and once for sedition. So far, he had escaped arrest, but she feared that before long he would overstep the mark; his periodical would be shut down, and he'd be incarcerated in the Fleet.

He smiled broadly. 'No trouble, my dear. Far from it. Will you be free in an hour?'

'About. I can't talk now, Father. I must get on.'

'I understand. I'll wait for you at the Chapter Coffee House. I must talk to you before you leave for Bury St Edmunds this evening.'

At Jane's recommendation, Sarah had been offered a position with a touring company based in Bury St Edmunds. She had an appointment the next day to meet the owner and decide whether the position suited her.

'Very well, Father.' She stood and clapped her hands. 'Come everyone. Let's get on. From Fidesco's entrance.'

Matthew left the theatre, and the rehearsal continued.

Two

When Sarah arrived at the Chapter Coffee House, the boisterous conversations among the many journalists, publishers and booksellers who frequented the place provided the necessary privacy for what her father had to say.

As soon as the servant girl had brought Sarah her coffee and meat pie, he came straight to the point. 'The Home Secretary summoned me because he wants me to publish a new periodical,' he said. '*The Weekly Police News.*'

'For the Government!' Sarah could not believe that her father would even consider doing such a thing. She had no time for politicians, nearly all of whom had either bought or inherited their seats in Parliament. Whig or Tory, they were all the same, concerned mainly with feathering their own nests or those of their relatives and friends.

Matthew shook his head. 'No. As an independent publication. He wants to do something about the amount of crime in the city. He maintains that it's out of control and that many of the Bow Street Runners are either corrupt or useless. Now he has introduced the new police offices with constables supervised by magistrates, he hopes that a weekly publication with news about reported crimes and the investigations into them, would be politically useful.'

Under her long lashes, Sarah looked searchingly at her father. 'It sounds to me much like a piece of government propaganda. Where would you get the information from?'

'There will be a constable in each of the new police offices who will provide the news. I will have a reporter at the Old Bailey and be free to use information from my own correspondents.'

'Censorship?'

'None. No restrictions.'

'That's hard to believe, Father.' Sarah frowned with suspicion. 'Is he offering you money?'

Although still a young woman with little experience of life outside the theatre, Sarah knew that most people could not be trusted. They had their own, usually hidden, reasons for doing things. In this, she was very much her father's daughter. His knowledge of the underworld and the apparently respectable men who inhabited it, especially the wealthy and high born, had made him one of the most sceptical men in the country.

'It is to be a wholly commercial venture. Which is why I'll need a partner.'

'You seem to have made up your mind already, Father,' Sarah said, a little testily. She did not like being presented with a fait accompli.

'Not so, my dear,' Matthew objected. 'I want your help. Unless I can have it, I shall pass on the proposition.'

'Me? Help you run a crime magazine? Father, you are surely joking,' Sarah replied, appalled. She had no interest in being a journalist of any kind. She had her own plans, and they were more than enough to occupy her life.

'Many crimes involve women,' Matthew explained. 'I need an intelligent and sympathetic woman who can talk to women in trouble. Get them to confide in her.' He leaned forward. 'Sarah, my dear, you are a playwright, and you have an ambition to be a successful novelist. You understand human character and the passions and desires that can lead to crime or to becoming its tragic victim.'

'But, Father—'

He held up his hand. 'If it is to be successful *The Weekly Police News* will need more than facts. It will need emotions. A serial crime story to attract readers.'

'Fiction!' Sarah exclaimed. 'So much for the truth.'

'Truth is as much what people feel as it is what they do.'

Sarah could not deny this.

Matthew hurried on while he had her accepting the logic of his argument. 'I ask only for strong stories—in serial form—about a woman who is either a victim or an accused person on trial. Perhaps including a character who is some kind of detective. Not necessarily a Bow Street Runner. A story that explores not only the "what" and the "how" of it all but also the "why".'

Sarah sipped her coffee and took a small bite of her pie to give herself time to think. She realized that her father's contact with the magistrates and constables could be an endless source of fascinating stories—the kind of human interest content that made many of the periodicals so popular. She would also find ideas for plays.

'I'm not going to try to persuade you to make a decision, Sarah,' Matthew said. 'I'm not fool enough to try to persuade you to do or not do anything.' He smiled to take the sting out of the remark. 'I just want you to consider what I'm offering before you decide to take the job in Bury St Edmunds. Will you do that?'

Sarah felt he had presented her with a fork in the road, one that, depending on which way she went, could change her life. She reached forward and touched his hand. She loved him dearly and did not want to disappoint him. However, she could say only, 'I will think about it, Father. I cannot promise anything.'

'I know, my dear.' He smiled ruefully. 'It will be a pity if you say no, but not the end of the world.'

Three

The long-distance mail coaches all left the Lombard Street post office at eight in the evening. Sarah needed to take the Norwich coach, which stopped at Bury St Edmunds for an hour to change horses at the livery stable attached to The Angel Inn. The distance as the crow flies was almost eighty miles with at least ten more for diversions due to roads damaged by one cause or another. Assuming that wheels falling off the coach, axles breaking, or an unlikely hold-up by the notorious highwaymen of Chelmsford district did not interrupt the journey, the coach would probably arrive at The Angel in time for breakfast. Sarah expected to be in good time for her ten o'clock appointment.

Unfortunately, punctuality was not one of her virtues. She arrived at Lombard Street only a few minutes before the coach's scheduled departure time, just as the coachman handed the last piece of luggage up to the guard to stow on the roof. The coach seated only four passengers—any other passengers sat sideways outside. The four inside places were already taken. Sarah sighed, realizing that she faced a ten-hour journey of extreme discomfort—and that assumed the unsettled weather held. Should it rain heavily, the journey would be utterly miserable, and she would be exposed to the likelihood of catching a chill.

She stood outside the coach, deliberating whether to risk the weather or cancel the trip. The four passengers inside consisted of an elderly couple so covered up that she could not place them socially—though had they been wealthy they would almost certainly be making the journey in a faster post-chaise or more likely their own equipage—a young girl with a red, sniffing nose, clearly a servant on her way to a new position; and an elegant young man, neatly but simply dressed, clean-shaven, with short, fair, curly hair. Noticing Sarah deliberating, being sufficiently perceptive to guess why, and being aware of how attractive she was, he leaned out the window towards her.

'Forgive my impertinence, madam, but are you travelling with us?'

'I'm considering doing so, sir, as far as Bury St Edmunds.'

The young man opened the door and climbed out. 'In that case, will you do me the honour of occupying my seat? I shall be content to pass the journey in conversation with the guard.'

Sarah hesitated, for he had presented her with a quandary. Her principle of not wishing to depend on anyone for anything fought with her desire to travel in comfort. Her principle quickly lost the uneven battle.

'You are most kind, sir.'

It took but a few moments for the exchange to take place, and then the coachman cracked his whip, the horses strained, and the coach moved off.

Although tired and reasonably comfortable, Sarah found it impossible to sleep. She already felt far from sure that a move to Bury St Edmunds was the most sensible course of action. One did not usually move from London to the provinces. Ambitious actors usually took the reverse route, so there had to be a good reason for taking such a step.

Sarah weighed up the advantages and disadvantages, noting as she did so the worn silk shawl of the old lady across from her and the cheap, almost threadbare coat of the girl who by now had stopped sniffling, and, clutching her sodden and none-too-clean handkerchief, stared morosely through the window. Sarah noticed that her hands looked older than the rest of her, no doubt due to years of scrubbing floors. How fortunate Sarah was to have had an education and, unlike most women, be earning her living in a demanding but wholly fulfilling way.

With regard to her present situation, she would almost certainly be offered more leading roles with the travelling company than she got at the Sans Pareil, but she would be acting with an inferior supporting cast. Although the theatre would probably have a loyal following in Bury St Edmunds, the income from the provincial audiences would not permit the management to employ many actors who could command reasonable fees.

These thoughts led to another problem. She thought it likely that the management of a touring company would be more concerned with offering well-established and popular works than untried plays from young dramatists. And, of course, poor acting could, and often did, ruin a new play. Inexperienced actors often had little idea how to make the most of their lines; they stressed the wrong words and often omitted meaningful pauses in their haste to reach the end of a scene before they forgot their words and dried up on stage.

Living in Bury would be cheaper than in London, Sarah knew, and this meant she might be able to save enough within a couple of years to live in Paris or another European capital. She would benefit greatly from experiencing the different theatrical styles the European theatres had to offer.

But, of equal, if not greater, importance, was the wholly unexpected possibility of writing a completely new kind of play—a mystery drama—and having it produced at the Sans Pareil with a cast of experienced and highly regarded actors.

The problem circled round and round in her mind, and by the time she arrived at The Angel, she almost felt ready to return immediately to London. However, she decided to postpone a decision until after she had met the management of the touring company and formed an opinion of what the position really had to offer.

As she left the coach, the young man climbed down from the rear.

'I do hope, sir,' she said to him, 'that you have not been too uncomfortable. I'm most obliged to you.'

'I've had far worse journeys, madam. The guard is a man full of interesting anecdotes about his experiences.' He bowed and smiled, and Sarah found his smile, his general appearance, his manners, and even his voice, quite attractive.

A porter carried her small bag into the inn, and after a brief visit to the privy where she adjusted her bonnet, washed the road dust off her face in cold water and rinsed her hands, she went to the dining room where breakfast was being served. She had just ordered her meal when the young man from the coach walked up to her table and bowed.

'I trust,' he said, 'you have recovered from your journey.'

'Indeed, I have. Thanks to your kindness, it was quite bearable.'

At this point in their conversation, she could either invite him to join her or make some mildly dismissive remark such as, 'I hope you will be as comfortable during the rest of your journey,' and then smile and say, 'I wish you a very good day, sir.' And that would be the end of it. However, being an inquisitive kind of young woman, Sarah said, 'Would you care to join me?'

In one smooth movement, he seated himself before her. 'James Brewster at your service, ma'am.'

'Miss Sarah Kedron. Please order your meal.'

Like most actresses, Sarah's social confidence was such that people found her easy to talk to, and before long, James Brewster was telling her a shortened version of the story of his life. He spoke quickly as if he knew he had but a brief time— the duration of the meal—in which to ingratiate himself in her eyes.

He was a law student, he explained, eating his dinners at an Inn of Court, prior to becoming a barrister. He presently earned his way by working for an attorney as a general legal dogsbody and was currently on his way to Norwich in an attempt to discover the whereabouts of a beneficiary to a will. His ambition was to work for the reform of the penal and criminal justice systems. The writings of Patrick Colquhoun and Matthew Kedron had much influenced and inspired him.

As he said the name Kedron, he stopped talking, and his mouth remained open and his eyes wide.

Sarah laughed. 'Yes, sir. My father is Matthew Kedron.'

'Bless my soul.'

'If you would like to meet him, I can arrange it,' she said, almost before she realized what she was doing.

Four

Sarah met with Mr William Wilkins, the proprietor of the Norwich circuit, who quickly explained that the Bury St Edmunds Company toured most of the year.

'The company is small, Miss Kedron,' he explained. 'It has to be because we play to only small audiences in mostly ill-equipped small theatres. The company undertakes an annual tour of six theatres, one each in Yarmouth, Ipswich, Cambridge, Colchester, King's Lynn and here. In each city we open for just one or two short seasons. In 1814, the first year of our operation, the company performed here only during the Great Fair from early October to mid-November.'

'So the company is on tour most of the time,' Sarah said, unable to keep her dismay out of her voice.

'That is so.'

Sarah had heard the stories of the circuits from actor acquaintances in London. It meant living in dirty and uncomfortable lodgings for most of the year. Worse, many days were spent packing and unpacking costumes and properties and transporting them with the rest of the company, in slow-moving wagons on bad roads and in all weathers. The prospect did not appeal. Apart from the hardship involved, the standard of actors willing to work in such conditions would likely not be very high. Such a company would not do justice to performances of her own writing—assuming there would be some—and would not advance her reputation as a playwright. Exchanging her position at the Sans Pareil in London for a touring company clearly had few—if any—advantages.

She thanked Mr Wilkins for his time and courtesy and explained that she needed time to consider the offer and all it entailed. Then she promised to give him her decision without delay.

Within the hour she sent him a brief note declining the position. She then took the next coach with a vacant inside seat back to London.

During the journey she considered her situation and became convinced that she had made a sensible decision. She would be able to continue as an actress and playwright at the Sans Pareil and have time to write a serial for her father.

Matthew was delighted and much relieved by her decision.

'I'm sure, my dear,' he said, 'that you will not regret remaining in London. I have already had a most encouraging meeting with an investor who is prepared to advance money to help finance *The Weekly Police News*. And I have already placed advertisements in a number of papers for an editor. Such a person will also be expected to write most of the content.'

'That's excellent news, Father,' Sarah said. Then, a little hesitantly, not wanting to seem too interested in her new acquaintance, she said, 'By chance, I have met someone who may suit the situation. I know little about him except that he is a law student, hoping in due course to be called to the Bar. At present, he is working as a clerk for an attorney.'

'A law student and possibly a future barrister? Hmm. He could be a suitable candidate.'

'He is also a great admirer of your work, Father. When I gave him my name, he immediately asked if I was related to *the* Matthew Kedron. He is a student of the penal and criminal justice systems and believes reform is essential.'

'Indeed.' Matthew savoured the compliment of being referred to as *the* Matthew Kedron. Then he said, 'I shall be pleased to meet this person. Where did you meet him? What is his name?'

'His name is Mr James Brewster, and we shared the mail coach to Bury St Edmunds.'

'And you had an opportunity to talk.' Matthew smiled. 'I assume he is a good-looking fellow?'

'Oh,' Sarah replied offhandedly, 'he is personable, I suppose. But highly intelligent and well-mannered.'

Matthew consulted his journal. 'I shall be free at ten o'clock on Wednesday. Perhaps I should meet this young man before I interview any other applicants.' He stood up. 'But you must be hungry after your journey, my dear. Let us find a quiet chophouse and have something to eat.'

Five

Three days later, James Brewster entered the office of *The Informer* carrying a copy of Matthew Kedron's most recent book, *Corruption Discovered*. He had received no communication from Sarah but quietly hoped this was simply because he had been travelling and that her letter had not yet caught up with him. He had decided in the meantime to ask for an interview with her father, on the off chance that she had mentioned him.

'My name is James Brewster,' he said to the clerk. 'I'm acquainted with Miss Sarah Kedron. Perhaps you would inquire of Mr Kedron whether he would do me the honour of autographing my copy of his splendid work.'

The clerk sniffed as clerks tended to do in such situations. 'I'll see if he is free,' he said, and walked towards the door of a back room. He knocked, received the single word, 'Come' and entered. He returned after being inside only a few moments.

'Mr Kedron will see you, sir,' he said.

James thought that the 'sir' sounded promising. He followed the clerk into Matthew's office.

Matthew stood to welcome him and offered his hand. 'I have been expecting you, Mr Brewster. I assume my daughter has spoken to you?'

'Not since we met in Bury St Edmunds, sir.' James shook Matthew's hand firmly.

'Then I need to inform you of the situation. Do please be seated.'

Wondering what the situation was and suspecting that he was about to be discouraged from paying his attentions to Sarah, James sat in one of the armchairs.

Matthew sat in the other. 'I understand you are a law student.'

'That is correct, sir.'

'At present employed as an attorney's clerk of some kind.'

'More of a messenger boy, in truth, sir.'

Matthew laughed. He considered the young man's self-deprecating honesty an attractive trait. 'I'm shortly to launch a new publication, *The Weekly Police News* or some such title. I need an editor for it. Someone with a knowledge of and interest in the law would be valuable. Tell me about yourself.'

And thus, from James's point of view, began a completely unexpected interview. He explained that he was the younger son of a naval captain now on half pay, and that his university education had been interrupted due to his father's change in financial circumstances. He was single, in good health, enjoyed a game of cricket when he had the opportunity, and hoped to be called to the Bar within a couple of years.

When Matthew asked him if he thought he would make a good barrister, James replied, 'I like to win, sir, and that, I believe, is what being a barrister is all about.'

'And you will do what is necessary in order to win your cases?'

'My responsibility will be to my clients, sir.'

'Prosecution or defence?'

'I would prefer to prosecute in case I had difficulty defending adequately an accused whom I believed to be guilty.'

Matthew knew that an essential characteristic of a good journalist, whether reporter or editor, was to win in the pursuit of the story. James Brewster seemed to have the potential of the kind of man he was looking for. He had no journalistic experience, but that was of little importance. He clearly had other skills, the right attitude and an engaging personality and manner. He had also shown considerable initiative in getting an audience for himself.

Within the hour he offered James the position. James accepted it eagerly.

It later occurred to Matthew that by employing Mr Brewster he might be creating complications in his daughter's life. However, he quickly dismissed any concern, confident that she would deal appropriately with any situation that might arise.

Six

Three months later, as Sarah left the Sans Pareil Theatre to return home for a brief rest before her final performance in her latest melodrama, *Lady Ellesmere's Revenge*, a young woman approached.

She dropped a quick curtsey and cried, 'Please help me, Miss Kedron. I'm desperate.'

Assuming the young woman was begging for money, Sarah said, 'Don't curtsey to me. It's demeaning to you and unnecessary. Is it money you want?'

The young woman stood up, and Sarah realized she was little more than a girl. Her clothes showed quality and fashionable good taste, so clearly, she was no common creature begging for a few coins. Unfortunately, her pallor and the dark, almost-black shadows beneath her eyes despoiled her otherwise lovely features.

'My name is Celia Browning,' the girl said. 'I beseech you, Miss Kedron, to spare me a short time to tell you my story. When we were staying in London, my husband took me to see your wonderful play. Angelica was so sympathetic to the poor, deserted wife whose husband left her for that awful woman. I think you will understand my situation.'

Sarah was used to having her writing praised, and audiences often identified her with the main character in her play, a woman with great experience of the world who had suffered and showed compassion for women less fortunate than herself.

Something about the girl intrigued her, so she said, 'There's a quiet little tea shop around the corner. We can talk there.'

They settled in a nook in the tea shop and Sarah ordered refreshment. Then she sat back and invited the girl to tell her story.

'Begin at the beginning and tell me what this is all about.'

'My husband has disappeared. He is Sir Charles Browning, and we live at Browning Hall in Hertfordshire, not far from the village of Langley.'

'So you are Lady Celia Browning,' Sarah said, trying not to show surprise.

'Just Lady Browning, ma'am,' the girl said. 'Charlie is only a baronet, but I prefer to be called Celia.'

'I understand.' Sarah smiled, amused and pleased by the girl's lack of social ambition—a rare condition. 'When you say that he's disappeared,' she said, 'what do you mean exactly?'

'He left the house early one evening a month ago, and no one has seen him since. It's as though he has just vanished.'

Not wanting to hurt the girl's feelings, but knowing that the possibility had to be faced, Sarah said, 'He could have just left you for another woman. Men do such things, you know.'

'I … I suppose it's possible. I know only that he started returning home late. He smelled of drink and … and cheap scent.' She blushed with embarrassment and looked down. Then pulling herself together, she took a deep breath and blurted out, 'Miss Kedron, you must help me find him. I'm sure something bad has happened to him.'

'But what do you expect me to do, Celia? I'm not some kind of constable.'

'Charlie takes *The Weekly Informer*. He often praises your father for his opinions. And he's a famous man. He must know many people of all kinds.'

Sarah didn't think there would be anything her father could do that would help the girl whom, she realized, was wholly unsophisticated. She may have been Lady Browning, but she seemed to be a simple country girl who had married into the gentry.

'Have you asked the Watch, the Constables or the Bow Street Runners for help?' she asked.

'Yes, but none were interested. They told me it's not their responsibility to find missing persons. They said Charlie had probably disappeared because he wanted to for some reason.'

'And could he have a reason?'

Celia choked back her sobs and spluttered, 'It's all my fault. It was my idea. I didn't mean any harm.'

Sarah knew her chance to rest before her final performance had now passed. She might as well hear the girl's story. Patiently, knowing that Celia needed to confide in her own way and that to hurry her would achieve nothing, Sarah asked gently, 'In what way?'

'I suggested we should spend a few weeks in Bath. Rent some rooms there. Enjoy the society, the waters and the entertainments. Everyone who goes says how wonderful it is.'

'And Sir Charles agreed?'

'Yes. And we had a lovely time. There were concerts and balls.'

'And people accepted you because your husband was a baronet,' Sarah said.

Celia didn't answer this question. Instead she said, 'I thought Charlie really enjoyed being in society. He said he'd met lots of interesting people.'

'But what was the harm in that?'

'He decided we should spend some time in London. Rent a house in Marylebone, somewhere nice like that.'

'I see.'

Sarah imagined what had probably happened. Like so many young bloods up from the country, Sir Charles would have been wholly innocent of the viciousness of the London underworld. He would have mixed with men far worldlier than himself—and probably a great deal wealthier. He would have been determined to be accepted by them, regardless of the cost.

'I suppose he gambled at the tables and lost a large amount,' she said. She did not add, though she suspected it, 'And visited brothels with them.'

'I don't know anything about his money. His banker, Thomas Coutts, won't tell me anything about his account.'

Sarah remained silent for several moments as she considered the likely effect on the girl of her husband's behaviour. Apart from the emotional hurt and confusion, there could be a problem with money.

Aware of the problems most married women faced financially, she said, 'Do you have any money of your own?'

'Very little. I'm wholly dependent on Charlie. It was his way to pay all our living expenses and the wages to the servants and farm workers. He gave me money as and when I needed it for … for personal expenses.'

'Then how have you been managing?'

'While I was still living in London, I pretended to be a single woman. I pawned my few items of jewellery. When there was nothing left, the coachman took me back to Browning Hall. He's a good man. He knows I can't pay his wages.' At this, Celia broke down.

Sarah realized that if her story were true, the girl's situation was serious. Unless her husband could be found or declared legally dead, she would be unable to access any of his wealth until probate of his will was proven. And this could take years if his body was never found. And if the estate was entailed, which it almost certainly would be, any younger brother would inherit it unless Celia had given birth to a male child since her marriage.

She thought that perhaps she ought to do something for the girl but felt unsure where to begin. Certainly, before committing herself to any course of action she needed to know a lot more about the girl and her situation, but she found it difficult to know what would be most useful to ask.

She started with the most obvious question: 'I think you said he's been missing for a month.'

'Yes. A month today. The last time I saw him was when he left the house at about six o'clock in the evening.'

'And you have no idea where he was going?'

'No. He often went out in the evenings.'

'But you didn't know where.'

The girl shook her head. 'I didn't like to ask.'

Her reply suggested that the couple were not particularly close. Sarah knew this was nothing unusual, especially in arranged marriages in the middle and upper classes, and even in many love matches. Many husbands preferred to lead private lives as far as their wives were concerned, especially among the nobility, where it was common for married men to have mistresses, at best, or consort with prostitutes, at worst. Unwilling to ask their wives, especially if of genteel birth, to indulge in the sexual practices they preferred, they resorted to paid sex of various kinds. The debauched antics of the aristocracy made good copy for the gossip columnists.

There was, therefore, nothing remarkable about the girl's ignorance of her husband's movements, especially as she gave the impression of being both young and innocent.

"How long have you been married?" Sarah asked.

"Barely six months. I am eighteen now, but seventeen when we married."

'And how old is Sir Charles?'

'He'll be twenty-six next birthday. That's in November.'

'I assume you have no children.'

'Not yet, but we will.' She burst into tears again.

Sarah reached out and touched the girl's hand and said softly, 'Where are you living now?'

'I had to leave the London house and return to Browning Hall. I've had to let most of the servants go. I've kept only the housekeeper and the groom who acts as my coachman, but I've no money for them.'

'Are there any tenants on the estate?'

'Yes, and when the rents are due, I hope to be able to use them to live on.'

Sarah understood the difficulty of the girl's situation. 'I can't promise to be of assistance, but you'd better tell me all about yourself, just in case I can help you in some way, Lady Browning.'

'Bless, you.' Celia sniffed back the tears. 'And please don't call me Lady. I'm just the daughter of a poor clergyman. My father was the vicar of St Andrew's Church on the Browning estate. He's been very ill and is rather frail. The living was the gift of whoever owns the estate. After my marriage, Charlie arranged a better living for him. It's near Watford, and it has a curate as well who does all the visiting and so on. Father rarely leaves the vicarage.'

'So there is a new clergyman at St Andrews?'

'Yes. Mr Somersby.'

'A family man?'

'No. He is single. But I think perhaps not for long. He has many admirers among the young ladies in the district.'

'I see. Not a profitable living for a young clergyman.'

'Perhaps he has an independence,' Celia said. 'And he is of a studious turn of mind. Charlie knew him at Oxford. They are good friends.'

'That explains why your husband gave him the living.'

Celia nodded. This topic of conversation didn't appear to interest her. Sarah could imagine that the two men held discussions on subjects several miles above her head. She said, 'Did you grow up in the village?'

'Oh, yes.'

'How did you get to know Sir Charles?'

'At church. He spoke to me one day and then asked my father if he could call on me. My father couldn't really say no.'

'And you became friends?'

'Yes. I was never invited to the hall or anything like that. He explained that his father, Sir Robert, wanted him to marry where there was money and would oppose a marriage to a village girl. I never thought for a second that we would ever be more than friends.'

'I understand.'

No doubt, Sarah thought, the possibility of the heir marrying a poor clergyman's daughter would have horrified Sir Charles's parents.

'How soon after Sir Robert's death did Sir Charles wait before he asked you to marry him?'

'About three months.'

'Presumably you expected opposition to the marriage?'

Celia began weeping again. 'Oh yes, it was horrible.' She sniffed back the tears. 'Lady Augusta refused to attend the wedding. Only the servants from the hall and people in the village came. Afterwards, Lady Augusta moved out of the hall into the dowager cottage and refused to speak to me. She's a horrible woman. No, I shouldn't say that. She's bed-ridden and is in much pain. I should be more understanding of her situation.'

'Does Sir Charles have any brothers and sisters?'

'A younger brother. Edward.'

'Didn't he attend the wedding?'

'No. He was already living overseas by then. You see, there had been a problem between Edward and his father. As soon as Edward was old enough, Sir Robert sent him abroad with barely more than the clothes he wore. Charlie said Lady Augusta had to persuade her own father to support him, and he gave Edward enough to buy a small sugar plantation in Antigua. He hasn't been back to England since he left.'

'This is all incredibly sad,' Sarah said, 'but surely it is not bad enough for you to be so desperate. You have the title and social position. Lady Augusta can't take that away from you, can she?'

Celia shook her head. 'No, I suppose not.'

The time had come to make a decision. The girl was either telling the truth or this was the beginning of a complicated confidence trick. In Sarah's theatrical world, they all looked out for one another, offering money or bread and board as needed. If Celia was telling the truth, Sarah felt she should at the least make further inquiries. If, on the other hand, the girl was a clever little liar, Sarah wanted to find out what she was after and how she intended going about getting it. In either case, Sarah realized that her curiosity was adequately aroused.

The girl's story was plausible. There was nothing unusual about a young aristocrat disappearing. Many got into debt in their attempts to live a fashionable life in the city and had to flee to the continent. The unusual part of Celia's story was that her husband had not confided his whereabouts to her. Sarah realized it was possible that the young baronet had met with a fatal accident.

'Come home with me, Celia,' she said. 'You can stay with us for the night. I'll arrange accommodation for your coachman and horses.'

Overcome with gratitude, the girl began to sob again. 'You're very kind, Miss Kedron. So very kind.'

'Nonsense. If I were ever in your situation—and God forbid I ever will be—I'd hope to find a friend.'

They left the tea shop together. Sarah hailed a hackney and gave her address in Portman Place.

As the hackney weaved its way through the heavy late-afternoon traffic, she said, 'As soon as we get home, my abigail will settle you in the guest room. Mrs Wells, our housekeeper, will arrange for a meal to be sent up to you on a tray. I suggest you try to have an early night. You must be exhausted.'

The girl nodded, too overcome with gratitude to speak.

'I shall return home as soon as I can from the theatre this evening and talk to my father then. We'll decide in the morning what is to be done.'

Seven

As good as her word, Sarah hurried home immediately after her play came to an end and she had taken her bows. Fortunately, her play had been the first item on the six-hour bill, and she returned to Portman Place before nine o'clock. Her father and James Brewster, the newly appointed editor of *The Weekly Police News*, sat in the library, discussing the next edition of the publication.

At first Sarah felt disappointed to find Mr Brewster there. She had hoped to be able to speak to her father privately. She knew he liked and already trusted Mr Brewster, who had turned out to be a most conscientious and competent editor, but she felt a little concerned that his ambition would one day result in a parting of the ways. When called to the Bar, as he would be in about two years, his income as a successful barrister would far exceed anything he could earn as the editor of a periodical. Sarah suspected that he might use her father as a stepping stone to a more important position, in the same way that he had used their casual acquaintance to achieve a meeting with her father.

Despite her reservations, however, she found him an attractive man, impeccably mannered and not without considerable charm. He, in turn, seemed attracted to her, though his behaviour towards her remained formal. They were both careful not to move onto a Christian-name basis too soon, even though they met at least once each day, and he often visited the house as well as the office. She was determined to retain this level of friendship and not allow stronger feelings to develop between them. She'd had several brief affairs, usually with actors, and once, distressingly, with a young lord. The experience had convinced her that the life of a wife or mistress was not one she was prepared to adopt. She had no wish to put her career priorities under those of her husband or lover, and the thought of bearing children year after year horrified her.

When Sarah entered the library, James Brewster stood and bowed. 'Good evening, Miss Kedron.'

'Good evening, Mr Brewster.'

'I trust the performance was greeted with the usual enthusiasm.'

'Ten curtain calls, Mr Brewster. I find all the bowing and curtsying quite exhausting.' She turned to her father, who sat behind his large desk. 'Can you spare me a little time, Father?'

'Of course, my dear. Have we finished for the day, James?'

'I think so, sir.'

At that moment, it occurred to Sarah that Mr Brewster would be able to advise on any legal implications of Lady Browning's situation. She decided to take him into her confidence concerning the young woman's situation.

'I shall be obliged if you will stay, Mr Brewster. If you have the time. It is possible you may be of some assistance to me.'

'Always at your service, Miss Kedron.'

Sarah sat down, and James arranged himself elegantly on a settee.

'I assume, my dear,' her father said, 'that this is about the young woman sleeping soundly in the guest room.'

'Yes. Lady Browning. Celia. Her husband, Sir Charles, is a baronet.' Concisely, Sarah described what she knew of Celia's plight. She concluded her narrative by saying, 'I don't know what we can or should do for the girl, but I do feel deeply sorry for her.'

Matthew Kedron nodded thoughtfully. 'Her situation is certainly unfortunate. What do you think, James?'

James had steadily taken notes throughout Sarah's narrative. Being a barrister in the making made him an inveterate, even obsessive, note-taker. Sarah sometimes wondered if one day he would quote verbatim something she or her father had said which would be to their disadvantage.

'There are far too many unanswered questions for me to even proffer a hesitant opinion, sir,' James replied. 'We do not know if the husband is dead or alive. If he is alive, we do not know if his disappearance is deliberate, an accident or some form of abduction. And if he is dead, we do not know how or why.'

'The only clue we have is that his wife smelt drink on his breath and scent on his clothes,' Sarah pointed out.

'Quite,' James agreed, then added, 'Forgive my indelicacy, Miss Kedron, but that little clue would suggest he had been to a club of some kind.' He paused and looked at the floor. 'Or a house of ill repute.'

'Please don't feel you must avoid calling a spade a spade, Mr Brewster,' Sarah objected. 'I'm in the theatre and not easily shocked. You think he may have been to a brothel.'

'It is highly likely. If he has made the acquaintance of young aristocrats and gentry—which he almost certainly has—they have little else to do but whore and gamble.'

'Ah, yes. Gambling debts,' Matthew said. 'The curse of our time.'

'There are unscrupulous men and women in the *haut ton*, sir, as I know you are aware. They make a living preying on innocent and inexperienced young men recently up from the country. If he has been gambling, you can be sure he has lost money. Probably a great deal.'

'So much that he would have to sell or mortgage his estate?' Sarah asked.

'Quite possibly. It is not at all rare for men to wager their inheritances at the tables.' He laughed ruefully. 'Or to have to pay the debts incurred by their wives or mistresses. There are gambling hells that cater especially for society women with nothing better to do.'

'And gambling debts have to be paid?' Sarah asked.

'They are considered debts of honour. Any man who does not pay his gambling debts will be ostracized—excluded for ever from society.'

'Even if payment results in penury?'

'Indeed. Or worse. He may have incurred a further debt to a bank or moneylender. And these can be recovered in law.'

'Can the courts enforce payment of a gambling debt, James?' Matthew asked.

'I don't believe they can, sir. There is something called the Statute of Anne, which was a law passed in Queen Anne's time. She was concerned that large estates were being transferred into the wrong hands because of gambling debts. I believe she hoped that an appropriate act of Parliament would prevent this from happening.'

'And did it?' Matthew asked.

'To a small extent, sir. Loss of reputation, blackmail, physical threats and other means of extortion can still be used, even if illegally, to enforce payment of a debt. As you know, the gambling clubs are technically illegal, but the law is rarely enforced.' He grinned mischievously. 'Especially as the Prince Regent spends much of his time in them and is one of the most reckless high-stakes gamblers of them all!'

'So,' Sarah said, wanting to bring the conversation back to Lady Browning's situation, 'Sir Charles may simply have decided to disappear to avoid payment of a gambling debt.'

'Or any other kind of debt. I suspect that is the most likely explanation,' James said. 'We should perhaps bear in mind that anyone to whom he is indebted would gain nothing by killing him. If, as we should assume, Miss Kedron, his estate is entailed, on his death it will automatically go to his younger brother. Lady Browning will probably inherit an annuity—no more.'

'Would she or her brother-in-law be under any obligation to pay the deceased's gambling debts, if that is all they were?' Sarah asked.

'Only if they considered it dishonourable not to.'

Sarah pulled her lower lip between her teeth and made a small grimace. 'I suppose in Sir Charles's case suicide might be considered preferable to dishonour.'

'I fear that is so, Miss Kedron.'

Matthew stood. It was now past his usual retiring time. 'I suggest we sleep on this sad matter,' he said. 'We will talk more in the morning.'

He walked towards Sarah, paused and kissed the top of her head. 'You have done well, my dear. I'm not surprised. I anticipated nothing but generosity and kindness from you.'

He nodded to James, who bowed and said, 'Good night, sir.' Then he turned, bowed to Sarah and followed his employer out of the library.

Sarah remained seated for a few moments in her father's study. She enjoyed the serenity of the space, the heavy silence, the smell of well-worn leather volumes lining the walls, the familiar sounds of the heavy wall clock. She feared that there would be little that could be done to help Celia. The girl's life was on the edge of ruin. And as James Brewster had said, there were so many unanswered questions.

Eight

When Sarah came down to breakfast the next morning, her father and James Brewster, who had breakfasted with him, had almost finished their meal and were about to leave for the office of *The Informer* and *The Weekly Police News*.

'Is our guest still asleep?' Sarah asked the housekeeper as she entered with additional dishes.

'I heard movements, Miss Sarah,' Mrs Wells replied. 'I'm sure she'll be down soon.'

The Kedron domestic establishment was small. Although the income from *The Weekly Informer* was steady and increasing, Matthew Kedron employed only the minimum of servants—a housekeeper, a cook, a maid, a skivvy for the kitchen, and a groom who maintained the carriage and looked after the horses. Sarah had her own abigail, Ellen, a twenty-five-year-old Irish woman who had been with her for ten years or so and had become as much a friend as a servant, despite her inability to read and write.

In defence of having such a small domestic staff, Matthew argued that the more people he employed, the more he would have to employ as he would have to employ people to look after the people he employed! Though an exaggeration, the argument had an element of truth.

The staff of his publishing business with its own print shop and distribution department, on the other hand, was much larger. He had quite enough trouble, he maintained, especially with the printers—temperamental to a man—without having to deal with all the usual staffing problems at home.

After greeting her father and Mr Brewster, Sarah said, as she accepted a plate of bacon, sausage and eggs, 'Before Celia comes down, I'd like to suggest a course of action.'

'You have decided to help the girl?' her father asked.

'I'd like to inquire further into her situation, Father. I think I should go back with her to Browning Hall and perhaps talk to a few people there.'

'If you intend becoming involved in any way, my dear, I agree that would be the sensible thing to do.'

'Would Mr Brewster be free to accompany me?' Sarah asked the question before giving it much thought. Even before the words left her mouth, however, she wondered if she had been wise. It was not, she told herself, that she had any qualms about making the journey to Browning Hall unaccompanied; but she simply felt it would be an advantage to have a companion with whom she could discuss whatever she discovered. James Brewster was the obvious choice. She hoped he would not read too much into the invitation.

A little surprised, but being careful not to reveal it, Matthew said, 'I'm sure we can spare him. The new assistant editor is working out well.'

'Are you agreeable to a jaunt into the country, Mr Brewster?' Sarah asked him.

'If Mr Kedron has no objection, I shall be pleased to accompany you.'

'Excellent. I am obliged,' Sarah said. 'I suggest we leave as soon as it is convenient for Lady Browning. I will take our coach, if that is acceptable, Father.'

'By all means, my dear.'

'When we arrive, Mr Brewster,' Sarah continued, determined to make the expedition as formal as possible, 'I shall try to speak privately to Lady Augusta, the dowager. I think it would be helpful if you spoke to the few servants who remain and to the tenant farmers. The more we can find out about the Browning family, the better it will be. Gossip can be so valuable. My main concern at present is to satisfy myself that we have not been selected as the target for a complicated confidence trick.'

Greatly pleased by Sarah's invitation to accompany her, James Brewster nodded his agreement. A journey together, he thought, might serve to lessen the degree of formality between them. Aware that a wrong word or move on his part could irretrievably damage their relationship, such as it was, he had so far comported himself with respectful reserve towards her.

Her success as an actress and playwright, he thought, had made her proud. He also observed her to be a voracious reader, particularly of the works of such women as Mary Wollstonecraft, whose publication *A Vindication of the Rights of Women* had surely strengthened her determination to maintain her independence from men. James knew Sarah would deeply resent the slightest suggestion that she was in any way inferior to or in need of a man. Stunningly attractive and amiable though she seemed, conversing with her could be rather like walking on eggshells.

Nine

After Celia had breakfasted, appearing to have lost none of a country girl's appetite, she accompanied Sarah in the carriage to the Kedron & Co office, where they collected James, who had gone ahead to the office to arrange matters during his absence.

All three travelled together in the Kedron carriage, followed by Celia's coachman with her curricle. The journey passed swiftly and trouble-free. They travelled through the village of Langley in mid-afternoon and were settled in Browning Hall shortly afterwards.

Built originally in Queen Anne's reign when the barony had been granted, the three-storey house had been added to and remodelled frequently over the years and now had what, Sarah thought, was best kindly described as a style of its own. It had a forest of chimneys, a great deal of stained glass, Corinthian columns astride the main entrance, and ivy-covered brickwork—a memorable house, if not an impressive one, modest for the size of the estate of almost two thousand acres.

As they approached the house up the long drive, Celia explained that Sir Charles's grandfather had been an avaricious landowner who had gradually acquired neighbouring farms and set about incorporating them into the home farm. However, Charles's father, Sir Robert Browning, had made no improvements during his tenure but allowed the farm cottages to fall in into disrepair. Charles, on the other hand, in the nine months since inheriting the estate, had set about the enormous task of modernizing the farms. He had introduced the latest crop rotation ideas and, to the wonder and excitement of the neighbourhood, acquired a steam-powered traction engine, which could be pulled from field to field by horses and used to drive a threshing machine.

Celia expressed the opinion that unlike his father, who had not been liked by his tenants and labourers, Sir Charles was both popular and respected. Whereas Sir Robert had been a proud, stubborn, severe and unapproachable man who had maintained the social chasm between himself and the lower orders, Sir Charles had done his best to make amends for his father's behaviour, even to the extent, Celia believed, of marrying a village girl. This latter action, she admitted, was considered by some to be taking amends rather too far. Many in the village disapproved most strongly of the marriage.

'Charlie wants to bring more of the land under cultivation,' Celia continued, 'and he has new ideas about farming methods. I don't understand them, of course, even though he has tried to explain them to me. He has many books on agriculture, but I don't read them. I mean, it's not a wife's work, is it, to read that kind of thing?'

The more she conversed with Celia, the more Sarah realized how limited the girl was intellectually. If she read at all, Sarah thought, it would be only the lightest romantic novels or fashion and gossip magazines. Sarah gathered her education had been limited to a few years at the parish school. There she would have learnt her letters, simple arithmetic and basic needlework. She would not have had the more sophisticated education expected of a future lady of the manor, such as musical or artistic instruction.

Sarah smiled to herself, thinking that Celia was probably typical of the readership of the most popular novels. Sweet-natured, gentle and pretty, she would have been a fish out of water in the social whirl of Bath and a London season of the *ton*. She would have been scorned and ignored by her contemporaries, pitied by her elders and, unless he was a saint of a man, an embarrassment to her husband. If she had already lied, Sarah thought, the lie would have been that their stay away from Browning Hall had been lovely. It would almost certainly have been agony for her. Sarah could not discount the possibility that Sir Charles's disappearance was connected to his wife's social ineptitude.

While Celia arranged with the housekeeper, Mrs Williams—the wife of one of the tenant farmers—for rooms to be prepared for her guests, Sarah and James discussed their next move.

'I shall visit Celia's mother-in-law, Lady Augusta,' Sarah said. 'If she will agree to talk to me, I think the conversation could be useful. I leave it to you, Mr Brewster, to ride around the estate, acquiring as much information about the family as you can. It will be interesting to compare what you discover with what Lady Browning has told us. I have the impression that she has given that little speech before, perhaps to people she met in Bath and London.'

James said. 'I assume we will be fed, so I shall find out what I can, and we can discuss it after dinner.'

'Yes. If we are fortunate, we shall be left alone afterwards in the library.' She smiled a little girlishly. 'It's all rather exciting, don't you think, Mr Brewster?'

'I hope, Miss Kedron,' he replied, 'that it does not become too exciting. I don't wish to alarm you, but we do not know what kind of situation we shall discover here.'

Laughing, Sarah said, 'I hope you are not suggesting that we may find a body in the barn, Mr Brewster.'

'If Sir Charles has met with foul play—and it is quite possible that he has—then there will be a body somewhere.'

'I suppose you are right,' Sarah said, somewhat disappointed that James had not played along. There were times when she liked to be a little frivolous. James Brewster always seemed to take life seriously.

Ten

Though almost a mile from Browning Hall, the dowager house still resided in the extensive grounds of the Browning estate, so Sarah asked the coachman to find her a suitable horse from the estate's stables. She loved to ride and welcomed the opportunity. Even though she had not brought a riding habit with her, this was not a problem. She was quite capable of tucking up her skirt and petticoat and riding bareback, even shoeless, if necessary.

On arrival, a maid admitted her to a parlour where she was kept waiting for at least half an hour. She tapped her foot impatiently as she looked around the room. Family portraits created a gallery on walls devoid of bookshelves, and the small bare table offered nothing to read.

At last, a plainly dressed, elderly woman entered. 'I am Miss Simmons, her ladyship's companion. She will see you, madam, but I must tell you that she is very ill indeed. She has no energy, and to alleviate the pain of her disease she must take frequent draughts of laudanum. Please do not stay longer than is really necessary.'

'I shall be as brief as I can,' Sarah said.

Miss Simmons then escorted her to a drawing room where Lady Augusta reclined on a day bed with a rug over her knees and a shawl across her shoulders. Though a woman in her late forties, she looked a great deal older. Her face was gaunt, and her arms were almost skeletal, so wasted was her flesh. Her hair, prematurely grey, hung dank and limp, without body or shape. She looked near death.

'It's kind of you to see me, Your Ladyship,' Sarah said.

'What is it that you want, Miss Kedron?'

Lady Augusta spoke so softly that Sarah could hardly make out the words, but her tone was far from welcoming and the woman clearly suspicious.

'Lady Browning is worried about the disappearance of her husband,' she said. 'My father is the author and publisher Matthew Kedron. He is acquainted with the Home Secretary and has contacts in the judiciary. We have offered to assist Lady Browning in the search for Sir Charles.'

The dowager looked at Sarah through half-closed eyes, her face taut with pain and anger. She almost hissed her response. 'And you've been taken in by that wicked slut of a girl, have you? More fool you.' A fit of coughing suddenly overcame her.

Miss Simmons, who must have been hovering outside the door in expectation of being needed, hurried in with a bowl and a cloth. Tenderly she wiped Lady Augusta's mouth, and placed the bowl and cloth in her lap, ready for immediate use.

Lady Augusta spat yellow, blood-spotted sputum into the bowl. Miss Simmons again gently wiped her mouth for her, behaving like a competent and experienced nurse.

When the coughing fit ceased, Lady Augusta, panting heavily with the effort, spoke into a scented lace handkerchief that she held to her mouth: 'She's done away with him. Murdered him. Had him buried somewhere on the estate. Why do you think she has sent all the servants away?'

'I understood that it is because she has no money with which to pay them,' Sarah said, trying not to sound argumentative.

'Of course she hasn't—that's what it's all about. Anyone with half a brain can see that. She wanted him dead. Now she can inherit the annuity she's been promised and then remarry.' She paused and breathed heavily, then sneered, as if no more needed to be said. 'Yes, marry a man of her own class. And there is one waiting in the wings. I'm not a fool.'

Sarah sat silently, knowing no comment was required.

After a short pause, Lady Augusta continued, seeming to summon up a burst of strength. 'I was opposed to the marriage from the beginning. She is just a common village girl. No good comes of mixing the classes. There were plenty of young women of good families who would have brought wealth and prestige to the family.' Lady Augusta closed her eyes, apparently exhausted.

Sarah wondered how much longer she had to live. Intuitively, she thought the old woman remained determined to stay alive to do something she believed she had to do. She would fight her disease, whatever it was, to the bitter end.

She decided to risk one more question: 'If Lady Browning has killed Sir Charles,' she said, 'or somehow arranged for him to be killed, why has she come to me, begging me to help her find him?'

Without opening her eyes, Lady Augusta murmured, 'That's where she is so clever! The devious, deceitful minx.

She thinks that approaching you will take suspicion away from her. She seems to have succeeded.'

'Have you informed the magistrate of your suspicions?' Sarah asked quietly.

'Don't be a fool, girl. What could he do?'

'Get a constable to search the estate, I suppose,' Sarah said, though she knew it was most unlikely that the local magistrate would order any such thing. Lady Augusta appeared to have reached an age and condition of mind and body when reality was of no consequence. Her fantasies fed her days. 'Did Lady Browning and Sir Charles quarrel?' she asked.

'She was much too clever for that. It was nauseating the way she fawned over him. The girl has no dignity. She is little more than a whore. Charles should have married someone more suited, a bride with either money or a superior title.' She opened her eyes, slowly raised a hand and waved it dismissively at Sarah. 'Go now. I have said all I have to say.' She closed her eyes again and lay back, totally exhausted.

Sarah said, 'You do realize, don't you, my lady, that Lady Browning cannot remarry or inherit anything until Sir Charles is declared deceased? That could take years unless his body is found. Her life is impossible at present and her situation can only get worse.'

But Lady Augusta had said all she cared to say or was capable of saying. Miss Simmons indicated that Sarah should leave. The interview was over.

As Miss Simmons led the way to the front door of the house, Sarah said, 'Her mind is disturbed. Has she been like this for long?'

'She has good cause to believe what she believes,' Miss Simmons replied. 'There is gossip in the village that shames the family.'

'I see. How did Sir Charles respond to his mother's suspicion?'

'There has always been a problem between them. His marriage to a village girl brought matters to a head.' Miss Simmons opened the front door for Sarah. 'I'm afraid that Lady Augusta will not be with us much longer. The consumption is far advanced. And there is a tumour on the lung.'

'Oh, dear. The poor woman.' Sarah offered Miss Simmons her hand. 'Thank you for your assistance. Lady Augusta is fortunate in having such a devoted friend. I bid you good day.'

Sarah mounted the horse which placidly grazed the grass outside the stone wall around the garden and rode slowly and thoughtfully back to Browning Hall.

Eleven

During her ride back to the Hall, Sarah went over in her mind everything Lady Augusta had said. She ought to ignore the ravings of a sick and bitter old woman, and yet she had to admit it was not beyond the bounds of possibility that Celia was in some way responsible for her husband's disappearance. If he were dead—and perhaps Mr Brewster was not far wrong in his concern—then when his body was found, her attorney could apply for probate and she would inherit the annuity. It could be substantial—several thousand a year. Her brother-in-law, Edward, would inherit the estate and title, but she would be a young, attractive and comfortably wealthy widow, an ideal catch for an ambitious man of social position in need of a wife, and even more desirable as the wife for a working man in the village.

If she were responsible for her husband's death, Sarah reasoned, it would not be difficult at an appropriate time for her to plant ideas in their minds as to where the body could be found. Unless she, or more likely an accomplice—a lover, perhaps—had been careless, the baronet's death would be attributed to just another violent robbery. There would be no inquiry, especially if he had been bludgeoned to death or shot with the kind of pistol commonly used by highwaymen.

The possibility that Celia could be so duplicitous intrigued Sarah. For the present, though, she did not want to give it too much attention. However, the seed had been sown. Over the coming week, she would revisit it again and again.

When she arrived at the hall, as James Brewster had not yet returned she went to her room to rest briefly and change from her travelling clothes to something more suitable for dinner at a country house, plain though the meal would almost certainly be. If they lingered over dinner, it would be late in the summer evening and inappropriate for her to walk in the garden to talk privately with Mr Brewster. It seemed likely they would have to postpone discussion of their meetings until the morning.

The only useful development during the evening came from Mr Brewster. During the dinner he said, 'Forgive me for suggesting this, Lady Browning, but if Miss Kedron and I are to assist you, we need all the information you can provide.'

'Of course. But I have told you everything I know.'

'I'm sure you have told us everything you can remember. But other memories may occur to you. In any case, there may be other clues as to what has caused Sir Charles to disappear. Would it be possible to look through the clothes you brought back from London? There may be a note of some kind—anything that could suggest where he might have been or intended going.'

'I didn't think of that,' Celia said. 'I'm sorry. I'll take you to his dressing room and show you the clothes he wore.'

'That will be excellent. And perhaps we may look through the papers in his bureau. There might be a letter that could provide a clue to the situation. If Miss Kedron would like to go with you to Sir Charles's dressing room, perhaps I may spend some time in the library.' He turned towards Sarah and raised his eyebrows questioningly.

With a smile, she said, 'I think that is a most useful suggestion, Mr Brewster. I should have thought of it myself.'

She felt both pleased and relieved that she had invited him to accompany her to Browning Hall. His involvement in the inquiry promised to be invaluable. And it would definitely be helpful to have a colleague with whom to discuss developments and possibilities.

Before the evening was out, they had both found documents that provided possible leads as to where Sir Charles had been: a name card that Sarah found in a pocket in one of his coats bore the name of a Miss Elizabeth Stockton with an address in Chelsea—and James found an account from Jenkins & Sons, Tailors and Haberdashers of Jermyn Street for half a dozen shirts. The tailor thanked Sir Charles for his esteemed custom and respectfully requested settlement within thirty days. Mr Brewster discovered it in an unopened envelope in the bureau in the library. Celia confirmed it had been forwarded from the address of the house they had rented in London and dated the last day she'd had any contact with her husband. She knew nothing about Miss Elizabeth Stockton.

'With your permission, Celia,' Sarah said, 'we shall visit both of these addresses. We have so little to go on that we must follow up every possible lead, no matter how unpromising.'

Celia agreed and thanked them profusely. She told them that she would have to remain at Browning Hall, but that she would write to them immediately if she had any news, further thoughts or information that might be of use. For their part, Sarah told her they would do their best to establish what had happened to Sir Charles and would let her know as soon as they had anything to report.

Celia wept with gratitude. Her habitual refuge in tears rather irritated Sarah but, overcoming this, she held the girl in an affectionate embrace. She found it hard to believe there could be any truth in Lady Augusta's accusation. If there were, Sarah thought, then the girl had to be the most consummate actress of all time.

With this in mind, she climbed into the carriage and, with fond waves from Celia until they were out of sight, they began the journey back to London.

Twelve

During the first part of the journey back to London, they passed the time exchanging details of their discoveries and speculating on possibilities.

James Brewster was tempted to dismiss Lady Augusta's ravings. 'From the gossip I heard,' he said, 'her marriage to Sir Robert was less than happy and perhaps, consequently, this has affected her relationship with Sir Charles. His marriage to a village girl has done nothing to alleviate her anger.'

'I find that very interesting, Ja ... Mr Brewster,' Sarah said, almost falling into the trap of referring to him by his Christian name—a trap because it would encourage him to respond to her in a similar fashion. Sarah knew from experience that one wrong step in a relationship could lead to many difficulties. It was safer not to risk anything.

'There is something not right about Lady Augusta,' she continued. 'I do not mean her present mental state. It is her manner and language that surprised me. Even though she is ill and clearly drugged with laudanum, they were not what I would have expected from a well-bred woman.' She laughed and added, 'Even her vowels slipped occasionally.'

'It is widely believed that Sir Robert married beneath him,' James observed.

Sarah nodded. 'Hmm, that might explain her attitude to Celia. I have heard it said that the lower the class the greater the pretension. What else did you hear?'

'Very little. I had only a short time at my disposal and was therefore limited in the number of people to whom I could speak. I also had to be circumspect in the way I phrased any questions. I believe it would be useful for me to return here shortly and spend time in the village tavern.'

'That's a sensible suggestion. There is bound to be someone who is aggrieved, with or without justification. Spending time in the tavern might enable you to hear such a person give vent to his feelings.' Sarah remained silent for several miles, then as the horses clattered through the cobbled street of Rickmansworth, she said, 'Tell me, do you think Sir Charles has been killed?'

'I think we need to keep an open mind and make as many inquiries as we can,' James replied. 'If we incline at this stage to a particular opinion, it could blind us to other possibilities. All we know for sure is that until Sir Charles is found, dead or alive, Celia will have a miserable existence. And that could continue for many years.'

'But there's no harm in speculating,' Sarah objected. With a background in the theatre rather than the courtroom, Sarah enjoyed considering as many fantastic possibilities as occurred to her. 'Assuming,' she continued with quiet determination, 'that he is dead, what are the possible causes of his demise?'

'Well,' James said, humouring her, 'there is accident and illness, of course. But I'm sure someone would have informed his wife if either of those situations had eventuated and his identity had been known. If he has been murdered, then we must ask ourselves why. *Cui bono?*'

'Who benefits? What if no one benefits?' Sarah replied, thoughtfully. 'We must also consider the possibility of suicide.'

'We can consider anything, Miss Kedron, but unless we know a great deal more about the man, there is little of value that any speculation will have to offer.'

'But what if he is in debt? What if he has lost great sums gambling and put his property and marriage at risk? Would not suicide be a way out? Would that not save his honour?'

'He may believe so in a desperate state of mind. But it would be a coward's way out.'

'Perhaps he was challenged to a duel?' Sarah conjured up a vision of pistols at a misty dawn in some silent wood or glade.

'That raises several possibilities,' James observed. 'He may well have been fatally injured, and duelling is illegal, of course, although still frequently occurs. His opponent could be charged with manslaughter, even murder. To avoid prosecution, Sir Charles's body could have been disposed of.'

'How?'

'Sold or given to a medical school for dissection.'

Sarah wrinkled her nose. She'd heard there was a brisk trade in recently dead bodies. Grave robbing was one of the more disgusting crimes.

'Or he could have been dismembered and thrown into the Thames. Burned. Buried somewhere,' James added, warming to the speculation.

'And is that also what could have happened to him if he had been killed during a robbery?' Sarah said.

'Quite so.'

'Hmm.' Sarah remained silent for several minutes. Then she said, 'I suppose he could always have disappeared deliberately, and is in hiding somewhere.'

'Indeed. Even on the continent. There are many tales of gamblers who have fled to France. The best known, of course, is that man of fashion, Beau Brummel. As far as I know, he intends to stay in France even if that means living in poverty and depending on the generosity of the few friends he has left.' He laughed, remembering an anecdote about the dandy. 'Do you know,' he said, 'that men of the *ton* actually paid to watch him dress? Extraordinary.'

'Nothing people do surprises me,' Sarah said, and then asked, 'Do you think we are foolish, even to attempt to discover what has occurred?'

'Probably. But, if we take care, what have we to lose? You may get the plot for a serial novel out of it. I could get a good article for *The Weekly Police News*. We shall not have wasted our time.'

'If we continue with our investigation,' Sarah said a little primly, 'it will be because we wish to be of service to Celia. For no other reason.'

'Quite.'

James turned and looked out the window to hide his expression of amusement. Much though he liked and respected Sarah, he thought she lacked a sense of humour.

Thirteen

Elizabeth Stockton's address in Chelsea was in Cheyne Walk, a short distance from the Cross Keys public house. Frequented mainly by artists and authors, the wine flowed freely, and the conversation was always lively. Strangers were also welcome, so long as they had intelligence or anecdotes to contribute and did not become too violent in their cups. If intense arguments on matters of artistic merit reached the point when only fisticuffs would suffice to settle the issue, the other patrons quickly brought the contestants under control. Pugilism was not a sport that was encouraged by the landlord of the Cross Keys.

Within moments of entering the hostelry, Sarah was noticed by the innkeeper, a heavily built man of about forty with a ruddy, smiling face. Recognizing her from the stage, he approached and gave an elaborate bow.

'Miss Kedron. Welcome, welcome, madam. George Belkins at your service. May I offer my congratulations on your last performance?'

Sarah smiled.

With a boisterous laugh, Belkins added, 'Many of my gentlemen patrons claim to recognize the original of your character, The Malevolent Mistress.'

'I can assure you, sir, she is a creature of my imagination,' Sarah said, still smiling.

'May I bring you a glass of wine? We have an excellent range of Bordeaux, recently arrived.'

'Thank you, Mr Belkins, but no. I have come hoping to find someone who can give me information about Miss Elizabeth Stockton. I believe she resides near here, but I do not have a house number.'

'Indeed, she does. A most talented and amiable lady. And beautiful. Oh, my goodness, yes. She resides at number 2A. Fifth floor.'

Sarah's immediate thought was that the woman might be Sir Charles's mistress. Although he had not been long married and, presumably, cared for his pretty young wife, Celia was wholly unworldly and might not be as imaginative and energetic in bed as a more experienced woman. The *ton* attached little opprobrium to having a mistress, or even being one, especially in the artistic and theatrical community. It was, therefore, quite possible that this was the nature of Elizabeth Stockton's relationship with Sir Charles.

'I should like to call on her,' Sarah said. 'Is she likely to be at home at this hour?'

'That is more than likely. If she is, no doubt she will be delighted to make your acquaintance, Miss Kedron. Your reputation precedes you.'

'Thank you.' Sarah smiled. 'I may well return and sample some of your Bordeaux.'

She left the inn and soon after rang the bell at 2A Cheyne Walk, a tall, narrow house that had been divided into apartments. Within a minute, an elderly servant answered the door.

Sarah offered the woman her card. 'Good morning. Is Miss Stockton at home? If she is, perhaps she will be kind enough to spare me a little time?'

'You had better come in, ma'am,' the woman said. 'She's in but working. I'll go up and see if she will take a break.'

She led the way into a small parlour, one shared by all the tenants of the building. Sarah wondered what Elizabeth Stockton's work could be. It could hardly be of a domestic nature.

The servant soon returned. 'Follow me, if you please, ma'am. I'm afraid we are on the top floor. It is a bit of a climb. But there, you are young. You do not have old bones to trouble you.'

Sarah followed the servant up the stairs. On the fifth floor, a woman of about Sarah's years stood at the door of an apartment, waiting for her. Plump but shapely, she wore a paint-spattered smock, and her thick, golden hair coiled on top of her head in what seemed an attempt at a nest for a large bird. Her generous lips curled into a broad smile. Sarah thought she looked delightful.

'Miss Kedron!' she exclaimed, clearly pleased to have such a famous visitor. 'What a lovely surprise. Come in.'

'I do hope I'm not intruding,' Sarah said.

'Not at all. I usually take a break about this time. Will you take tea?'

'Thank you.'

To the servant, Elizabeth Stockton said, 'Tea for two, please, Edith. And perhaps we might have some of your delicious little biscuits.'

She stood back to allow Sarah to enter the apartment—a large attic room, clearly a busy artist's studio. Bright afternoon sunlight streamed through windows at the far end, and paintings and canvasses were stacked along the walls. Several tables bore pots of paint and jars of brushes. The room smelt strongly of turpentine.

Unable to help herself, Sarah blurted out, 'You're an artist!'

'I try to be. But you, Miss Kedron, are rapidly on the way to becoming London's most successful playwright. I adored *The Malevolent Mistress*. It's so lovely to meet you. Have you come to arrange for your portrait to be painted? I would dearly love to be the artist whose portrait of you hangs in the foyer of the Sans Pareil.'

Smiling, Sarah said, 'I think it would be a little presumptuous of me to sit for a portrait yet. Perhaps if my reputation continues to enjoy respect, I may commission one in the future.' She laughed. 'Or the theatre may be persuaded to part with the necessary cost, Miss Stockton.'

'Please call me Elizabeth,' the artist said. 'I hate formality; it makes me nervous. It is so easy to say and do the wrong thing.'

'I do so agree,' Sarah replied, disarmed. 'And I shall be happy if you will call me Sarah.'

Elizabeth indicated an empty chair and removed a pile of books from another chair next to a small table. The two women sat down.

Sarah glanced at an easel on which sat a half-finished portrait of an elderly woman, clearly an aristocrat. 'I'm sure you're busy, Elizabeth,' she said, 'so I'll come to the purpose of my visit. Do you know Sir Charles Browning?'

'Sir Charles! Oh, yes. I've almost finished his portrait. Just a little more work around the eyes. He was due for another sitting about ... oh, at least a month ago. But I've neither seen nor heard anything. Is he unwell?'

'I'm sorry to have to tell you this, but he has disappeared.'

'Disappeared? Do you mean he has vanished?'

'In a word, yes. His wife has asked me to try to find out what has happened to him. My father is Matthew Kedron, publisher of *The Weekly Police News*. She thinks his connections may be helpful. May I see the portrait? I have no idea what Sir Charles looks like. I've seen a portrait of his late father, but there might not be a strong family likeness.'

'Of course you may. It's over here.' Elizabeth stood and led the way across the studio to where a portrait of a young man leaned against the wall. Instead of wearing formal clothes, as in the usual kind of portrait, the subject wore clothes more suited to a working man than a gentleman. But his simple clothing did not disguise his good looks. He had a fine, ascetic face with a firm, well-shaped mouth and strong, rather staring eyes. Sarah thought him a man to swoon over, reminiscent perhaps of the Mr Darcy, who a recently published novel described as a fine, tall person, handsome features, noble mien.

'My goodness,' she said, 'isn't he just ...?'

She stopped, and while she searched for a more appropriate word, Elizabeth giggled and said, 'I suppose he is good-looking. In a rather severe way. Is his wife young and pretty?'

'Very, and completely unspoiled. Childlike really. She's desperately concerned.'

'I'm not surprised,' Elizabeth said. 'Do you have any idea where he might be?'

'Not one.'

The arrival of tea and biscuits interrupted further conversation. When the servant had left, and Elizabeth was pouring, Sarah said, 'Apart from the unexpected pleasure of your company, Elizabeth, I think you can be of vital importance to me in my quest.'

'Anything I can do, I'll do willingly.'

'May I borrow the portrait of Sir Charles? My father employs an engraver and apprentices. If I have an engraving made of the portrait and have it printed, I can show Sir Charles's likeness in places where he may have visited. Someone may recognize him and set me in the right direction.'

'What a splendid idea,' Elizabeth exclaimed. 'Of course you may borrow it.'

'Perhaps you would also tell me anything about him that you think might be relevant. Presumably while he was sitting you had conversation.'

Elizabeth smiled ruefully. 'Hardly conversation, Sarah. He is the master of the monologue. A determined young man who appears to have read every significant book published in the last century.' Quickly she added, 'excluding fiction and poetry, of course. In these he has no interest. No, he reads only works by such authors as Thomas Paine, Adam Smith, Rousseau, John Locke, John Wilkes, Jeremy Bentham and other learned or opinionated gentlemen of that ilk. I cannot remember all their names. He liked to quote from them ... at length.'

She gave Sarah a mischievous smile. 'He is a profoundly serious young gentleman with a mission in life.'

'Not the kind of man,' Sarah suggested, 'who would commit suicide.'

'Good heavens, no. The last man on earth to take his own life.'

'Unless he has gambled away his inheritance and the shame of dishonouring a debt is too great for him to bear, perhaps.'

Elizabeth nodded. 'That is always possible. But I do not think he is the kind of man to get himself into such a situation. The temptation in London is great, of course, especially for a young gentleman set on achieving social acceptance among the nobility. But if he did gamble, I'm confident he would not be tempted to risk more than he could afford.'

'Is that not what they all say?'

'You are probably right. But my instincts tell me that if he has disappeared, then something worse has happened. Life is so cheap nowadays. There are men—and women—out there who will kill for a few shillings.'

Unexpectedly, tears flooded Elizabeth's eyes. Hardly able to speak, she whispered, 'My brother was killed by a drunken sot in a tavern brawl. At any moment, it can all come to an end for any of us. We have so little charge over our lives.'

Sarah reached out and took Elizabeth's hands. 'My dear, I'm so sorry. I do know how bad things are. My father is a vigorous campaigner for better law and order. He maintains that crime of all kinds is out of control. He argues that we must have more constables and a proper police force, one that will prevent crime, not the Runners, who will just chase after known criminals when they are pointed out to them.'

Elizabeth dried her eyes. 'I'm so sorry to embarrass you.'

'You have done nothing of the kind.'

Elizabeth stood. Thinking about her dead brother made her unable to continue the interview. 'I will arrange for the portrait of Sir Charles to be packed and delivered to your address.'

'Thank you.' Sarah realized that Elizabeth was too upset to continue their conversation. She wondered if her sensibilities were a problem for her. She perceived something warm-hearted and sensitive about the artist, and it was this, apart from her physical appearance, that appealed to Sarah. 'I do hope we meet again,' she said.

'And so do I.' Elizabeth impulsively seemed about to put her arms around Sarah in an embrace, but embarrassed and ashamed at being so forward to a stranger, she held back. 'And I do so want to paint you.'

She picked up a shawl and threw it over her shoulder. Then she escorted Sarah down the stairs to the front door of the house, insisting that she needed to get out of the studio into the fresh air and that a walk along the Thames embankment would be good for her.

'Please let me know immediately if you think of anything that Sir Charles said that might help me find him,' Sarah said as they parted.

'I will, Sarah. Be sure that I will. I promise. Oh, I have so enjoyed meeting you.'

Sarah smiled and walked away. Then she stopped and turned. Elizabeth stood at the door of the apartment building, waving to her. She waved in return. Clearly the woman had taken an instant liking to her. For her part, Sarah already looked forward to meeting Elizabeth again and, she hoped, making a friend of her. She'd never had an artist as a friend. All the women she knew were actresses, authors or poets. Sometimes, Sarah found their self-obsession and need for admiration quite overwhelming.

Fourteen

While Sarah called on Elizabeth Stockton, James Brewster visited Sir Charles's tailor in Jermyn Street.

After the initial exchange of the usual courtesies, James came to the point. He took the tailor's account out of his pocket and handed it to Mr Jenkins, the elderly proprietor of the establishment.

'I'm calling on you, Mr Jenkins, at the request of Lady Browning. Sir Charles is presently travelling on the continent and she is concerned that he may have overlooked your account prior to his departure. Perhaps you would be so kind as to consult your ledger.'

'Of course, sir. If you will excuse me for a few moments. Pray be seated.'

James took a seat while the tailor hurried to the rear of his shop where an even more elderly man sat hunched over a large volume, on a high chair before a clerk's desk. They engaged in a whispered conversation and turned pages, and then, with a slightly sorrowful expression, Mr Jenkins returned to the front of his establishment.

'The account is still outstanding, sir,' he said. 'I trust the shirts are to Sir Charles's satisfaction. They are of the finest material.'

'I believe so,' James said, and then rather cunningly, he added, 'I understand from Lady Browning that Sir Charles was introduced to your establishment by a friend whose judgement he trusts.'

'Indeed he was, sir,' the tailor exclaimed. And then, unable to resist the opportunity to aggrandize his business, he added, 'Captain Fanshaw of the Royal Artillery. Currently stationed at Woolwich. A most valued customer. We have been honoured to dress the gentlemen of the Fanshaw family for three generations.'

Mr Jenkins seemed about to launch into a detailed account of the history of his firm's connection with the Fanshaws, but James, having obtained the kind of information he had been seeking, cut the visit short.

'You must excuse me, sir, but I have a hackney waiting, taking up the entire road for all I know. I am most obliged to you. I will inform Lady Browning of the state of Sir Charles's account with you.'

And with a short, barely perceptible bow, he left the premises.

If Captain Fanshaw was a friend of Sir Charles, then it was necessary, James knew, to talk to him. He could have invaluable information about the baronet's situation.

He hailed a chair and was carried quickly to Paternoster Row, there to put in a day's work on the new edition of *The Weekly Police News*. Celia's problem was important, but the periodical had to be published on time.

***

At dinner that evening, Sarah and James informed Matthew of the little they had discovered.

Matthew said, 'I fear you are not very advanced in your investigation. I think another visit to Browning Hall will be necessary. On this occasion, I suggest you have specific questions to which you require answers.'

'Such as, Father?' Sarah asked, aware that he was not impressed by the paucity of information they had acquired.

'Well,' he said, 'two obvious matters come to mind. Firstly, who are Sir Charles's bankers? If the man is alive, he'll need money. Secondly, does Lady Browning know of anyone who might wish her husband harm? Few of us are able to go through life without making enemies of one kind or another.'

'Of course!' James exclaimed. 'His banker would know if he has drawn funds from his account, and if so, whether the amounts have been unusual.'

'Not only drawn funds,' Matthew said, 'but he may have deposited them. Any activity on the account—or none—could be significant.'

James agreed. 'Indeed, it could be helpful, sir, to know if he has deposited a large sum. If he has, this could indicate that he had a run of luck at the tables. If he left a gambling club with a large amount of currency on his person, he would be ripe for the picking.'

'And you are correct, Father,' Sarah said, 'that if he is alive, he will need money to meet even ordinary expenses. I think Celia said her husband banked with Thomas Coutts in the Strand.'

'I'll call on Mr Coutts tomorrow,' Matthew declared. 'He is a very old man now—he must be almost eighty—but I have banked with him for some years. He may be prepared to let me have the information we need.'

Sarah frowned. 'I should have asked Celia what friends or acquaintances they made during their sojourn in town. She is naïve and innocent, but she may have noticed someone who acted towards them in a suspicious manner. They may have asked too many questions about their movements and so on.'

Matthew smiled. 'You are beginning to understand the basics of research into a crime, my dear. The skill is in knowing the most important questions to ask and then asking them in the most appropriate way to the most likely sources of information. I would hazard a guess that the landlord of the village inn would know as much about the Browning family as anyone. Servants and labourers would gossip at the inn, and the landlord would overhear a great deal. And servants, of course, are a rich source of information. I have noticed in my limited social contacts with the nobility that they completely ignore the presence of servants. Footmen, coachmen, maids—they all overhear conversations that are conducted in their presence as if they were made of stone.'

'It is clear, Father, that we should return to Browning Hall as soon as possible,' Sarah said decisively. Then she asked, 'Would it be possible for Mr Brewster to accompany me again?'

His daughter's request did not surprise Matthew Kedron. He found the young man's quiet confidence and amiable manner admirable. He would be a valuable colleague for Sarah in her investigation. 'Well, I suppose I can spare him for another day,' he said with a gentle smile.

With great courtesy, James said, 'If you wish me to accompany you, Miss Kedron, I shall be most pleased to. But could we wait a day? I need to seek a meeting with Captain Fanshaw, the gentleman who recommended the tailor to Sir Charles. Apparently, he is in the Royal Artillery and their barracks are in Woolwich. I'm planning to hire a shallop and travel there on the river. I understand the journey is about two hours each way from London Bridge. Perhaps the good captain will have significant information to impart.'

At this moment, the housekeeper entered with a letter, interrupting the conversation. 'Excuse me, sir,' she said, 'but this was delivered by messenger for Miss Sarah. And there is a large parcel. Could be a picture. Don't know where we can hang it.' She handed Sarah the letter.

Sarah opened it. 'It's from Elizabeth Stockton. She's as good as her word. The parcel will be the portrait of Sir Charles.' She scanned the contents of the letter briefly, and then reported, 'She wants me to have luncheon with her tomorrow at Vauxhall. She has remembered something about Sir Charles that she thinks might be important.'

'That settles it then,' her father said. 'Your next visit to Browning Hall must wait until the day after tomorrow. I assume you will not be required at the theatre.'

'Not until my new play goes into rehearsal next week, Father. I have decided to resign from my various management responsibilities.'

'Ah! So you are about to become a full-time writer.'

Sarah smiled happily. 'Yes, Father. And I never dreamed that would happen. I thought that, at the most, writing would be little more than a pastime.'

James smiled. 'Don't forget, Miss Kedron, that you are also a detective now.'

'Only an occasional one, I hope, Mr Brewster, though I must confess that as an occupation it has its attractions. One never knows what one will discover.'

Contentedly enjoying his daughter's happiness, Matthew Kedron dabbed his lips with his napkin and rose from the table. The day's work had begun.

Fifteen

When Sarah arrived at Elizabeth Stockton's studio the next day, only a little after the appointed time, Elizabeth was already dressed and ready to go out. She answered the door to her apartment herself and warmly embraced Sarah. Women in the *ton* would have found her behaviour inappropriate on such a short acquaintance, but for Sarah, who spent her days with emotional actors and actresses, most of whom were usually desperate for admiration, affection and assurance, her behaviour was perfectly acceptable. Indeed, Sarah welcomed it, knowing that she was capable, even eager to respond in the same way. She was finding the necessity of maintaining formality with Mr Brewster rather a strain.

Neither woman had made any attempt to impress the other by means of fashionable clothes, but both wore ludicrous hats for the fun of it. Elizabeth's was broad brimmed, topped with a forest of feathers of various shapes, sizes and colours. Sarah's bore what amounted to a sculpture of twisted and knotted coloured ribbons.

As one, both women burst out, 'I love your hat!'

'Do you mind if I say we're so alike?' Elizabeth added. 'So much of fashion is ludicrous these days. I fear, though, that without it many women's lives would be completely empty. Goodness knows how they would fill the hours and have something to talk about.'

'There's always gossip,' Sarah said. 'And scandal and slander.'

'And accounts of the appalling behaviour of men,' Elizabeth added, laughing.

They left the apartment building and walked arm in arm towards the embankment.

Elizabeth said, 'I have been thinking of nothing else but how to paint you.'

'And I, Elizabeth,' Sarah rejoined, 'have been thinking not only of what you may be able to tell me about Sir Charles, but also how I can introduce a character as gentle and charming as you into a play. If you will forgive my saying so, I see you as the sensitive heroine beset with unhappiness because of your sensibilities. But I'm intrigued ... tell me, what set you on the path to becoming an artist?'

'Oh, I knew it was what I wanted to be when I was about fifteen,' Elizabeth told her. 'I was educated at home by a governess, and for a short time I had a visiting drawing master who encouraged me. He'd worked in the studios of a number of successful landscape artists and was attempting to make a living from his own work. He was finding it difficult, so he had acquired pupils. I was one. He believed I had ability and took a special interest in teaching me as much as he knew.' She paused and smiled with contentment. 'It was a great deal.'

'You lived at home?'

'Yes. Until I was eighteen. Then I went to Florence and lived with an Italian family for a year as a kind of governess-English tutor while I studied there.'

'An unusual education for a woman,' Sarah said.

'I had unusual parents.' Elizabeth began a little hesitantly but soon warmed to her narrative. 'My father was the master of an East Indiaman. I suspect he was also a privateer as we always seemed to have plenty of money. It is quite romantic being a pirate's daughter until one thinks about how they behaved. He was, of course, a kind of licensed pirate, encouraged by the government to sink as many French ships as he could and keep the spoils for himself and officers and crew. Anyway, I saw very little of him. He was away at sea most of the time. But he was a good husband to my mother in his way. He always made sure that his employer sent money to her regularly. We had a pretty cottage near Exeter in Devon. Then one day his ship was attacked by a French frigate. It sank with all hands. Our lives suddenly changed. I had to earn a living or marry. I could not bear the thought of marrying, of becoming dependent on a man, on anyone really. My father's employer, a merchant in Cheapside, was kind enough to provide me with an introduction to a periodical publisher he knew. I was fortunate in obtaining from him work as an engraver. I earned but a pittance, but I survived while I developed my ability as a portrait artist. But what about you? Your father is a famous man in some quarters.'

'I was also educated at home,' Sarah said. 'My mother died when I was three, and my father never remarried. Fortunately, he believed girls should receive as sound an education as boys. When I became too old for my governess, he looked for a boarding school to send me to. Being the kind of man he is, he visited every possible seminary within a hundred miles of London. He could not find one that he deemed acceptable, so he decided to start his own. He talked to friends and acquaintances—mostly authors and journalists—and invited them to send their daughters to his establishment. He began with eight girls between the ages of twelve and fifteen, and he engaged experts in the different subjects to tutor us.'

'How wonderful. And you were happy there?'

'We had one lesson a day on a different subject each day. The remainder of the time we spent in my father's library. He insisted that we read all the important authors.'

'And playwrights?' Elizabeth queried.

'When I was sixteen, he took me to the theatre for the first time. To Drury Lane. I saw a production of Mr Sheridan's *The School for Scandal*. It changed my life. I decided then that I would become a playwright, and from then on, I read every play I could lay my hands on. And, of course, I acted many roles to an audience of one in the mirror in my bedroom.'

Laughing, Elizabeth asked, 'When did you become a professional actress?'

'When I was seventeen, my father met Miss Jane Scott at a dinner, and he told her of my interest in the stage. She offered to accept me as an assistant to the stage manager at the San Pareil which she and her father owned and managed. I could not have had a better education as a playwright.'

'Oh, we are so alike, Sarah. We both live uncertain lives,' Elizabeth said.

'Painters and writers have to live with rejection, and so many are living in poverty. But we persevere despite all the disappointments and the many, many hours wasted on works that we cannot sell. And as women, of course, we are seriously disadvantaged. Men dominate my profession. You may not believe this, but the two women painters who were among the founding members of the Royal Academy of Arts were excluded from the group painting of all the founders.'

'Because they were women?'

With a snort of indignant laughter, Elizabeth said, 'The explanation given was that they were excluded because the painting also contained nude male models. It was considered indecorous for the women to be in the same painting as the models. Have you ever heard of such hypocrisy?'

'It does not surprise me,' Sarah said. 'And I have no doubt that every male member of the Royal Academy of Arts has a young mistress under his protection. It's what one would expect.'

They reached the embankment and looked for a jetty from which they could hire a wherry to take them across the river.

Elizabeth said, 'Do you find that women are deliberately excluded from the theatre as playwrights?'

'At one time I'm sure they were. And, of course, in the Elizabethan theatre there were not even actresses. Men played all the female roles. But the situation has been much better for the past fifty years or so. There are now dozens of women playwrights—many of them actresses as well. And thanks to Mrs Siddons—who is a great lady as well as actress—it is now almost respectable to be an actress. She has done so much by the example of her life to improve the position of the actress in society.'

'Women have always busily painted their little watercolours, of course,' Elizabeth said, 'but only for their personal amusement. I think this situation is changing slowly, though we still find it difficult to get our works exhibited.'

A ferryman hailed them, and they walked carefully down the steps into his boat. When they were settled, and the wherry was moving well against the strong current, Elizabeth exclaimed, blushing with embarrassment at her uncontrolled enthusiasm, 'I'm so enjoying myself, Sarah. It is such a pleasure being with you.'

'And I am enjoying your company, my dear.' Sarah squeezed her hand affectionately. She wanted to indicate that she appreciated her new friend's courage in expressing herself. She suspected that Elizabeth usually took care to hide her feelings in case they gave offence, seemed inappropriate or were too revealing of her emotions. Sarah thought that although they were about the same age, Elizabeth behaved more like a young girl than an adult woman living an independent life in what was very much a man's world. She felt protective towards her.

Sixteen

While Sarah lunched with Elizabeth Stockton, James travelled from London Bridge to Woolwich, a journey of just over two hours by the fastest boat available, a six-oar shallop. The amount of traffic was extraordinary, James thought, but the oarsmen maintained a steady pace through the congestion of boats, barges and sailing ships. As James's shallop approached the East India Docks, it slowed, and he watched a huge East Indiaman being unloaded. Stevedores and merchants lined the wharf where warehouses received all manner of goods from the Orient, the exotic aromas from which wafted across the water, almost masking the usual stench of pollution from the tanneries and the raw sewage discharged into the river.

During the short walk from the Woolwich jetty to the Royal Artillery barracks, James pondered the possibility that the officer could in some way be responsible for Sir Charles's disappearance. Frequent confrontations occurred at cards when one of the players accused another of cheating. A man could receive no greater insult, and as a matter of honour, the offended player had to demand satisfaction. To not do so was to admit to guilt.

Had there, perhaps, James wondered, been a quarrel between the two men, resulting in a duel in which the baronet had been killed and his body disposed of? Or perhaps he had just been wounded and left languishing unconscious somewhere and was alive but suffering from shame or amnesia.

As he walked, James debated with himself how best to approach Fanshaw. He finally settled for a note written on the back of his name card stating, 'In connection with Sir Charles Browning.'

When he presented the card to the sergeant on duty in the guard room and asked for it to be taken to the officer, the NCO said, 'Captain Fanshaw is the adjutant of the Second Battalion, sir. He took passage with the battalion to the West Indies three weeks ago. If you care to leave a letter for him, it will be forwarded with the next regimental mail.'

Hiding his disappointment, James thanked the sergeant and said he would have a letter posted to Captain Fanshaw the next day. Then, just as he turned away to leave the barracks, the sergeant said, 'It may not be of any interest to you, sir, but I understand that Captain Fanshaw has a wife and child in the neighbourhood.'

'Indeed!' James said. 'Do you have an address?'

'If you will excuse me, sir, I will look it up in the book.' Turning smartly, he marched into the guard room, emerging a few minutes later with a piece of paper, which he handed to James.

'Fourteen Crooms Hill, Greenwich, sir. The lady has a small school for girls. Some senior NCOs with families send their daughters there.'

'Thank you, sergeant. I'm most obliged to you.'

James knew that a letter to the West Indies would take at least a month, and any reply at least a further month; and this assumed that there were regular and frequent sailings. He would be fortunate to receive a reply in much less than three months. A promising lead had led him nowhere. But, while in the district, he had nothing to lose by calling on Mrs Fanshaw. The captain's wife could have information of value.

Without further delay he set out to walk the couple of miles to Greenwich.

Seventeen

Though in a respectable neighbourhood, Crooms Hill showed no evidence of wealth. The four-storey terraces were drab and poorly maintained and, James assumed, consisted mainly of rooms rented out to artisans and craftsmen employed in the arsenal and shipyards. A notice pinned to the door of number eleven stated simply *Mrs Fanshaw's School*. James knocked on the door.

Before long the door opened, revealing a woman of about thirty years of age, plainly dressed in a grey dress and a white lace bonnet.

She looked at James suspiciously. 'Yes?'

'Are you Mrs Fanshaw?' he asked. 'Captain Fanshaw's wife?'

'He has been posted abroad,' she snapped, then moved to close the door.

James put into practice lesson one of the journalist's craft. He inserted his foot in the doorway. 'I am calling on behalf of Lady Browning,' he declared. 'I understand Captain Fanshaw was acquainted with Sir Charles Browning.'

Considerably relieved—James suspected he had been mistaken for a debt collector—the woman said, 'I cannot talk to you now. I have children to attend to. There is a coffee shop around the corner. I will see you there in about half an hour.'

'Thank you, madam. I am obliged.' James bowed. 'I will await you there.'

He removed his foot from the door and walked away.

He knew little about the dame schools—of which many thousands dotted the country—except that they were usually single-teacher establishments conducted in the front room of the teacher's residence. The teachers were all women, often poorly educated, and either spinsters—and likely to remain so—or women whose men had died or deserted them, leaving them in poverty. The education they provided was rudimentary and consisted of spelling, a little handwriting, the simplest sums and basic needlework. Whereas there were proper schools for boys of all ages, the only education available for girls was in the few boarding seminaries for older girls or in the shilling or so a week dame schools for the younger ones.

The fact that Captain Fanshaw's wife was obviously short of money suggested that he found an officer's life beyond his means. Not only would his family have had to purchase his commission, but his army pay would barely cover the cost of his uniform and mess bills. Had he been in the cavalry, he would have had to pay for the purchase and maintenance of his horse.

James settled in the coffee shop with a hot chocolate and wondered, not for the first time, why any man in his right mind would decide on a career in the army. Unless they were fortunate enough to win a battle and relieve their dead or wounded enemies of their property, only men from wealthy families could enjoy the kind of life it had to offer.

He did not have to wait more than a few minutes for Mrs Fanshaw and guessed that she'd decided to send the children home early or had left them in the care of a servant girl. Sir Charles Browning's name had clearly meant something to her.

She accepted his offer of refreshment, and thinking she looked in need of nourishment, he ordered a hot chocolate for her. He wondered if she had been just a temporary 'wife' for Captain Fanshaw and that he had abandoned her. It was not unusual for army officers to behave in this way.

He said, 'I am sure, madam, that you are missing your husband. Will he be overseas for long?'

'Several years.'

'May I inquire where he met Sir Charles?'

'In a coffee shop somewhere. You know how it is, sir. People talk to strangers in such places. Friendships are not uncommon from such beginnings.'

'Indeed.'

James thought the woman spoke well, which suggested she had received some education and may even have come from a respectable middle-class family. A young, innocent, romantic girl, he thought, had fallen for the splendours of an army uniform. She had then probably run away from home to be with him and now found herself cut off from her family and almost destitute. He wondered if any of the children in the school were hers.

'Did Captain Fanshaw know Sir Charles well?' he asked.

'They socialized occasionally.' She paused, then added—rather bitterly, James thought— 'My husband has an unmarried sister. He discovered that Sir Charles has a younger, unmarried brother. I think my husband hoped to establish a friendship between the families.'

James smiled. 'I understand.' He decided not to inform her that Edward Browning lived in Antigua. Instead he asked 'How did the two men spend their time together? Did they have mutual friends?'

'Why are you asking all these questions, sir? Are you a constable? A man from the Government?'

'I'm a journalist, madam. Sir Charles has disappeared. Lady Browning has asked me to try to find out what has happened to him.'

'Disappeared! That must be worrying for her. The poor lady.'

Mrs Fanshaw's hot chocolate arrived. She sipped it slowly for a few moments and then said, 'I understand my husband and Sir Charles went to a number of gambling clubs and such places.'

James felt a little surprised that the woman was prepared to talk to him. Then it occurred to him that she was probably doing so because she hoped to find out more about her husband's activities. He began to think that she had indeed been abandoned and made only a meagre living from her little school.

'And they gambled. And lost money,' James said.

'My husband had no money to lose. He acted only as a guide to Sir Charles, who wanted a tour of the gambling clubs. High and low. I don't know if he lost or won at the tables. I expect he lost. They usually do.'

'Did your husband tell you the names of the clubs they went to?'

'I can't remember most of them, but I know he mentioned a club called White's. My husband is not a member, but he had friends who are members and could have signed him in as a guest. Having a baronet with him would have helped.'

'Do you know why Sir Charles was interested in the gambling establishments?'

'My husband told me he was some kind of reformer and wanted to have personal experience of these clubs. For all I know, they visited brothels as well.'

James opened his card case, took out his card and offered it to Mrs Fanshaw. 'If you can remember any of the other clubs they went to, madam, I'd be most obliged if you would send me a note.'

Mrs Fanshaw looked at the card and frowned. 'You are from the police.'

'No, madam. *The Weekly Police News* is a wholly independent periodical. It is published by Kedron and Co., the publishers of *The Informer*.'

'I see.' She stood up. 'I have stayed long enough. I have children to attend to. Good day to you, sir.'

James remained in the coffee shop for a little longer and bought a pasty. He had a two-hour river journey ahead of him and was already hungry. He had not learned a great deal about Sir Charles but thought that the morning had not been completely wasted.

He had a dinner appointment later but decided to return to the office and inform Matthew Kedron what he had found so far, little though it was. He had one definite lead to follow up—White's—but he knew he would get no information from anyone there unless he had a contact. Matthew Kedron might know such a person, someone who contributed gossip items about activities in the club to *The Informer*.

His assumption proved correct.

'White's,' Matthew said, 'is one of the most luxurious and expensive clubs in London, probably in the world. It's one of the "golden halls" and membership is open only to men of wealth or political influence.'

'No doubt,' James said, 'the two go together.'

'That is certainly the case. Men who are unable to enjoy the benefits of such clubs as White's—dubious though in some respects they are—frequent the "copper hells" where it is equally easy to lose a fortune, though not in so large or salubrious surroundings. White's is the oldest of the gentleman's clubs and, along with Brooks's and Boodle's, well-known for the recklessness of its gamblers. Cards are preferred to dice, but White's also has a betting book that records details of bets placed by members. Perhaps it could be of interest to you.'

Matthew left his desk and moved to a shelf that housed back issues of *The Informer*. 'Last year we published an article on the betting book. We have a source of information in the club. Not a member, but one of the club servants.'

He sorted through the periodicals until he found the issue he was looking for. 'Here we are!' He opened it at the article in question. 'What do you think of these, James? "Mr Greville bets Lord Clanwilliam ten guineas that Lord Stewart will be married to Lady F. Vane in six months. Clanwilliam paid. Mr Mills bets Lieutenant General Mackenzie a pony that Lord Stewart goes to Vienna before he marries Lady Frances Vane. Mills paid. Lieutenant General Mackenzie bets Lord Yarmouth sixty guineas to fifty that the Duke of Cambridge has a child before the Duke of Clarence."'

'I'm surprised they do not have something more important to bet on,' James said.

'Oh, but they do.' Matthew scanned the article and found a different kind of bet. 'What about this one from 1809? "Lord Sefton bets Sir Joseph Copley fifty guineas that Lisbon and Cadiz will be in Bonaparte's possession on or before the first of April next. Copley paid."'

'How extraordinary! But would Sir Charles, as a visitor, have been allowed to make such bets?'

'That is most unlikely. But if there was a member prepared to guarantee payment of any gambling debts he incurred, he would have been welcomed at the tables.'

'He would surely not have been so foolish,' James said. 'From what we know of the man, he has no experience of cards.'

'I will make inquiries,' Matthew said. 'My source will be able to find out if anything of interest occurred during Sir Charles's visit to the club.'

He returned the periodical to the shelf, saying, as he did so, 'Are you attending dinner at Lincoln's Inn this evening?'

'I was planning to, sir.'

'I asked only in case you would be free to dine with Sarah and me. But we can do that another day.'

James was entered as a clerk at the Honourable Society of Lincoln's Inn, one of the four qualifying institutions for barristers in London. As such, he was required to eat twenty-four dinners a year at the Inn before he could be called to the Bar and commence his readership. Apart from the cost, which had at one time been a problem for him, but which he could now accommodate from his emoluments as editor of *The Weekly Police News*, he enjoyed the social encounters that the dinners provided. He mixed easily with most of the other students and was well thought of by several of the tutors.

Eighteen

Although content with his work as editor of *The Weekly Police News,* James was aware that the financial rewards from journalism, irrespective of how successful he might be, would be as nothing compared to the income he could expect as even a moderately successful barrister. But combining the two occupations was also a possibility: as a barrister he would be well qualified to write learnedly on new legislation and its implications.

James also benefitted from the experience of his mentor, one of the older gentlemen, a Mr Joshua Fielding, a pleasant and greatly experienced barrister, who had been practising in the criminal courts for almost twenty years. Impressed by James's ability and diligence, he invariably made himself available to the young man. He was one of the few men James had met in London whom he trusted.

That evening, James approached him as they filed out of the dining hall. 'Mr Fielding, sir, a good evening to you. I trust you are keeping well.'

Joshua Fielding halted and turned, a large smile lighting up his face as he recognized James. 'My dear boy, how good to see you. Come, we will drink a bumper.'

A short, round man with a comfortable belly and a drinker's complexion, he always wore a full wig, often at a rakish angle to indicate that he was in truth a jolly sort of fellow—an impression that belied his ruthless determination to win his cases. He led the way to his favourite public house in nearby Chancery Lane and ordered a bottle of claret. As soon as he had tasted the wine and pronounced it acceptable, he said, 'Well, James, this periodical of yours is the talk of the Bar.'

'It is hardly mine, sir. I am but the editor, much assisted by the proprietor, Mr Kedron.'

'A most interesting man. He should enter politics. Has he any new book in preparation?'

'I don't think so. He is too occupied with *The Informer*.'

'Very radical, James. Very radical. No doubt you are influenced by the gentleman.'

James's politics were as radical as his employer's, though he knew better than to advertise them at this stage of his career. Even as an undergraduate, he had been careful not to associate with the more extreme end of the radical movement.

The two men discussed several cases currently being heard at the Old Bailey, and then, halfway through the bottle, James said, 'Would it be impertinent, sir, and overly presumptuous, if I sought your advice on a confidential matter?'

Joshua Fielding beamed. He liked nothing better than to be consulted. It provided him with an opportunity to hold forth at length without fear of interruption. 'I shall be delighted, dear boy.' Then, like a cloud passing over the sun, his face darkened. 'You are not in any sort of trouble, I trust. Or have fallen in love with a wholly unsuitable young woman. Which, I suppose, is the same thing.'

'It is nothing of a personal matter, sir. It concerns Sir Charles Browning.'

Succinctly, he explained the situation and completed his narrative saying, 'I was wondering, sir, if in your career, you had experienced anything similar.'

'No. It is most unusual. If he has not disappeared of his own free will, then we have to assume he has either committed suicide or been killed or abducted.'

'For the present we have discounted suicide,' James said. 'We know of no circumstance that would explain it.'

'Well, dear boy, I must not even consider offering an opinion based on such a paucity of information.'

'We have followed up all the leads we have,' James said, a little defensively.

'Then you must discover more leads. And if you are to make any progress with your investigation you need to have a strategy. I suggest you follow my own—it has stood me in good stead in preparing my advocacy—either to prosecute or to defend. A barrister, my boy, needs to be as fully informed as possible. He should know the background to every case. There is nothing more dangerous when cross-examining a witness than to ask a question to which one does not know the answer, or not know the questions that your opponent will ask and the answers he will receive to them. Knowledge, my boy, knowledge is the route to victory. And we are in this game to win. Is that not so?'

'Indeed it is. And what may I be permitted to ask, sir, is your strategy?'

'My rule of the four levels. It is essential, as a first step, to discover as much as possible about the victim—his or her character, circumstances and so on and so forth. This knowledge, unless the victim has suffered an opportunistic attack, such as a highway robbery gone wrong, will lead usually to the second circle, the victim's family. Women murder husbands or lovers; men murder wives or mistresses, and so on. Even patricide and fratricide are found, especially among the nobility and royalty.'

'Lady Augusta would agree with you, sir. She considers Sir Charles's disappearance to be no mystery. But what are the other levels?'

'Employees. At all levels. A footman may have stolen an item and taken steps to prevent being accused of the crime. A clerk may have been embezzling and done the same. With so many offences carrying the death penalty, criminals often take extreme action to prevent discovery. The criminal has nothing to lose, you see, by taking the murderous course of action. I believe the expression is "to be hung as a sheep as well as a lamb".'

'And the third level?'

'Rivals and competitors of all kinds. Among these I include, where the male sex is concerned, acquaintances who have been, or believe they have been, insulted and their honour impugned. Though illegal, duelling is still not uncommon, especially among the gentry, whose sense of honour is often exaggerated. Women, of course, have their own means of destroying a rival—death by a thousand lies. A reputation thoroughly besmirched.'

'This is fascinating, sir. And the fourth level?'

'Surprisingly, where serious crime is involved, it is the least likely. Most thieves and robbers, especially the professionals, take great pains to get away with their loot without seriously wounding their victims. A prostitute, for example, will rarely murder to obtain the purse of her client. She has other means of lifting it without getting caught in the act.'

Pleased with his exposition, Joshua Fielding chortled. 'There, my boy. A strategy for you in a nutshell. Begin with the family, and then move through the levels until you end up with strangers. In my experience, the victim of a murder usually knows his assailant. And, perhaps, to coin an expression, it is a good idea to "follow the money". Now I suggest we sink another bottle. The most attractive quality of a good wine is that it never satisfies one's thirst!'

Nineteen

The matter most on Elizabeth Stockton's mind during lunch at a fashionable pastry-cook shop in the Strand was Sarah's portrait.

'I shall need at least five sittings to do you justice,' Elizabeth said. 'The light in my studio is at its best in the mornings when the sun is still rising from the east. May I suggest two hours from ten until midday?'

'I shall be honoured to sit for you,' Sarah replied, 'but at the moment, I cannot confirm on which days I shall have responsibilities at the theatre.'

She did not add that investigating the disappearance of Sir Charles would probably also make considerable demands on her time.

'I can wait for your convenience,' Elizabeth said. 'I have no other commissions at present, and I can occupy myself tidying my studio. Now, the next thing to decide is what you will wear.'

'I confess I have not given it any thought.'

'Do you have a favourite gown?'

Sarah shook her head. She rarely bought clothes. The wardrobe at the theatre was extensive. She could always borrow from it whenever she needed something for a special occasion, such as a first night of a new play when she would be required to respond to the shouts of 'Author! Author!' from the audience—or if not from them, from members of the cast.

'A favourite fictional character then,' Elizabeth suggested.

Immediately Sarah knew how she wanted to be dressed: as Lady Teazle in *The School for Scandal*. An appropriate choice for many reasons.

'Do you know Lady Teazle?' she asked, a smile creeping across her face. Wagging a finger at an imaginary Sir Peter Teazle, she declared, 'Sir Peter, you may bear it or not as you please; but I ought to have my own way in everything, and what is more, I will, too. What! Though I was educated in the country, I know well that women of fashion in London are accountable to nobody after they are married. … If you wanted authority over me, you should have adopted me; I'm sure you were old enough.'

Elizabeth clapped her hands and exclaimed delightedly, 'Bravo! A performance for my own special benefit. How fortunate I am. And you have the costume?'

'I can obtain it. And the wig. And the make-up. I have never performed the role, but I have always wanted to.'

Elizabeth put down her knife and laid a hand on Sarah's arm. 'Sarah, do we both share Lady Teazle's philosophy?'

'A large part of it,' Sarah agreed. 'And I'm sure it is a subject we shall no doubt discuss at length another time, even though we do not have husbands to apply it to. But now I need to know what you have remembered about Sir Charles.'

Elizabeth shrugged, trying not to show her disappointment at the change of subject. 'Perhaps it is nothing of significance,' she said. 'You may already be aware of it. I can tell you only that he expressed very radical opinions, unusual, I'm sure, in a member of the gentry. He also mentioned that he intended standing for Parliament should there be an election.'

'Interesting,' Sarah said. 'Thank you. Did he give any details about his plans?'

'I have to confess that I listened with only half an ear, concentrating as I was on my work. But he said something about Parliament needing to be reformed. I think he called the electorate in which he lives a rotten borough.'

Sarah remembered her father holding forth, as was his wont, about the disgrace of the rotten boroughs. These were constituencies with so few eligible voters, most of whose votes could be purchased for a few pounds, that the seat was for all practical purposes the gift of the lord of the manor. In *The Informer*, Matthew frequently agitated editorially for electoral reform—another reason why the Home Secretary thought highly of him.

'That could be very significant indeed,' Sarah said. 'Did Sir Charles indicate which political party he supported?'

'If he did, I did not take it in. I'm so sorry.'

'There's nothing to apologize for. How were you to know that you would be interrogated about him?'

Elizabeth smiled gratefully and moved on to the matter that was of much greater interest to her than Sir Charles's political affiliation. She was anxious to know more about Sarah's private life, in particular whether she presently had a serious interest in any man.

Sarah assured her that she had not. 'I'm much too busy to concern myself with romance and the possibility of marriage. Indeed, there is nothing further from my mind than the idea of marriage. I have worked hard to establish my independence. Why should I sacrifice that for life with a man who will as likely as not take a mistress when he soon tires of me and for whom I will be little more than a child-bearing service?'

'You don't believe in happy, loving marriages?' Elizabeth asked, probing as deeply as she dared.

'Oh, they can exist. My father and mother were happy, I believe, but he is an exceptionally good man. And, of course, my mother died young. No, my dear, I will manage very well without having a man to control my life. But what about you?'

Elizabeth blushed slightly and took a little time to answer the question. Then quietly she said, 'I do not find men attractive, Sarah.' She stood, quickly adjusting her hat to hide her confusion and then said, 'But come. Let us go shopping. It is what women do, is it not?'

Sarah smiled. 'It is, indeed, my dear.'

She joined Elizabeth and took her arm.

As they walked towards Bond Street, where many of the most fashionable shops were, Sarah wondered to what extent Elizabeth preferred women to men. But she said nothing. She was not ready yet to enter into any serious exchange of confidences with Elizabeth, though she already knew that she wanted her as a close friend. Elizabeth was beautiful and lively, and there was something about her that Sarah found enchanting—perhaps mainly her honesty and dislike of all pretension.

At that moment an idea occurred to her. It would provide them both with an outing, she thought, and be a little harmless fun. At the same time, it would advance the investigation. She would suggest it to James the next time she saw him.

Twenty

That afternoon, Matthew Kedron took time off from his work on the next edition of *The Informer* and walked from his office in Paternoster Row to visit Thomas Coutts's bank in the Strand. At last, the sun had broken through the clouds to bring a hint of summer. Despite the preceding days being dull and overcast, no rain had fallen so the traffic still sent up billows of dirt and dust, much of it being dried horse dung.

Thomas Coutts himself, though elderly, attended the bank every day to ensure that all was well. He also enjoyed welcoming his many aristocratic clients, some of whom were of the highest social position. His quiet boast was that he was the banker to some of the nation's most influential personages.

Matthew was not among this illustrious number but, nevertheless, he was a respected customer. Thomas Coutts admired his reforming beliefs in so far as they did not conflict with what the banker considered to be the natural pursuit of profit. Accordingly, when Matthew presented his card to one of the clerks, he was immediately conducted to Mr Coutts's office.

'Mr Kedron, welcome,' the frail old man exclaimed, half rising from his chair behind a large desk completely free of all documents and ledgers. 'Your business is prospering, and deservedly so. *The Weekly Police News* is an excellent publication. I was discussing it with Viscount Sidmouth, the Home Secretary, only the other day. I am sure you are aware that many are pressing him to recruit more constables in the city and organise them into a proper police institution. An uphill struggle, but its time will come. In what way may I be of service to you, Mr Kedron? We are always prepared to consider an accommodation to such as your good self.'

'I have an unusual request, Mr Coutts,' Matthew said. 'It concerns Sir Charles Browning. I fully appreciate the necessity of confidentiality, but it is most important that I know whether there has been any activity on his accounts with you.'

'That is indeed an unusual request, sir,' Thomas Coutts said. 'May I ask the reason for it?'

'Of course. The nub of it is, sir, that Sir Charles has disappeared. His wife, Lady Browning, has neither seen nor heard anything from or of him for a month. She is naturally distraught.'

'Is a kidnapping suspected? A ransom demanded?'

'No ransom has been requested as yet. My daughter, assisted by Mr Brewster, the editor of *The Weekly Police News*, is making inquiries on Lady Browning's behalf. We need to know only whether Sir Charles has either drawn or deposited money recently. If he has, that will suggest that he is alive and is not the victim of foul play.'

'Precisely. Well, sir,' Thomas Coutts said, 'this is not the kind of information we would usually reveal to any inquirer, but I have no hesitation in being of assistance to you.'

He rang a small silver bell on his desk. The door soon opened, and a clerk appeared.

'Bring the ledger for Sir Charles Browning,' Mr Coutts commanded. The clerk bowed and hurried away to do his bidding.

'Do you have any possible explanations for Sir Charles's disappearance?' the banker asked.

Matthew shook his head. 'There are many possibilities, but we have no preference for any of them. We are at the beginning of our investigation and trust information will come to hand that throws some light on the situation. Our worst fear, of course, is that he has been murdered. The city is averaging about thirty convictions for murder a year at present. That figure does not include, of course, all the murders for which suspects have not been brought to trial for lack of evidence or for which no likely offender has been named. And people are disappearing all the time. If Sir Charles has disappeared of his own free will for some reason, he could be anywhere. The colonies are full of men who do not want to be found.'

'Quite,' the elderly banker agreed, nodding his head sagely.

'Especially worrying,' Matthew continued, 'is the increasing number of murders connected with life assurance. This situation will continue until there is legislation making it impossible to take out a policy on a person with whom one does not have a family connection. As you will be aware, sir, as things are, one can take out a life policy on anyone.'

'Another recent development, sir, is robbery from bank messengers in broad daylight,' Mr Coutts exclaimed. 'Numbered bank notes or bearer bonds are the preferred items. A person acting on behalf of the thieves—often it is believed to be an attorney of the worst kind—then negotiates the return of the stolen property for a reward. It is most troubling.'

The arrival of the clerk with a ledger interrupted further complaint. Thomas Coutts soon found the appropriate page.

'Interesting,' he said. 'There has been no activity on the account since May fourth—over a month ago. No withdrawals. No deposits.' He smiled wryly. 'Somebody must be feeding Sir Charles if he is alive.'

'I see. Would it be possible for you to inform me if there is any change to this situation?'

'Most certainly, I will. Have you the reported the matter to the constables?'

'Not yet. They do not have the training or the resources to deal with a case of this nature. I am anxious, also, not to—shall I say—muddy the waters with a clumsy investigation.'

'Quite.'

The clock of the nearby church of St Mary Le Strand struck four. This being Mr Coutts's dinner time, and it being his most desired part of the day, he stood and offered Matthew his hand.

'It has been a pleasure to be of service to you, Mr Kedron. Be assured that we shall watch Sir Charles's account with great diligence.'

Matthew shook the old man's hand, bowed and left the bank. Of only one thing was he confident: he now thought it most unlikely that Sir Charles had disappeared of his own free will unless he had committed suicide.

What was he living on? Matthew asked himself. He had almost certainly met with foul play unless he was living on borrowed money. And why he would do this when he was the owner of a substantial country property, it was difficult to understand. If he had left the country for the continent to avoid paying a gambling debt or for some other embarrassing reason, then why had he not sent a note to his wife to the effect that he was safe and that she need not worry? It would be strange and cruel behaviour to allow his young wife to suffer such anxiety.

The more Matthew thought about Sir Charles, the more likely he thought that the man had been murdered. Following on from his concern expressed to Mr Coutts, he wondered who might have taken out a life policy on the baronet. There were so many companies, large and small, genuine and fraudulent, that it would be difficult to trace the beneficiary of such a policy. And if such a person were traced, it would be difficult to prove that he—or she—was responsible for the death of the person insured.

Twenty-one

James and Sarah could not decide what to do next until breakfast the next morning. Sarah had been far from idle, however. The previous evening, she had spent much of her time at the theatre, putting together a collection of costumes, wigs, beards and make-up that she thought would be useful for their investigation. She had decided that it may be necessary for one or both of them to be incognito when questioning certain people. She thought that this should apply immediately to James during their next visit to Browning Hall.

When James concluded the account of his meeting with Mr Fielding, Sarah said, 'I'm sure he is absolutely correct in his assumptions. It is the first level we must attend to immediately. We have already agreed that we should make another visit to Browning Hall today. Can you drive a carriage and four, Mr Brewster?'

'I'm not an expert, but if the horses have been properly trained, I do not think I will have any problem on a turnpike. Cross-country could be a different matter.'

'Excellent. I'm sure my father will release you from your editorial responsibilities to be my coachman, and in such a guise you will drive me to Browning Hall, and then have a full day's gossip in the village. I suggest you pass yourself off as an ostler or groom or some such who is considering applying for a position at the hall. This will explain your curiosity about the family.'

James was far from pleased by Sarah's tone of voice. She seemed to think she was commanding a servant. He had not previously experienced her assertiveness, and as a reasonably senior employee, not a domestic servant or labourer, he resented her autocratic manner.

Speaking as calmly and lightly as he could, he said, 'I shall need different clothing, and even if differently dressed I fear the landlord of the inn may recognize me.'

In her next utterance, Sarah made James feel even more imposed upon. 'Not by the time I have finished with you, James,' she exclaimed with a laugh, and then realizing that she'd used his Christian name, she thought, *Oh, well, it had to happen sooner or later. I'd better deal with it.*

She said quickly, 'I hope you do not think it either forward or impertinent of me to address you in such a familiar way, but I am not used to formality with the people I work with—my colleagues in the theatre. And I do think of you as a colleague in this matter. But please do not read more into this than I intend. And I shall appreciate it if you will call me Sarah.'

'I am honoured, Sarah,' he said, considerably mollified. He now felt it would be ungracious to object to her plan. 'May I ask how you intend to disguise me?'

'Come with me. In the storeroom I have a basket of costumes I've brought home from the theatre. I think you will look splendid in a full black beard.'

While James sorted through the clothing and selected what a coachman would wear, Sarah went to the kitchen. Sitting at the table, she prepared a thick, black beard from the assortment of hair available. She also tested on the housekeeper, much to the woman's amusement, a stick of make-up that would create a ruddy, weather-beaten effect. The two women giggled with the fun of it all.

When James came in, fully attired as a coachman, Sarah controlled her giggles and exclaimed, 'The tradesman's entrance if you please, my man.'

Grinning, James rejoined in his best yokel's accent, 'I be damned if I will, missus. Not 'til I be behind that there beard.'

'Come and sit down then, James, and let's put it on. Mrs Wells can decide if it is an adequate disguise.'

The beard was a great success, and there was now nothing to delay their departure.

James asked, 'Is it correct for you to call on Lady Browning without warning or invitation?'

'I have thought about that. My instincts tell me that there is nothing to be lost by arriving unexpectedly. We are, when all is said, doing her a favour. She will hardly have any cause to complain.'

Accordingly, they left Portman Place half-an-hour later. Their coachman, fearing that his position was at risk, had argued that the horses might not respond to a strange hand, but a quick trip up and down the mews made it clear that James was a capable driver. Without further delay, with Sarah sitting back comfortably inside and James holding the reins, they set off for Browning Hall.

***

The journey passed uneventfully, and at each stop to rest the horses, they rehearsed and discussed the questions they would seek answers to at the hall and in the village. Then at the final stop just after passing through Langley, James said, if only for the pleasure of using her first name again, 'It isn't appropriate for your coachman to sit inside with you. I suggest we walk the horses for a while and then I will mount the lead horse before we arrive at Browning Hall.'

'James, that's very thoughtful of you. I'm sure you are right, but I am concerned for your safety.'

'As a boy I often rode bareback on an uncle's farm,' he said. 'I shall not have any difficulty, especially as there should not be anything that will frighten the horses. When we arrive, I will deposit you at the front entrance, wait until you are admitted, and then trot off to the village. I will put up at the inn and stable the horses there. I may get them re-shod. There is a blacksmith in the village.'

Sarah agreed, so he halted the carriage and moved to the lead horse.

When they arrived at Browning Hall, the gates were open, presumably, Sarah thought, because the gate-keeper had been dismissed. As the carriage moved through them, a horseman, riding as if all the devils from hell were after him, approached and raced by, his head down and turned away from them as if he were most anxious not to be recognized.

'He was in a hurry,' Sarah called to James.

'He was indeed. And he did not want us to know who he was, I'll wager. I wonder why.'

As conversation was difficult above the noise of the horses' hooves on the gravel drive and the rattle of the carriage, it was not until much later that they were able to discuss the behaviour of the horseman.

At the main entrance to the house, James dismounted and pulled the bell rope. Then he assisted Sarah to the ground. The housekeeper soon opened the door.

'Good day,' Sarah said. 'Please inform Lady Browning of my arrival and that I would be obliged if I could speak to her.'

'She's not too well, madam,' the housekeeper said, 'but I'm sure she will be happy to see you. Come in, if you please. You can wait in the library while she gets dressed.'

'I do hope her indisposition is nothing serious.'

'She frets, madam,' the housekeeper explained, closing the door and following Sarah into the house. She escorted her to the library, then hurried away to inform her mistress of Sarah Kedron's arrival.

James drove the carriage away, making a mental note to inquire in the village who the horseman could have been. There had to be a reason why he had been in such a hurry and had taken such care to hide his face.

Twenty-two

Sarah was not alone in the library for more than five minutes before the housekeeper returned.

'My lady apologies for keeping you waiting, madam,' she said. 'She will be with you soon. May I get you some refreshment?'

'Nothing for me, thank you, Mrs ...?'

'Williams, madam. Mrs Williams.'

'It must be lonely for you here now, Mrs Williams,' Sarah said, feeling her way into a conversation. 'I assume you have no one to talk to, all the other servants having left.'

'It does get lonely, I must admit. The house is like a grave. It is no mystery that my mistress keeps to her bedroom most of the time. Do you have news of Sir Charles?'

'I am afraid not.'

Sarah wondered to which member of the family the housekeeper felt the greatest loyalty. She remembered that Celia had mentioned the woman had been in the Browning family's service for over forty years. She would have known Charles and Edward as children. She could be a mine of information about the family.

'Do sit down, Mrs Williams,' she said with a smile. 'Perhaps we can pass the time in conversation.'

'You are most kind, madam. At my age, it is not good to spend too much time on my feet.'

The housekeeper perched precariously on the edge of a chair as if expecting any moment to have to leap to her feet.

Sarah, too, sat and said, 'That is much better.' Then deciding on what she thought would be a topic that would not arouse the woman's suspicions in any way, she said, 'Tell me about Sir Charles and his brother when they were boys. Were they close?'

'Inseparable, madam. Sir Charles is the eldest, of course. Edward is a year younger. A sickly child, hesitant in everything.' She shook her head. 'Lady Augusta adored him. A bit too much if you want my opinion. Sir Robert now, oh my goodness, that was another matter. He could not stand the sight of the boy. I suppose because he was such a disappointment. He would not ride to hounds, shoot, fish, do any of the things a normal boy will want to do. Spent all his time brooding and moping about the place. If it had not been for Sir Charles, the boy's life would have been a misery.'

'In what ways did Sir Charles help his younger brother?'

'They spent hours together, mostly just walking and talking. They both read a lot, and I suppose they talked about what they'd read. Edward liked to paint, and he'd go out with his little box of watercolours. Charles would go with him, book in hand. They would sit down by the canal. Usually with a picnic that cook had made for them. Edward would paint for hours while Charles read. And wrote too, I reckon. He always had a notebook and pencil with him.'

'Did they have a tutor?'

'At first. Then they were sent to boarding school. Different ones. Charles went to Eton. Edward to somewhere the name I forget. Twice Edward ran away. He wanted to be with Charles. He was soon found, of course, and given a thrashing by his father. His howls were something terrible.'

'That would not have pleased Lady Augusta.'

'She and Sir Robert did not get on, madam. It was not a happy home.'

'I suppose it was an arranged marriage,' Sarah said.

'No doubt, madam. And Sir Robert was not an easy man to get on with. Very stern. Unbending. Insisted on his own way in everything.'

'You think something must have happened to damage the marriage,' Sarah said.

'Oh, in truth, it never was a marriage. Right from the start, they lived their separate lives and barely spoke a word to one another. Lady Augusta was a spirited young woman and, no mistake, had a mind of her own.'

'You preferred her to Sir Robert?'

'We all did. Tragic the way she went down. Soon after Edward was sent to the West Indies. She missed him so. She was a great beauty in her time, you know. Sir Joshua Reynolds painted her the year she came out. We all reckoned she could have married a duke if she had set her mind to it.'

'But she had to settle for a minor barony,' Sarah said with a smile.

'That was probably part of it, but she loved the land, not the title.'

Celia's arrival interrupted further conversation, and Mrs Williams sprang to her feet in an instant.

Sarah rose to embrace Celia, saying, 'Mrs Williams has been entertaining me with a little local history. One of these days I must set a story in a small village. So much goes on.'

Holding Celia's hands, Sarah stood back to study her. She had obviously been crying. She looked pale, haggard and exhausted.

'I'm so sorry to keep you waiting, Sarah,' Celia said. 'I have not been sleeping well, and after being awake all night, I had fallen into a deep sleep. Is there any news?'

Before Sarah could reply, Celia turned to Mrs Williams, who hovered near the door. 'Bring us tea, please, Mrs Williams, and make up a room for Miss Kedron.' She turned to Sarah. 'Is Mr Brewster with you?'

'No. My coachman will stay in the village. The horses need shoeing.'

The housekeeper left. Celia took Sarah's hand and led her to a padded bench in the bay window, where they sat down.

'No news I'm afraid, Celia,' Sarah said. 'And this is my main reason for returning to Browning Hall. My father has suggested that the more we know about Sir Charles—his friends, habits, interests and so on—the more likely we are to discover what has happened to him and where he is. I'm sure you understand.'

Celia sniffed back tears and nodded. 'I understand. But what can I tell you?'

'Sir Charles disappeared while you were residing in London. Begin there. Tell me about your life there. And please, Celia, tell me what it was really like for you, not what you had hoped it would be.'

'But—'

'No buts, my dear. If I am to help you, I must know the truth.'

'If you must, though I don't see how—'

'Let me decide what is relevant and what is not. Now, tell me, did you enjoy your sojourn in London?'

After a long pause, Celia said, 'I hated it. I had been looking forward to it so much. Bath had been lovely. Everyone had been so friendly there. Charlie had cousins there. Girls of my own age. A great-uncle on his mother's side kept a haberdasher's establishment there. I felt comfortable and was made very welcome. London society was completely different.'

'You were not invited to things?'

'Oh, we were invited—balls, dinners, soirees, everything. But I was included under sufferance. It was Charlie people wanted to see. He was so popular. But no one wanted to see me again. Not one lady called or even left a card. It was as though I did not exist.'

Sarah touched her arm. 'My dear, I am so sorry.'

Now that the flood gates had opened, memories poured out of Celia. For so long she had been desperate for someone to confide in. She revealed to Sarah that the girls in the village she had grown up with now thought her too grand to remain close friends, yet there were no middle or upper-class young women in the neighbourhood to call on.

'After three weeks of it,' she explained, 'I wanted to return home, but Charlie had leased the house for the season and he was enjoying London so much. It wasn't the *ton* he liked. He thought all the dandies, and especially what he called the macaronis, were awful. "Empty headed, vain and shallow" was how he described them. It was the writers he liked and the men from the universities. And his favourite place was the British Library. Charlie told me that the king had given it all his books, thousands and thousands of them. And anyone could go there to read. He also spent a lot of time in the Chapter Coffee House where writers liked to meet. And he attended lectures, especially those at the Royal Society at Somerset House. And there was a sort of club calling itself The London Abolition Society. They met at different public houses and coffee shops and talked about politics and, you know, reform. I don't know much about them.'

Sarah had heard of The London Abolition Society but knew only that its members wanted to abolish slavery. She thought that her father would be fully informed about it. He might even be a member.

'And while Sir Charles was having the time of his life, you were left at home.'

'Yes. I know he felt sorry for me, but what could he do? He was so enjoying himself. I just put on a brave face, you know, for him.'

'He was not angry with you because you were not, well, being accepted by the other women?'

'Oh no. That is, I don't think so. He was always considerate and sympathetic. He just said that I should try to be patient as we would be going home before long.'

'Did he make any special friends?'

'If he did, he did not introduce me to them or bring them home. It was as though he were leading a completely separate life from me.'

'But you did attend some functions.'

'At first. But then we stopped going to anything that Charlie was not really interested in. But we went to all kinds of places together for a while: Vauxhall Gardens, Ranelagh. Oh, and we went to Almack's several times. That was interesting. We danced and had supper and listened to the music. And there were people there who weren't too grand. We met a friendly couple and ate supper with them. And the next day I went shopping with her.'

'Can you remember their names, or the names of any of the people you met?'

'Her name was Frances. Yes, that's right, Frances Wetherby. I think her husband's name is Arthur.'

'What about the people to whom you were introduced at dinners and balls?'

'Oh, it was always Lady this and Lady that. Sir this and Lord that. I forgot them within seconds of being told them.'

'Have you seen Frances Wetherby since? Do you have her address?'

'No. Silly of me. I never asked. I was afraid of seeming too forward, you see. And she never asked me where we lived away from London. I think they lived somewhere south of the river.'

'Did they know you were titled, Celia?'

'I don't think Mr Wetherby knew. I mentioned it to Fanny, that is Mrs Wetherby, but she promised not to tell her husband. Charlie told me he wanted to meet some ordinary people. He wanted to get their opinions about things. You know, politics and all that kind of thing.'

Sarah knew that her next question would probably be painful to Celia, but she had to ask it. 'Celia, I must know the answer to this question. Was there another woman in Sir Charles's life? A mistress?'

Celia bit her lip and remained silent for a few moments. Then she said, 'There could have been. He was out such a lot without me. And there was the one occasion when I smelt another woman on him.'

'Did you say anything to him about it?'

'No. What could I do if he had been with another woman? Even if he had a mistress and was keeping her? It is what men do. Sarah, believe me, I did not want to lose Charlie. I love him, and if he had been tempted, then it was for me to accept and forgive. London is full of … loose women,' she said, avoiding the word prostitute, 'and many of them are very attractive to men, much more attractive than their wives.'

Sarah found it easy to understand how Celia felt and what her existence had been like during their stay in London. She was pretty and sweet in her way, but she spoke with such a strong Hertfordshire accent that society ladies would have found her difficult to understand at times. She had had little education and knew nothing about art, music, literature or the theatre. Neither was she interested or knowledgeable about politics—clearly her husband's passion. And she had no idea how to dress for a formal or even an informal London social occasion. In short, the society women would not have wanted anything to do with her.

Although Sir Charles would have been invited to various functions and events because of his good looks, breeding, education and barony, he would have been happier among the kind of society that Sarah and her father preferred—mostly men and women interested in politics and the arts but with little money or social aspirations.

'Everything you have told me has been most helpful,' Sarah said. 'I'm sure I can contact some of the men he met in London. Did you know he was having his portrait painted?'

Celia's eyes opened wide, and her mouth dropped open.

'My dear, there's nothing to worry about. It was almost certainly as a surprise present for you. The artist assures me it is a good likeness, and I have borrowed it. I'm having prints made from it to show around at the places he may have attended. If you can remember any of the addresses, that would be most helpful.'

She smiled and took Celia's hand. 'Just one more question. His brother, Edward. They were close, you said.'

'Very.'

'But he lives abroad. In Antigua.'

Celia nodded, but a frown formed on her forehead.

'Are there letters from him to his brother?'

Celia shook her head. 'They were close when they were children, young men, but now … Oh, Sarah, I don't know what happened between them, but they are, what is the word?'

'Estranged?'

'Yes, yes. They are estranged. I did not know Edward at all. He left home before Charlie and I were married. Charlie never talked about him, and I did not like to ask what had happened between them. Everything I know I heard from

Mrs Williams. She said that when Edward announced he was leaving for the West Indies to make a life for himself as a planter there, Charlie was horrified. He objected strongly. He did not want Edward to go. That's all I know.'

'No letters from him?'

'Not as far as I know. I believe it was a terrible quarrel.'

'How did Lady Augusta respond to that?'

'I don't know. She refuses to have anything to do with me.'

Celia began to cry, and Sarah realized that the time had come to bring the questioning to an end. Somewhere among all the information she had gleaned there would be indications of where to continue the investigation.

'Now, my dear, you are looking tired after your sleepless night,' Sarah said. 'I suggest you rest. Perhaps I may enjoy browsing the library. It may tell me more about Sir Charles. We can talk more at dinner.'

'Yes, I would like to rest. Thank you.'

'Good. Oh, just one more thing. As my carriage was coming through the gate, we were passed by a man riding like the wind. I hope he was not a thief making his escape.'

A blush crept slowly across the pallor of Celia's face, turning it a bright shade of pink. Flustered, she said, 'Oh, no. No, no. Nothing like that. It was just someone delivering something from the village for Mrs Williams. That's all. Nothing important. Something for Mrs Williams.'

'That's all right, then,' Sarah said, thinking how strange it was that Celia was, apparently, capable of noting the comings and goings of errand boys while asleep.

It occurred to her that the horseman riding by could be the clue they needed. She hoped that James would be able to establish the rider's identity.

Twenty-three

As soon as Sarah had been admitted to Browning Hall, James drove to the village. There he left the horses and carriage with the blacksmith. Then walked through the village to the George and Dragon, which was the larger of the two inns and looked as if it had at least basic accommodation and stabling. The time was still early afternoon, and the only drinkers were a few old men nursing their tankards while they half dozed or played desultory games of draughts or dominoes. One or two of them looked up as he approached the bar, but they soon returned to their dreams or games. They had no interest in a stranger.

James decided that a broad London accent would probably be the safest. It was also the one he thought he knew best.

'Gotta bed for the night?' he asked the landlord.

'Two shillin'.'

When he appeared to be considering this, the landlord quickly added, 'Another shillin' gets you breakfast thrown in.'

'I'll take it. And an ale now.'

As the landlord pulled the ale, he asked, 'Going far?'

'There's a job goin' at the big 'ouse, I 'ear.'

'Could be. All the servants 'cept one 'ave been dismissed. No money. Squire's disappeared. Where you from, then?'

'Clerkenwell. A bleedin' good place to get out of.'

Having established sufficient credentials to start asking questions, he said, 'Wot they like, then, up at the 'all? Good to work for?'

'Sir Charles is all right. His wife's a village girl. 'Is father was a bastard, though. And 'is mother's crazy. 'As been for years.'

He pushed the full tankard towards James, who picked it up and downed the contents in a series of gurgles. Then he put the tankard back on the bar.

'Another. Good ale.' He wiped his mouth with the back of his sleeve, thoroughly enjoying his performance. *Sarah would be proud of me,* he thought. 'Any idea why the squire's gone missing?' he asked.

'Everyone in the village 'as an idea. Mostly rubbish. Murdered. Done a runner.'

'What d'you think? Oh, 'ave one on me.'

'Thanks.' The innkeeper drew himself an ale and prepared to give his opinion in considerable detail. 'Well now,' he said. 'If you want my opinion, it's all to do with the father, Sir Robert. You know what it says in the Bible: the sins of the father shall be visited on the sons a thousand times.'

'You're sayin' revenge for somefin' the squire's old man did?'

'Right. Two things. Sir Robert was a magistrate, see. One of the village lads, Jack Harness, got caught poaching and was taken before 'im. Sir Robert could 'ave dealt with it and given 'im a fine or a few years inside. But no, what did he do? He remanded the case to the Assizes at 'Ertford.'

'And they 'anged 'im?'

'Transported for seven years. Australia. It just weren't necessary. Sir Robert should've dealt with it. Bastard.'

'When was this?'

'Oh, it would've been 1808. About that.'

'And you're suggesting the lad's family's taken revenge?'

'Wouldn't surprise me. He's got a brother. George. Big fella. He'd get a few of the lads together. They'd do the highwayman act one dark night.'

The innkeeper pulled a hand across his throat. 'Just like that. Then bury him in the forest somewhere. Who's going to search it? Not the local constable, that's for sure. Lazy sod that 'e is.'

James nearly said, 'But Sir Charles went missing in London, didn't he?' and only just stopped himself in time. Instead he said, 'Makes a lot of sense.'

'Course it does. No one in the village is going to inform on George. Broke 'is mother's 'eart, it did. See, it weren't just that. There was the girl.'

'The girl?'

'Mary Short. Parlour maid at the 'all. Village girl. Sir Robert, 'e took a fancy to 'er, the bastard did. Got 'er pregnant. Gave 'er ten pounds to clear out. That's what she said, anyways. Could 'ave been another bloke, of course. A footman. Groom. There was plenty to choose from up there. She weren't no better than she ought to be.'

'What happened to her?'

'She went to London. S'far as I know, she 'ad the baby there.'

'Is 'er still there?'

'If 'er's still alive. She thought she'd get a place in London. But pregnant? An unmarried chit of a girl with a kid inside her? Not a chance.'

'When did this happen?'

'Must 'ave been about the same time Sir Robert did for Jack. I tell you, he was a right sod, that man.'

'What about Mary's family?'

'What could they do? They couldn't prove anything. They only 'ad 'er word for what 'appened. Sir Robert was their landlord. If he evicted them, where would they live? Her father couldn't work. Lost a leg in an accident on the estate. Her mother took in a bit of sewing and laundry, and that was just enough to keep them alive, no more. Mary 'as a brother, if 'e's still alive. At the time, 'e was away, fightin' in some bloody war.'

'Is he back in England now?'

'Could be. But he don't live 'ere. No one's seen 'im about.'

'What was he like?'

'Rough. Temper like a maddened bull. Not a man anyone wanted to cross. 'E'd 'ave killed a few Frenchies; I'd wager this pub on it.'

'Name?'

'Sam. Sam Short. Short by name, short by temper.'

'This is all very interesting,' James said. 'And what about Sir Charles? Chip off the old block?'

'Not on your life,' the innkeeper exclaimed. 'As decent a man as you can find. The tenants won't 'ear a word against 'im. 'E's a real gent. Gawd, if only they were all like 'im. It's a tragedy for the village that 'e's gone missing. Church is full every Sunday. Vicar leading prayers that 'e'll be found safe and sound. Another?'

James indicated that both their tankards should be refilled, but there was to be no more conversation with the innkeeper. The labourers were coming in from their day's work in the fields expecting to be served instantly.

Twenty-four

The next morning, a little after ten o'clock, James drove the carriage up to the entrance of Browning Hall as arranged. Sarah was ready to leave, and after a tearful farewell from Celia, she let him assist her into the carriage, whispering to him as he did, 'When we're through Langley, come and join me inside. I can take off your beard then.'

James did as he was bid, and half an hour later sat comfortably beside Sarah in the carriage. He then summarized his conversation with the landlord of the inn.

'There are at least two families in the village who have a reason for wishing to harm Sir Charles,' he began. 'In both cases, it would be as revenge for his father's behaviour. Sir Robert was not a popular man, and I don't think that his death was mourned by his tenants or the people of the village. The two families who suffered most from what I have gleaned so far are the family of a young poacher whom Sir Robert is held responsible for having transported to Australia and the family of a disgraced parlour maid whom, it is believed, Sir Robert seduced and got with child. I can establish when the poacher was transported, and I can probably discover whether he has completed his sentence and returned to England. As for the seduced girl, it is possible that her family may know where she is and what has happened to her and her child.'

'If one of the family intended to harm Sir Charles,' Sarah interjected, 'he would probably do so regardless of whether he knew where the girl is and the nature of her situation.'

James nodded. 'You could be right. But if she has recently died in a workhouse or prison, such an event would stimulate an act of revenge, would it not? Actually, the innkeeper didn't seem all that convinced Sir Robert had fathered the child. Apparently, the girl had a reputation for being less than chaste. He thought there could be several candidates for the fatherhood in the village.'

'Then we probably shouldn't waste too much time on her,' Sarah said. She then told him everything she had discovered.

'The most significant items, in my opinion,' she concluded, 'are Charlie's quarrel with his brother, his dislike—even contempt—for his father and everything he stood for, his less than affectionate relationship with his mother, Lady Augusta and—I regret to say this, James—the possibility that Celia has not been entirely frank with me. She lied about the man on horseback. I have no doubt of this. Why would she do such a thing unless she has a reason to dissemble? And if she has such a reason, what is it? And does it have any bearing on her husband's disappearance?'

'We shall not know the answer to these questions until we establish who the rider is,' James said. 'This must surely be an important line of inquiry. If there is evidence that Celia has lied to you, it changes everything. We must doubt the veracity of her entire story.'

Then he added thoughtfully, the possibility just occurring to him, 'I suppose it is not out of the question that it was Edward who seduced the maid, not his father. It would be an additional reason for the young man leaving and for the two brothers quarrelling.'

'But you were told—'

'We need to be careful, Sarah,' James interrupted, 'that we do not assume that everything we hear is the truth. You fear that Celia may be lying. My experience of the courts, slight though it is, suggests that in every case, civil or criminal, at least one person, and often several, are lying. Village gossip prefers to hold Sir Robert responsible as he is disliked far more than his son. The girl, having to blame someone, may have accused the father not the son for whom she may have had some affection, and who may by then have left the country. I need to check dates.'

Sarah frowned. 'You are right, James. I'm too trusting. It is also possible, of course, that my informant, Mrs Williams, has not been completely truthful. Her main loyalty, I suspect, may be to Lady Augusta. And goodness knows what is going on in that woman's mind.'

James nodded. 'Gossip, rumour, sick fantasy, deliberate falsifications—we must expect and be suspicious of them all. I certainly believe that we shall find at least part of the truth in the village. But there is still the possibility, the probability even, that the poster bearing Charles's likeness will produce a useful response.'

'Of course, I had almost forgotten that. Well, one thing is certain,' Sarah said, 'we are beginning to accumulate a surfeit of suspects! The problem, of course, is that the possibilities seem to be almost endless, and we are only at the beginning of our investigation. Who knows what we shall discover before we have finished!'

Twenty-five

While Sarah and James had been in Langley, Matthew Kedron had arranged for a poster bearing Sir Charles's likeness to be distributed to many of the places in the city that the baronet might have visited personally, or that were frequented by people who might have encountered him. Not everyone who was approached agreed to pin up the poster. Some who did accept it, so as not to give the impression that they did not wish to cooperate, tore it into pieces as soon as the messenger was out of sight. Many, however, were prepared to display it, and before the day was out, it could be seen in various gambling clubs, coffee houses, the more expensive brothels, bathhouses, bagnios, pawn-brokers and money-lenders, and the waiting rooms of the magistrates' courts. The text proclaimed simply that a reward would be paid for any information leading to the whereabouts of Sir Charles Browning and gave the address of *The Weekly Police News*.

Immediately on his arrival in London, James went to his office. A new issue of *The Weekly Police News* was due for press that evening, and he wanted to ensure that the contents were up to standard. He knew that his assistant was competent, but he took his own editorial responsibilities seriously.

When he presented himself to Matthew, his employer told him what he had arranged and then added, 'Most of the responses will be of no value, James, and many will be no more than deliberate attempts to obtain money by false pretences. Be suspicious of any demands for ransom. Kidnapping seems to be unknown; that is to say, other than the few occasions of child kidnapping, no cases have been reported during the past ten years.'

'Isn't that strange, sir?' James said. 'I would have thought it was a common crime.'

'If it is, it is never reported. And even if it were, the Runners would not be in a position to pursue any kind of inquiry. No, I suspect that potential kidnappers realize that the difficulty in collecting the ransom money is too great. No one will pay a ransom unless there is evidence that the victim is alive. To do so would be most foolish. To provide such evidence, the kidnapper would have to present himself at a certain place at a certain time accompanied by the victim. It would be a simple matter for even the Runners to lay a trap and achieve an arrest—or at the very least rescue the victim.'

'Could not a body part—an ear or a finger, say—be included with the ransom note?'

'Certainly, but they would prove nothing. Even if the part had markings that were peculiar to the victim, which would be unusual, they would not prove that they had been taken from a person who was still alive. No, I strongly suggest that you do not waste time on any demands for payment before the value of the information provided has been ascertained.' He smiled broadly. 'Excessive optimism is a characteristic of the criminal mind.'

James did not argue, especially as he was confident that Matthew Kedron would be aware of the latest crime statistics.

'So we concentrate on information from someone who claims to have seen Sir Charles, but does not demand immediate payment,' he said.

'That is all you can reasonably do. And try to obtain information about Sir Charles that cannot have been gleaned from the portrait. I deliberately instructed the engraver to include only the head and shoulders on the print. Sir Charles's height, weight, body shape, clothing and so on, cannot be assumed from the poster. We know that he is slim and of above average height. Try to give the impression that you believe him to be short and fat. If the informants agree with you, then you can be sure they have no knowledge of Sir Charles's whereabouts.'

'Very good, sir. It shall be done.'

James then returned to his office and spent the rest of the day and most of the night making changes to the editorial copy of *The Weekly Police News*. The changes were minor, but he was a perfectionist.

Sarah, who wanted to talk to Elizabeth Stockton without delay, hired a chair to Cheyne Walk. Elizabeth was at home and delighted to see her. As she had explained, she was between commissions and was passing the time making desultory attempts to tidy her studio. She embraced Sarah warmly and then immediately ordered tea, hoping for prolonged conversation.

When the two women were settled, Sarah came to the purpose of her visit. It concerned the idea she'd had at the end of their last meeting.

'I'm wondering, Elizabeth, if you would be able to do me a favour.'

'Oh, anything, Sarah.'

'It is in connection with Sir Charles. We are not making much progress in our investigation. I have spent more time at Browning Hall, talking to Lady Augusta Browning and, on this occasion, at length with her housekeeper, Mrs Williams. James Brewster has obtained possibly useful information from the landlord of the village inn. But there are other people I should question about the Browning family. I believe that I'm likely to enjoy a better reception from them if they do not think my questions have any connection with Sir Charles's disappearance.'

Possessing a quick intelligence, Elizabeth immediately understood Sarah's problem. She said, 'And you would like me to visit the village and glean as much gossip about the family as I can.'

'I thought we might go together,' Sarah replied. 'You in your persona as an artist, perhaps interested in sketching or making watercolours of the Norman church in the village. I would be your aunt and chaperone—an elderly, naturally inquisitive spinster who cannot control herself from asking questions.'

Elizabeth laughed delightedly. 'A character from one of Mary Robinson's novels,' she exclaimed.

Also laughing, Sarah said, 'And, I'm sure, one from a novel I shall write sometime in the future.'

'Oh, Sarah, your plan is wonderful. I cannot think of anything I would rather do more.'

She put her hand on Sarah's arms. 'But where would we stay?'

'I will write to the vicar of the little church. I think it's called St Andrews. He is a young man, and unmarried. I understand he was at university with Sir Charles and has been a close confidante. The vicarage is large, and I'm sure he would accommodate us for a day or two.' She smiled and added, 'He might even be willing to accept as payment a watercolour of his church.'

'Then if he agrees,' Elizabeth exclaimed excitedly, 'it is settled. Oh, what fun we shall have. I can just see you all dressed up as a maiden aunt! Hmm, I'm not at all religious, but deceiving a religious man doesn't seem right. What does Mr Brewster say?'

Sarah sighed. 'Why should he say anything?'

'It never does any harm to get a man's opinion; even if we then choose to ignore it. When shall we leave?'

'Just as soon as we receive a favourable reply to the letter, which, my dear, I think will be more appropriate coming from you. If the clergyman knows that you have been painting Sir Charles's portrait, this would be in your favour. You are correct, though. At least, I should let James know our plans.'

'I shall write the letter referring to you simply as "my companion", rather than "my maiden aunt", that allows us to change the plan should Mr Brewster take issue with the idea. Will he be our coachman?'

'Oh, yes. He has already been a success in the role.'

The two friends spent an enjoyable hour or so sorting through Elizabeth's somewhat idiosyncratic wardrobe.

Sarah began to feel a little guilty for treating the investigation of the baronet's disappearance as a game, but she argued with herself that this did not mean that she was not doing everything possible to help Celia find out what had happened to her husband. Games, she reasoned, could be played seriously.

Twenty-six

James fell asleep at his desk shortly after midnight. He slept until the clatter of the night-soil man pushing his small trolley to the privy awakened him. A nearby clock struck five. James got to his feet, walked to a sideboard, poured water from the jug into a basin and splashed a little onto his face to freshen it. He was still tired but even more hungry than tired. He'd been so concentrated on his work the previous evening that he had forgone supper. He decided to walk from Paternoster Row to Covent Garden where there were market stalls which sold all kinds of hot food to the merchants and costermongers. After breakfast, he would go to his rented room nearby and change his shirt.

To his surprise, on his return to the office about two hours later, a long line of poorly dressed men and women of all ages confronted him—not a few of whom where the worse for drink. For a moment, he wondered what they were doing lined up outside the office at such an hour. Surely, they could not all be anxious to purchase the latest edition of *The Weekly Police News*. Then, his mind clearing from its usual early morning confusion, he realized who they were and what they wanted: respondents to the poster concerning Sir Charles.

Before he could be accosted, he hurried into the office, closing the door firmly behind him. Once inside, he was amazed to see two of the clerks attending to piles of letters.

'We have no small cash left, sir,' one of them declared. 'We have had to pay the postage on every one of these letters. And we have been advised that there will be more to come in a later delivery.'

Neither Matthew nor James had taken into consideration the cost of receiving letters. James wondered how his employer would react to this expenditure. It could amount to a month's wages for a clerk, depending on how many hundreds of letters they accepted. And the problem was, he realized, that they would have to accept them all in case one or more of the letters they declined contained the information they sought.

He considered whether to instruct the clerks to divide the letters into two piles: one pile for those of possible interest and one pile for those of none. But then he realized that at this stage he did not know what the selection criteria should be. He needed to read at least some of the letters before making such a decision. That would take time.

And there were all the people waiting outside. He had no doubt that as every minute passed the line would grow longer and longer. At his door he turned and said to one of the clerks, 'Tell the people outside I'll start seeing them in ten minutes.'

He sat at his desk and began to look quickly through the letters. It soon became obvious that most, if not all of them, would have nothing to offer. Badly written, the simple message of most of them was along the lines of 'I saw this man yesterday. A shilling will tell you where.'

London was full of old, sick and destitute men and women with no means of support or of earning a living. And many idle young men preferred to cadge and sponge rather than seek brutal and poorly paid labouring work of various kinds. And to the thousands of prostitutes who plied their trade in the streets for a coin or two—a shilling in a filthy room, six pence in a lane—the possibility of earning at least twice this sum for an invented tale about a missing gentleman would be too attractive to pass by.

James was not looking forward to his day, especially as he had other work to do. To aggravate his mood, the black pudding he had eaten at the market was giving him fierce indigestion and might well cause even more discomfort later. He would need to be within a few minutes' walk of a privy. He felt irritated, therefore, when one of the clerks opened the door and an elderly woman strode in.

'I'm sorry, sir,' the clerk said, 'but the lady insisted on seeing you. She is a relative of Mr Kedron. She said you would want to see her.'

James studied the woman. She was in her fifties, he assumed, and respectably dressed in an overcoat and bonnet. She wore a pince-nez attached to a black silken thread and carried an umbrella—as much a weapon, he thought, as a protection against rain.

He half rose from his chair. 'Please be seated, madam, and tell me what I can do for you. Mr Kedron does not attend his office until ten. Perhaps you would care to wait in his room or return later.'

In an abrupt and commanding voice, the woman said, 'Don't you recognize me, James?'

'Recognize you?'

The woman took off her bonnet and let her pince-nez drop down onto her coat. She shook her head, and her long hair fell to her shoulders.

'Sarah!'

'Who else? Do you like my disguise?'

'I do not understand. Why are you—?'

'We are returning to Hertfordshire. Elizabeth Stockton will accompany us. She will be an artist, interested in sketching historic churches. I shall be her aunt, collecting information for an essay I'm writing on life in an English village in these changing times. You will be the coachman as before. We shall make further inquiries in the village.' She clapped her hands happily. 'We shall depart as soon as Elizabeth receives a reply from the vicar of the church, agreeing to offer us accommodation. Isn't it such fun?'

Barely controlling his anger at her assumption that he was again expected to put his work on hold to be a pawn in her little game, James said through clenched teeth, 'And I suppose I'm again to be the bearded yokel?'

'Your performance was exemplary,' Sarah replied, insensitive to his feelings, so carried away was she by her enthusiasm for her project. With a laugh she added, 'And should you ever require a change of profession, be assured the theatre will welcome you.'

James thought about all the letters he had to read and all the people he had to interview. His stomach churned, and he felt the acid rise in his throat. He told himself that Sarah was behaving like a spoilt and impulsive child, that she was not treating him like a colleague in the investigation, and that she was a slave to her imagination.

'I shall not be accompanying you,' he said coldly.

'Of course you will.' Her voice had a sharp edge to it, which did nothing to alleviate his irritation.

He got to his feet. 'I shall do nothing of the kind. I have better things to do than indulge in pointless charades. You forget that I am a senior employee of your father's business, not a menial to be instructed to do this and that.'

Unused to such opposition to her wishes, Sarah got quickly to her feet, her mouth tight and her eyes blazing. 'How dare you speak to me like that!'

'I dare to speak the truth,' he said, speaking slowly now and barely managing to keep anger and insolence out of his voice. 'I can see no possible justification for this act of dishonesty towards the cleric, especially if he is, as you say, a confidant of Sir Charles. I would have thought that he would have been more disposed to communicate what he knows about Sir Charles and his family to the person who is actively assisting Lady Browning than to an elderly busybody who is, as far as he is aware, a stranger to him and to the Browning family.'

'Furthermore, though the investigation into Sir Charles's disappearance may be fun and a game to you and your new friend, to me it is an unwelcome chore that interferes with the performance of the duties for which I am employed. I am the editor of *The Weekly Police News*, Sarah, not a police spy. And now, if you will excuse me, I will resume my work.' He stood and walked to open the door.

This is what comes from being too informal, Sarah thought, breathing heavily to control her temper. *He is taking advantage of my good nature. Very well, if that is what he wants.*

'I shall not require your assistance in future in the matter of Sir Charles's disappearance,' she declared acidly. 'Not for one minute did I think that you would ever behave towards me in this way.' Without giving him another glance, she strode out of his room.

James returned to his desk and sighed heavily. Not only did he feel angry but also the quarrel, brief though it had been, deeply distressed him. He knew it was its intensity, not its duration, that was important. He had grievously offended Sarah. Instead of quietly excusing himself from accompanying her and explaining that he needed to attend to all the letters and the people lined up outside, he had insulted her. He had allowed his emotions to overcome his good manners and sense of propriety. And she was his employer's daughter. If she complained to her father, it was possible that Matthew Kedron, who adored her, would decide that he had no option but to dismiss him from his employment.

James knew he was a good editor, as good as Matthew would be able to find, but he would not be irreplaceable. London was full of journalists who would apply for his position should it become vacant. He felt sure that his outburst had put his career in jeopardy.

The question was, what, if anything should he do? He had his pride, and he would not be able to bring himself to grovel to Sarah, to beg forgiveness, even to admit to being wrong. The problem being that he had not been in the wrong. He had been correct in his accusation. She was playing a game, acting out the imagined plot of a novel or play, indulging in being a detective, even giving Elizabeth Stockton, whom she had only recently met, a part to play. She had assumed total charge of the investigation and allocated him the role of doing little more than moving the scenery and sweeping the stage as required. They were supposed to be colleagues, he told himself, but clearly that was not how she regarded him. Rather she saw him as her assistant, available, regardless of his other responsibilities, at her beck and call.

Round and round in his head went the arguments for and against the stand he had taken, and all the while, he knew that more letters would be arriving, and more people would be joining the line outside. He wanted to ignore them. He was not paid to attend to the letters or to the people in the line. He could instruct the clerks to have the letters taken to Sarah's home and for the names and addresses to be taken of the people lining up. Sarah could then decide what to do about them on her return from her fun excursion to the village. He would get on with his work and await developments.

He thought—he hoped—Sarah would not inform her father about their quarrel, at least until she returned from the village. By that time, it was possible, just possible, that she would have calmed down. She might have realized that she had been in the wrong. If so, he thought, she would probably say nothing to her father. In the future, their relationship would never be as it had been, and any greater intimacy between them, he was sure, was now out of the question. He could not help but feel that a friendship he had come to cherish had been shattered in less than a minute.

Twenty-seven

No more than ten minutes after Sarah had left the office of Kedron & Co, her father arrived. Alerted by a somewhat dramatic message from his chief clerk that the office was under siege, Matthew had cut short his breakfast and leisurely perusal of *The Times* and hurried to the office. Guessing the purpose of the long line of men and women, a line that now extended as far as the end of Paternoster Row and around the corner into Ave Maria Lane, he went straight to James's room.

To his dismay, the young man was sitting at his desk, almost surrounded by piles of letters, his head in his hands.

'Good morning, James,' he said. 'The poster appears to have achieved a result. Whether it is the desired one remains to be seen.'

James raised his head, and, seeing Matthew, got quickly to his feet. 'I'm sorry, sir. It's all a little too much for me to know what to do.'

'Sit down, my boy, and we will discuss the situation.'

A little surprised at the extent of James's obvious distress, he added, 'Is there anything else worrying you?'

James inferred from the question that Matthew Kedron had not yet spoken to his daughter. Presumably their hackneys had passed one another, probably in Oxford Street.

He decided to take the initiative. Convinced that eventually Sarah would confide in her father, he thought he would have nothing to lose from presenting his side of the argument before she had an opportunity to state hers.

'I regret to tell you, sir,' he said, 'that I have deeply offended Miss Sarah.'

'Have you indeed? You had better tell me about it.'

Choosing his words carefully, James explained that Sarah had requested him to accompany her on her return to Langley, this time with her artist friend, Elizabeth Stockton, with him again incognito as the coachman and Sarah disguised as her friend's maiden aunt. He confessed that instead of politely declining because of the extraordinary response to the missing-person poster, he had been not only abrupt but also insulting. He had even accused Sarah of indulging in play-acting and treating the investigation as a game. Sarah, he concluded, with a serious understatement, had not been pleased by his lack of courtesy and cooperation.

Much to James's surprise and relief, his employer's face creased into a smile and he nodded knowingly. He had, in truth, known that sooner or later there would be such an outbreak of temper from Sarah. Deeply though he loved and admired his daughter, he was aware of her faults, knowing her to be wilful, obstinate, impulsive and demanding. In such a mood, she could be as unpleasant as the most imperious aristocrat. In short, she could be impossible to deal with. Although disappointed in the breach between her and James, Matthew felt relieved that James had not allowed himself to be dictated to by his daughter. He needed as a senior employee a man who was strong-willed, who knew his own mind, and would not allow himself to be overruled on matters of importance.

He said, 'Your decision was the correct one, James. And I concur with the explanation you gave to Sarah. A childish disguise is sheer foolishness. A problem with actors, my boy, is that they never really grow up. They remain as children, playing dress-ups for family theatricals. As for the general tenor of your speech, you must decide whether it requires an apology. Sarah does not hold grudges, and I'm sure she will be forgiving. Who knows? She may even admit that you were correct to put your employment with me ahead of the matter of Sir Charles's disappearance.'

'You are too kind, sir. I am much obliged to you.'

'Good. Now let us talk of the response to the poster. I suggest that you leave the clerks to deal with it. In my opinion, it is most unlikely that anything of real value will be discovered from people who have responded so quickly. The possibility of earning a shilling or two for admitting to having seen such a person as Sir Charles would be difficult for them to pass by. The clerks can take a short statement from each of them, and we can consider these at our leisure.'

'I'm sure you are correct in your assumption, sir. And there are other lines of inquiry that I would like to pursue with your permission.'

'Which are?'

'Sarah, sir, is concerned with family and village matters. It is likely that she is correct. However, I think it is possible that there are wider issues that should be considered. Apparently, Sir Charles mentioned to Miss Stockton that he had attended meetings of The London Abolition Society.'

'Now that, James, is very interesting indeed. The winds of change are blowing. The revolution in France, the wars, the flood of labour from the farms to the new factories, the growing influence and popularity of the press, and a clamour for education for their children by the poor all herald huge changes in the nature of English society. They are causing considerable activity among the more radical members of Parliament. Among the reforms of particular concern, especially among the Quakers and other Dissenters, is the abolition of slavery. They are even having some success. As you may know, in 1807 legislation was enacted making it illegal for any ship sailing under the British flag to carry slaves. Although this has reduced the international trade in slaves, it has not freed many thousands of Africans who are still forced to work for their bare subsistence on the farms and plantations in the colonies owned þy British companies and individuals. The fortunes of too many of the members of the aristocracy and nobility are based on the income derived from slavery.'

James remembered that Edward, Sir Charles's younger brother, was in Antigua, managing a plantation. Such an enterprise would depend heavily on slave labour. Perhaps, he thought, this was the basis of the brothers' quarrel.

'Were you ever a member of The Abolition Society, sir?' James risked the inquiry.

'A member? No. Though I have attended a few meetings. And I strongly support the objective of the society. Eventually there will be total abolition; mark my words.'

'If Sir Charles supports the aims of the society—' James began, but Matthew Kedron finished his sentence for him.

'By some he would be accused of being a traitor to his class.'

'Precisely.'

Matthew's mention of class reminded James of what Sarah had told him about Lady Augusta. 'I think you know that Sir Charles's mother has accused her daughter-in-law of being responsible for her husband's disappearance. She maintains that the girl wants to be widowed so that she can inherit an income and be free to marry a man of her own class with whom she will be more at ease.'

'All very possible, especially if she already has a candidate for the position, even a lover. And there is also a younger brother, I believe.'

'Edward. He lives in Antigua.'

'Hmm.' Matthew grew thoughtful. After a few moments, he surmised, 'Presumably, if informed that Charles is missing, he would return to Britain to claim his inheritance as soon as Charles was officially declared deceased. I believe the brothers have been estranged for some time. Do we know why?'

'No, but it occurs to me that it may have something to do with their different views on slavery.'

Mathew nodded. 'Indeed, it is quite possible that there is a political as well as a familial element in the equation. Of course, Edward may have already secretly returned and murdered his brother—or more likely, have paid to have him killed.'

'Fratricide!'

'My dear James, murder within families is far from unknown. Especially where an inheritance is involved.

Indeed, you can be sure that anything that you are capable of imagining has already occurred somewhere, at some time.'

'But Sir Charles has been missing for only a month, sir. The journey to the West Indies takes at least three weeks, often longer, depending on the winds. Even if a letter informing Edward of his brother's disappearance was dispatched within a few days, Edward would have only just received it in Antigua. He would certainly not have had time to return to England and be responsible for it.'

'True,' Matthew said. 'But surely it is possible that he returned secretly to England before his brother disappeared and was, therefore, a party to it.'

'What an idiot I am!' James exclaimed. 'You are correct, sir. How foolish of me. It is perfectly possible. Oh, dear! The problem with this investigation is not only that there are so many known suspects, but also that there is probably an equal or even greater number of unknown ones. It is difficult to decide which avenue of inquiry to pursue.'

'Why not begin with that which you can pursue in London?' Matthew suggested. 'Leave Browning Hall and the village to Sarah, as you proposed. You will achieve more by working independently as long as you keep one another fully informed of anything you discover.'

'An excellent suggestion, sir.'

'Good. Now, a young apprentice reporter starts work on *The Informer* today. Jack Godwin is his name. I don't know much about him except that he seems to have had a good education and is desperately keen. He'll willingly do any task you give him. You may have him as your assistant. Dealing with the bureaucracy and learning how to ferret out the information he needs from official documents will be good for him.'

'I am greatly obliged to you, sir,' James murmured with feeling. Not a day passed that he was not aware of how fortunate he was to have Matthew Kedron as his employer.

For his part, Matthew was anxious to retain James's services. He had no son, and although Sarah was extremely capable, gaining business experience was not high on her list of priorities.

He smiled, stood up and turned as if to leave the room. He walked a few steps towards the door and then turned back. 'When you have a free evening, James,' he said, 'let us have a leisurely dinner together. A number of gentlemen with capital to risk want me to establish a new daily newspaper of a radical disposition. It will need an editor.' He smiled again and left the room.

James realized that the crisis in his relationship with his employer was over, and, in fact, there had never been one.

Twenty-eight

Immediately after leaving James, Sarah took a hackney home to Portman Place. During the short journey, her anger dissipated, and distress and guilt replaced it. Although still offended by James's outburst, she realized that she had provoked it. Not only had she decided on a plan of action without consulting him, she had not even offered to assist him in dealing with the piles of mail and the queue of people. As this situation was a direct result of her borrowing the portrait of Sir Charles from Elizabeth and having a likeness of the man distributed throughout the City and West End, she was now calm enough to accept that she was partly to blame for the quarrel, though not for his rudeness towards her.

This acceptance of her fault, though alleviating her anger, did nothing to lighten her mood. James's contribution to the investigation had been invaluable, and she realized with no little dismay that she would be incapable of continuing it without him. Having told him that she no longer required his assistance, she knew that if she were to regain his cooperation, she would have to apologize and hope that he would be forgiving. Also, apart from his usefulness, she could not deny that she had come to feel both affection and respect for him. Unlike most of the men she knew, he was secure in his confidence in himself, interested in other people, not only in his own concerns, and, in short, a very pleasant companion. His face, pleasant rather than handsome, and his usually gentle manner added to his agreeable personality. And the fact that her father thought so highly of him was confirmation of his good character.

The knowledge that she had even revealed the warmth of her friendship for James by inviting him to call her by her Christian name further discombobulated Sarah. Her relationship with him, at first easy and trouble-free, was now fraught with emotion—on both sides, she was sure.

Knowing that she would brood on her problem with James and that this brooding would achieve nothing but further unhappiness and dismay, she decided that she had to confide in someone. She had many female friends at the theatre, but they were all actresses and would seize any opportunity she gave them to turn the conversation quickly to their own emotional concerns, entertaining though they would no doubt be. No, this time she needed a friend who would not only listen and sympathize but who would also have sufficient life experience to offer sound advice.

The obvious choice was Elizabeth.

After changing into clothes more suitable to her age, she took another hackney to Cheyne Walk. Fortunately, Elizabeth was at home and, as usual, delighted to see her. Elizabeth immediately realized that something was amiss.

As they embraced, she said, 'Oh, Sarah, you look so sad. What has made you so?'

'I've quarrelled with James Brewster,' Sarah said, just holding back her tears. 'He has grievously insulted me, but it is largely my own fault. If I'm to regain his friendship I must apologize, but that will not be easy to do. It is not appropriate that I, his employer's daughter, should grovel.'

'I hope grovelling will not be either necessary or desirable,' Elizabeth observed. 'Any man who requires a woman to grovel to him deserves only contempt. But we'll have tea, and you can tell me all about it.'

Elizabeth rang for her maid and ordered tea, and then she sat next to Sarah on the settee and took her hand. 'Begin at the beginning,' she said. 'Omit nothing. I want to know what you said, what he said, what you feel and what you believe he feels.'

Sarah took a deep breath and began.

Elizabeth said not a word until her friend had concluded her narrative. Then she said, 'The worst part is over, surely. You have accepted that you were in error. If James is the man of sensitivity and sensibility that you believe him to be, then I suggest a simple, "I'm sorry, James." If he requires more or declines to accept the apology, then what is he worth?'

Before Sarah could reply, the maid entered with the tea. While she poured, Elizabeth continued, 'I have not yet received a response to my letter to the good clergyman, but since I referred to you simply as my companion, there is no need to use the disguise if you feel not to.'

'That is a relief,' Sarah said.

'While we wait,' Elizabeth continued, 'I suggest that, if you are free, we entertain ourselves with a visit to the gardens at Ranelagh House. There will be music there, the overdressed ladies of the *haut ton* to gawp at and all the bucks and macaronis in their ridiculous finery to amuse us.'

'What a splendid plan, Elizabeth!' Sarah exclaimed, brightening a little. 'We can take an early dinner there and even dance if we feel so inclined. We'll be mistaken for ladies of pleasure, but there's no harm in that.'

Elizabeth laughed with delight.

'I'm an actress. You are an artist,' Sarah continued. 'Neither of us has a reputation to protect. With our professions, even to imagine that we could be mistaken for respectable women would be futile.'

'We could be mistaken for frails,' Elizabeth exclaimed, 'and have fun!'

She knew Sarah spoke the truth. Many women in the arts had such meagre earnings that they became courtesans in order to survive. Only a few ever managed to marry well, even fewer into the nobility. Society widely assumed that all women in the arts were willing to provide sexual favours in return for protection, so both actresses and artists found it difficult to achieve respectability and social acceptance.

'If we want to be treated with respect, we could wear nuns' habits,' Elizabeth joked.

'And risk being accosted by priests and monks!' Sarah exclaimed. 'Oh, no! No, a thousand times no. I can imagine little worse than having to wait for a lover who kneels by the bed and says his prayers before demonstrating his passion.'

Overcome with laughter, the two women held one another.

Sarah recovered first and continued the conversation, 'But in spite of all that, I think a visit to Ranelagh Gardens is a splendid suggestion. Though not dressed as religious.'

Elizabeth nodded. 'As we walk in the gardens, we can decide what to do if the reverend gentleman offers us hospitality, assuming that you still want to meet him.'

'Oh, yes. But as myself. James was correct in pointing out that a man who is a friend of Sir Charles is more likely to be forthcoming to a friend of his wife's than to a total stranger.'

'I agree.'

'And I'd be grateful, Elizabeth, for any suggestions you may care to make concerning what I should ask him.'

'Of course. That is something we can discuss as we wander through the gardens. Shall we hire a chaise for our journey to Langley?'

'My father will let us use his carriage, and the coachman he employs. He is a pleasant and reliable man.'

And thus it was arranged.

Twenty-nine

Following Matthew Kedron's advice, James set two of the clerks to work dealing with the respondents to the engraving of Sir Charles's portrait; one to make a pile of the letters that might be of interest and the other to take down the necessary details of the men and women in line outside the office.

James then asked Jack Godwin to come into his office.

It was immediately obvious that Matthew Kedron's description of the young man as being keen was a most accurate choice of words. He oozed enthusiasm. Skeletally thin—presumably because his nervous engine burnt up as much nourishment as he could consume—the young man stood almost on tiptoe as if poised to dart in whichever direction was required of him. His entire body seemed to be quivering with excited expectation.

'Well, Jack,' James said, 'Mr Kedron has told me that you are to assist me in an investigation.'

'Yes, sir. Whatever you want me to do, sir, it shall be done instantly.'

'Good. But tell me about yourself. What education have you had?'

'Six years at Merchant Taylors' School, sir.'

'Indeed. A famous establishment. And not always for the best reasons.'

'We were not at fault, sir. We were set upon.'

Five years previously, as the boys were on their way to school, there had been a pitched battle in Old Change at the western end of Cheapside between the boys of St Paul's and those of Merchant Taylors' schools. There had also been riots at other boys' schools in recent years, including Eton and Harrow. Some had been so serious that troops had been called in to quell them.

'Were you there on a scholarship, Jack?' James asked.

'Yes, sir.'

'And what did you study?'

'The classics, sir.'

'Hmm. And what is your father's occupation?'

'He is Lord Belvedere's valet, sir.'

'And you lived on the Belvedere estate?'

'Yes, sir.'

'Why do you want to be a journalist?'

'Lord Belvedere subscribed to many periodicals, sir, and when he had finished with them, he generously gave them to my father. I always had the absolute best journals to read, and I have known for some years that journalism is what I want to do.'

'Good.' James thought it all sounded promising. 'Well, today you are going to discover that writing articles for the press is, for most journalists, the final element of the work. Establishing facts is the first and most important part. Do you understand?'

'Yes, sir.'

It occurred to James that if he did not quickly reach the moment of climax of this interview, Jack might rise into the air, rather like a hot-air balloon that had become untethered. 'In about 1808 or 1809 a man by the name of Jack Harness—'

'Would you spell that, please, sir?' As if by magic from nowhere a notebook had appeared in one of the young man's hands. A pencil was poised for action in the other.

'H.A.R.N.E.S.S.'

'Thank you, sir.'

'A man by the name of Jack Harness,' James continued, 'was found guilty at Hertford Assizes of poaching. I have been given to understand that he was sentenced to transportation to Australia.'

'What did he poach, sir?'

'I don't know. Probably pheasant. Even a hare or a rabbit or two. I want you to take the mail coach to Hertford and check the court records. If Harness was sentenced to transportation, he would have been sent first to the hulks in the Thames to await a ship. Yes?'

'Yes, sir.'

'The Home Office will have a record stating whether Harness died in the hulks, as so many prisoners did, conditions being so bad, whether he died at sea, or whether he reached his destination.'

'I understand, sir.'

'Good. The next step will be to establish what happened to him in Australia. If he was imprisoned at Norfolk Island, the chances are that he died there, if not from being flogged, then from poor food and hard labour. If he survived his term in prison, he would have either remained in Australia and made a life for himself or risked another long sea voyage to return to England.'

'A shipping company may have a record of his passage if he did, sir,' Jack said, now so eager that he seemed to be halfway out of the door already.

'Good lad.' James threw him two half crowns, which Jack neatly caught. 'This should cover your expenses— transport, food, overnight accommodation in Hertford if necessary and, erm, any appropriate …'

'Gratuities, sir?'

'Precisely, Jack. And you may introduce yourself as a reporter from *The Weekly Police News*. One more thing. While you are at the docks, you might visit the offices of the shipping companies dealing with the West Indies. Try to establish whether their manifests for sailings from these— especially any ship that has called at Antigua—lists a Mr Edward Browning bound for London. Have you got that?'

'Edward Browning, embarking Antigua for London. Any dates, sir?'

'Try the last six months. Now go to it.'

'Very good, sir.'

Jack's face held a beatific expression, as if he had suddenly found himself at the gates of heaven. He bowed and was out of the room in a flash.

Somewhat exhausted by the encounter, but in no way displeased, James sat back in his chair and murmured, 'Well, there's a young man in a hurry.'

His problem now was to decide which line of inquiry to pursue next. He assumed that, in spite of the situation with

Sarah, it would be appropriate for him to continue to involve himself in the investigation. He did not wish to appear petty or spiteful, and he could think of no good reason why Lady Browning should suffer from a quarrel that was none of her making. In delegating Jack Godwin to the inquiry, Matthew Kedron had implied that he thought the baronet's disappearance worthy of James's continued attention, and this knowledge assisted James in his decision to ignore, if only temporarily, the difficulty with Sarah.

He thought it clear that, at least for the time being, he needed to avoid confusing matters by questioning the same people in whom Sarah had expressed interest and to whom she might soon speak: Mr Somersby, the clergyman friend of Sir Charles; Mrs Williams, the Browning Hall housekeeper; Lady Augusta, the dowager; Lady Browning herself and probably the relatives of the transported poacher and anyone connected with the servant girl. If the clergyman was forthcoming with information about the Browning family, the tenant farmers, smallholders and the villagers, this would further narrow the field available to James, which could be a considerable advantage.

Apart from anything useful that might arise from the respondents to the poster, the only remaining avenue to explore immediately was Sir Charles's membership of The Abolition Society. Past issues of *The Informer* held abundant information about this organization, so James began his research without leaving the office.

He soon discovered that *The Informer*, unsurprisingly, had been very supportive of the Society, especially for the activities of its London Committee. This group of people, both men and women, had been active in mounting an ongoing campaign for the abolition of slavery. The driving force had been, and still was, William Wilberforce, an MP. The London Committee and its fraternal committees in many provincial cities had drummed up considerable national support for the cause, especially among members of the dissenting faiths such as the Methodists and the Quakers. Concern was growing among the middle classes that Britain should lead the world in abolishing what many now believed to be a shameful trade.

The London Committee operated from a printers and bookshop at George Yard in the City, a few minutes' walk away. James decided to call in the hope that the secretary, a Mr Herbert Reed, would be in attendance and have some knowledge of Sir Charles Browning.

He was in luck. Herbert Reed, a quiet, clerkly man in his fifties, had a desk in the shop, and from this, he conducted the daily business of the Abolition Society. James introduced himself and proffered his card.

'A splendid publication, sir,' Mr Reed observed. 'Pray be seated and tell me how I can be of assistance.'

'Thank you, sir. I am obliged to you.' James sat and placed his cane—his only concession to dandyism—on the floor. 'I believe Sir Charles Browning is a member of the society.'

'May I inquire why you are interested in this particular gentleman?' Mr Reed asked, being careful to whom and for what purpose he revealed the membership of the society.

'Certainly. I must tell you that Sir Charles has disappeared. It is possible, even likely, that he is the victim of foul play. Miss Kedron—Mr Matthew Kedron's daughter—and I have been asked by his wife, Lady Browning, to try and establish what has happened to her husband.'

'Dear me, that is indeed sad news. Sir Charles is a most pleasant gentleman. And dedicated to the aims of the society. I can confirm, sir, that Sir Charles is a member, and he joined about a month ago. Perhaps six weeks. Time moves so quickly. I have not seen him since the meeting at which he joined. It will be tragic indeed if he has suffered a serious accident.'

'Do you know if he was introduced to the society by a friend? An acquaintance?'

'Not to my knowledge. But that is possible, of course, and it is often the case. Alternatively, he may have read about our work in the press.' He smiled. 'Mr Kedron's other publication, *The Informer*, has been most supportive of our campaign. And for this we are much obliged.'

'You say it will be "tragic indeed" if some kind of calamity has befallen Sir Charles. May I ask why you express yourself so strongly?'

'At the meeting he attended, Sir Charles made an emotional speech. He declared that he was dedicated to the abolition of slavery and to other social reforms. If I remember correctly—it was a somewhat rambling and at times incoherent speech, sir, but of intense sincerity and passion—he also expressed his concern at the amount of prostitution, drunkenness and gambling of all kinds in the city. It was a speech rich in conviction, Mr Brewster, but it attempted to embrace too many issues at the same time, if I may express an opinion.'

'This is most interesting, sir,' James said, 'but has not the slave trade already been abolished?'

'Not exactly, sir. Legislation has been enacted prohibiting Britons from trading or transporting slaves, but slavery continues on the plantations. You see, sir, many of the present slaves have been born into slavery from slave mothers. And there is still trading among the plantation owners.'

'Ah. Quite. I understand.'

'We have repeatedly sent petitions to Parliament—to both the Commons and the Lords—but the influence of the merchants and the nobility is too powerful for further bills to succeed. Most of the Tories are opposed to total abolition, of course, even though there are many throughout the nation who are desperate for all kinds of reform. Sadly, little will be achieved until Parliament is more representative of the majority of the people, not only of the merchants and nobility.'

James knew that Matthew Kedron held similar views. 'Mr Reed, you have been most helpful,' he said. 'Just one more thing. Can you think of anyone I could talk to who might have information about Sir Charles that could be relevant to my inquiry?'

Herbert Reed bent his head and placed a hand against his brow. 'I need to think. To visualize, sir, the meeting at which Sir Charles spoke.'

He remained silent for a few moments as if in prayer, and then said, 'It may be of no significance, sir, but I seem to recall that he sat next to a lady at the meeting. As far as I recollect, it was Mrs Bradshaw, a Quaker lady, the widow of

Mr Ebenezer Bradshaw. You may have heard of Bradshaw's Tea.'

'Indeed, I have.'

Bradshaw's was the nation's largest importer and wholesaler of a variety of teas. Advertisements for them appeared wherever it was possible for an advertisement to appear.

'Whether or not Sir Charles entered or left the meeting in the company of Mrs Bradshaw, I'm afraid I cannot say,' Mr Reed continued. 'At the time I was engaged in conversation with our chairman.'

'I understand. Do you have an address for Mrs Bradshaw?'

The clerk consulted a ledger, then stood. 'Four Marylebone Place, sir, when she is in London. Otherwise she resides near Bristol where the late Mr Bradshaw established a model village and his business premises.'

James bent down to retrieve his cane, then getting to his feet, said, 'That is all most helpful, sir. I will attempt to obtain an audience with Mrs Bradshaw.'

'I am happy to have been of assistance. And it has been a pleasure meeting you, Mr Brewster.'

The two men bowed to one another, and James left the office of The Abolition Society, extremely pleased with everything he had heard.

Thirty

James decided he would dine at Lincoln's Inn, where, if he were fortunate, his tutor and mentor Mr Joshua Fielding would be in attendance. He felt the need to seek the barrister's further advice.

Before then, however, he had time to call on Mrs Bradshaw, and if she were not at home or unable to speak to him, then he would return to his office, where sorting the letters and interviewing the riff-raff in the queue outside would be well under way.

On arriving at Marylebone Place, a row of recently built and distinguished four-storey terrace houses, James sent in his card with the words 'In connection with Sir Charles Browning' written on the reverse. A servant showed him into the library on the first floor, where Mrs Katherine Bradshaw sat at her escritoire, writing letters. As he entered the large room in which crowded, glass-fronted bookshelves rose from floor to ceiling, Mrs Bradshaw rose to her feet and walked towards him, hand outstretched.

'Good day, Mr Brewster.'

'It is most obliging of you to grant me an interview, madam.'

Mrs Bradshaw sat, neatly sweeping her long, grey silk dress under herself as she did, and then invited James to take a seat opposite.

A soberly dressed woman in her middle to late fifties, she wore a high-necked dress with just a thin frill of Nottingham lace at the collar, her hair tightly drawn back in a bun and no cosmetics or jewellery. The warmth of her smile, however, belied the severity of her appearance.

'Your publication is of great value, Mr Brewster,' she said. 'In what way is it connected with Sir Charles Browning?'

'He has disappeared, madam, and I am inquiring into this situation. It is possible that you may be one of the last persons to see him before he vanished.'

'Dear me! How very strange,' Mrs Bradshaw said. 'But, tell me, I was not aware that *The Weekly Police News* also offered a missing-persons inquiry service.'

'We do not usually, madam.' James launched into the explanation for his involvement in the investigation.

When he had finished, Mrs Bradshaw said with a smile, 'The complexity of your explanation, Mr Brewster, adds to its plausibility. How can I help you?'

'We have decided that the more we know about Sir Charles, the more likely we are to discover what has happened to him. I was wondering, therefore, what you can tell me about him.'

'I'm not sure if my impressions will be helpful,' Mrs Bradshaw replied. 'I met the young gentleman only once. He spoke passionately at a meeting of The Abolition Society where I sat next to him. I thought he might have something of value to offer the society, and at the conclusion of the meeting I invited him to return here with me so that we could talk about his concerns at our leisure. He holds very radical opinions, Mr Brewster, especially for a baronet. And although he is undoubtedly sincere, I believe him to be troubled. As you may know, my late husband was, and I am, a Quaker. Apart from our interest in social and political reform, we are very concerned with our religious life. I hoped that Sir Charles would attend our meetings, where the emphasis is on peace and quiet contemplation, and that he might receive spiritual guidance and solace.'

'Did he say anything that explained why he was troubled?' James asked.

'I think his main problem stems from his inheritance. He gave me to understand that part of his income is derived from a sugar plantation in the West Indies. These investments were inherited through his maternal grandfather. He also has a younger brother who even now manages such a plantation in Antigua.'

'And yet he believes in and is anxious to campaign on behalf of the abolitionist movement,' James said. 'An unusual situation surely. It could be considered hypocritical.'

'Precisely. He feels profoundly guilty and that his only possible honest course of action is to devote any of the income his family derives from slave labour to the abolition campaign and other social issues. And, of course, he has little or no control over the income his brother enjoys from the plantation. I understand that the brothers are estranged because of this matter. Sir Charles feels the rift between them deeply. He told me that they were very close as children.'

'I suppose he could dispose of any family financial interest in the plantations,' James suggested. 'Other than his brother's.'

'This is true. But he feels that would be simply to pass on the responsibility to another person. It is a serious problem for him.'

'The secretary of your society,' James said, 'believes that the abolitionist campaign will have no further success until there are major changes to the electoral system. As a parliamentarian, Sir Charles would be in a strong position to promote the cause. I understand it is possible that he might be a candidate at the next general election.'

'That is correct. I discussed with Sir Charles the value to the society of his pursuing a parliamentary career. It is widely believed that the present government will soon fall and that a general election is imminent.'

'In your opinion, madam, would Sir Charles make a good MP?'

Katherine Bradshaw remained quiet for several moments, and then said, 'His heart is in the right place, and he means so well, but I fear his extreme radical approach to many social problems and his apparent inability to concentrate his efforts on one issue at a time will not stand him in good stead. He is also—and I intend to be sympathetic not critical—excessively emotional and even erratic in his speech. I am in no way an expert on the diseases of the brain, but I could not avoid wondering whether his level of excitement was not at the level of mania. I also had the impression that he suffers greatly from melancholy. Reformers, you know, Mr Brewster, have to accept years of failure. They must be mentally strong so that they can manage disappointment and frustration without it destroying their mental stability. Perhaps, above all else, they need the comfort and support of an affectionate and understanding family life.'

James nodded. 'Yes. Yes, I can understand that.'

James found so much to absorb from this speech that he remained silent for a while. The elegant French carriage clock on the mantelpiece above the fireplace quietly ticked away the seconds. At last he said, 'Should I infer from your last observation, Mrs Bradshaw, that you do think Sir Charles is not well served by his wife and mother?'

'He said nothing about them to me, and I know nothing about either lady or of any of his relations. I was simply making a general observation.' Katherine Bradshaw stood up, pulled a bell rope, and said 'And now, Mr Brewster, I must ask you to excuse me. I have several letters to write that I must finish in time for this evening's post.'

As he stood, James said, 'You have been most helpful, madam, and I am deeply obliged to you. May I have your permission to call on you again should anything occur to me that you may be willing to discuss?'

'Most certainly.'

The maid entered, and Katherine Bradshaw indicated that she should show James out.

Once back on the street, James hailed a hackney and travelled to his office. During the journey he pondered everything Katherine Bradshaw had said. An educated, enlightened woman, she was the widow of one of the most successful businessmen in the country—a man, moreover, who had led the way in providing his employees with improved living and working conditions. Men like him—Josiah Wedgewood, the potter, had been another, and James felt sure there would be many more—who were harbingers of beneficial change. James suspected that other less-beneficial changes caused the increasing incidence of melancholia among people of all classes: changes such as the loss of religious certainty, the insecurities caused by the massive movement of population from the stability of rural life to the chaos of urban living, and the burgeoning industrial towns with their dirt, bad air, over-crowding and wholly different way of life.

Since Sir Charles apparently suffered from distressing mood changes, the possibility that he had taken his own life could not be ignored.

Thirty-one

Sarah and Elizabeth spent an enjoyable afternoon window shopping in Bond Street, then crossed the river to wander through Vauxhall Gardens, listen to the music, take refreshments and make caustic remarks to one another about the young bucks who were attempting to disport themselves to maximum effect. Their similarity to peacocks putting on a display to attract the hens was undeniable, except that their extravagant mode of dress and the turn of a well-shaped leg had to suffice for the missing tail feathers.

The friends became too tired to stay for dinner at the gardens, they also had other matters to attend to. Elizabeth was eager to return to Cheyne Walk where there might already be a reply from the clergyman. Sarah had the unfortunate incident with James on her mind and felt a strong need to make amends before leaving town for several days. Accordingly, although they recrossed the river together, the women took separate hackneys to their respective destinations: Elizabeth to her studio and apartment; Sarah to the offices of Kedron and Co.

Before she approached James, Sarah decided to confide in her father her anxiety concerning her quarrel with his obviously highly regarded employee.

She found Matthew in his room, writing an editorial for the forthcoming issue of *The Informer*. He looked up as she entered, smiled and put down his pen.

'May I disturb you, Father?'

'You are always a welcome disturbance, my dear.'

He left his desk, and they sat in the armchairs, facing one another.

'I have made rather a fool of myself, Father,' she said.

Showing little surprise, but raising his eyebrows slightly, he said, 'That, my dear, is something we all do from time to time.'

'I have been very unkind to James. Insulted him, I fear.'

Her use of James's Christian name told Matthew a great deal. With a smile, he said, 'I'm sure he will not demand satisfaction. Do you wish to tell me about it?'

She nodded and described what had taken place, being both fair and accurate in her recollection.

Matthew knew of his daughter's fiery temperament and the tendency to want her own way. She gave the servants instructions at home, and the stage hands and cleaners at the theatre were required to do her bidding. He said, 'James is a most able young man, Sarah. He is also proud. I believe him to have the potential to be not just a good journalist and editor, but also a great one. The qualities he will need, and possesses, apart from intelligence, are determination, confidence in his own ability and opinions, and an unwillingness to be, dare I say it so bluntly, pushed around.'

Realizing that James had almost certainly confided in her father, who she suspected had already begun to think of

James as the son he'd always wanted but never had, Sarah said, 'I did not intend to address him as if he were a servant.'

'I have been expecting a problem of this nature, my dear. I'm relieved that it has occurred now when it can be dealt with before there have been important commitments.'

'I don't understand, Father. What do you mean?'

'It would be more than embarrassing; it would be disastrous,' he explained, 'if, for example, at some time in the future I were to offer James a partnership in the business and you two suddenly ceased speaking to one another. If there are any clouds in your relationship, they need disbursing before they darken into a storm. We all need to know where we stand with one another.'

'I don't understand why James's involvement in the business need affect me or my relationship with him,' Sarah exclaimed.

'One's expectation of life is uncertain,' Matthew said. 'Hardly a day passes without someone in the neighbourhood being knocked down and killed by a recklessly driven horse, and the London air is little more than a diseased effluent. When I die, you will inherit the business. If James is a partner, you will, as my heir and the senior partner, be in the position of his employer. I do not think I need elaborate.'

Sarah fell silent and remained so for several moments. Her father's decision came as a shock to her, though she could understand why he'd decided to take the action he had in mind. He was not young and took little care of his health, often eating and drinking to excess with friends to relieve the stress of his occupation. He needed to groom a capable editor to assume responsibility for the business in the event of his incapacitation or death. However, she did not want to feel pressured into greater intimacy with James than she felt ready for. At times she even wondered if she would ever be ready for more than an affectionate friendship with him, or with any man. She suspected, too, that he felt the same about her, though almost certainly for different reasons. They were like a blind couple, feeling their way slowly into a greater knowledge and appreciation of one another.

'I understand, Father,' she said, standing up. 'Whether or not we have a future as friends and colleagues will depend, I believe, on how he responds to my apology and how well we continue to work as colleagues in the investigation into Sir Charles's disappearance. It will be a testing time for both of us. I will speak to him now.' Bending down, she kissed her father's head, then left the room, closing the door behind her.

Matthew returned to his desk and took a large pinch of his favourite snuff. He hoped he had not been too precipitate in informing his daughter of his plans for James. He had a somewhat vague, and at times, he thought, a foolish and premature ambition to establish a publishing dynasty. If Sarah and James became man and wife, it would simplify the partnership situation and make a dynasty possible. Also, and of equal importance, Sarah had achieved much in her career already and, he was sure, would achieve much more, but it would all be worthless unless she was also emotionally fulfilled.

***

After leaving her father, Sarah went straight to James's room and knocked on his door.

'Come in,' he called.

She entered and found him sitting at his desk, staring at a pile of letters. It appeared as if he had remained where she'd left him that morning.

He rose to his feet. 'Miss Kedron.'

'Please sit down, James. We need to talk.'

He resumed his seat as she sat on the chair in front of his desk.

'I was unreasonable this morning, and I apologize. You are not a servant. You are a valued friend and colleague. And you were, I suspect, correct to oppose my "dress up" as you so scathingly referred to it.'

James felt almost too overcome with surprise, relief and joy to respond, but quickly recovering his composure, he said, 'You are very gracious, Sarah. I humbly apologize for my rudeness. I was not myself.' He smiled wryly. 'Well, I hope I wasn't.'

'I have decided,' she said, 'not to play dress-ups, but if we receive an invitation from the clergyman, I will go with Elizabeth, as Celia's friend, not as an artist's eccentric maiden aunt.'

'If you are Celia's friend, though, will she and the clergyman not think it strange that you are not staying with her at the big house?'

'Possibly. And I have thought of that. I will explain that I want to be near my artist friend who wishes to stay as near to the church as possible so that she can take advantage of the fine weather and sketch outdoors. To the clergyman, I will add that Lady Browning will probably prefer to be without house guests, since only the housekeeper is presently employed.'

'I'm sure you have made a wise decision. May I tell you what I have discovered this morning? The knowledge is, I think, relevant to the purpose of your visit to the clergyman.'

'Please do.'

Feeling relaxed now in her company, and aware, not for the first time, that standing up for oneself, though risky, was by far the most sensible way to behave, James said, 'Sir Charles attended a meeting of The Abolition Society. At that meeting, he met Mrs Katherine Bradshaw, the wife of the tea merchant.'

James continued by summarizing the conversation he'd had with the lady. He concluded by saying, 'Sir Charles's mania and melancholy could explain many things, Sarah.'

'Indeed they could,' Sarah exclaimed. 'It is well established that during manic periods people behave in rash and often irrational ways. They go on shopping sprees, make unwise investments, enter into inappropriate relationships ...'

'And gamble recklessly,' James added. 'If Mrs Bradshaw is correct in her description of Sir Charles, the explanation for his disappearance could lie in his mental state.'

Sarah nodded, although her thoughts had taken a different track. 'Celia,' she said, 'is young, immature and of a timid disposition. She would surely find marriage to a man who suffers from mental instability most distressing. Not only would she not know how to manage him, but she would inevitably, I think, regret having married him. Of course, we cannot be sure of this as we don't know the nature of their relationship. Perhaps it was a love match, perhaps not.'

'Her father,' James observed, 'would probably have encouraged, even required it. A wealthy son-in-law would assure his comfort in retirement. As an obedient child of a clergyman, she would have thought it her duty to marry the man her father had chosen.'

'Even though she already had a sweetheart in the village and had to abandon him,' Sarah said, thinking of the horseman riding so swiftly by.

'Lady Augusta's suspicions, therefore, may not be as outrageous as we assumed,' James said. 'Even if Celia was not directly responsible for her husband's disappearance ...'

'... and possible death.'

'Exactly. But she may be the cause of it. A desperately unhappy woman, trapped in a marriage she bitterly regrets, would not have to promise much to a lover to persuade him to remove the husband, the obstacle to his own happiness.'

Sarah clapped her hands together in excitement. 'Especially as it would mean marriage to a young and wealthy widow. It is all there, James. The motivation for the crime is powerful.'

'And the opportunities limitless, not so much in the village, but in London, where violence is an everyday occurrence.'

Sarah and James looked at one another, their eyes wide with excitement. Then James brought them back to earth.

'However, it could be impossible to prove,' he said, 'and it is still only speculation. Until we know more about the

Browning family and any possible enemies that Sir Charles has made, we should not risk following a false trail.'

He then reported that young Jack Godwin was spending the day visiting shipping companies to establish whether the convict Jack Harness, or Edward, or both men, had returned to England.

'And there may be communications of interest from the respondents to the poster,' he concluded. 'It is early days, Sarah, but we can be confident that we are making progress.'

She stood up. 'James, I'm so relieved that we are working together. I greatly value your assistance and friendship.'

She offered her hand, which, in an unusually gallant gesture, he bent down and kissed.

'I'm sure the clergyman is awaiting you with great expectations,' he said. 'I hope to meet my tutor this evening. No doubt, he will be brimming over with advice.'

Laughing, Sarah left the room and departed from the office to Cheyne Walk where she hoped Elizabeth had received good news. She could now look forward to the expedition with her new friend without having the worry of her quarrel with James on her mind.

For his part, James set out for Lincoln's Inn and walked the short journey with a spring in his step.

Thirty-two

James was in luck at Lincoln's Inn. During the meal his tutor, Mr Joshua Fielding, approached and tapped him on the shoulder.

'Same time, same place, Mr Brewster?'

Quickly James got to his feet. 'Of course, sir. It's good to see you here. I trust you are keeping well.'

'I shall be a great deal better after a bumper or two of claret.' And with this hint that he expected to be James's guest for the rest of the evening, he bustled away.

James finished his meal as quickly as he could, then hurried away to meet him at his favourite public house in Chancery Lane. When he arrived, the barrister was already halfway down the first bottle. A full glass awaited him.

'Drink up, my boy, and tell me all your news. Your investigation should be much advanced by now.'

James sipped his wine and then leaned towards his tutor so that their conversation would not be overheard by other men in the bar—though this was hardly necessary. A group of barristers celebrating an unexpected win by one of their colleagues were making a great deal of boisterous noise. An evening of conviviality, no doubt at the client's expense, would occupy them until their coachmen helped them into their carriages and drove them home.

James quickly brought Mr Fielding up to date, concluding with a description of the response to the print of Sir Charles's portrait.

'The problem, sir,' he said, 'is to sort the wheat from the chaff. I'm sure you have had similar difficulties with the communications from informers.'

''Pon my word, yes. Wretches, most of them. Time wasters.' He then launched into a detailed lecture on the habits and types of informers. 'The only ones you can reasonably rely on are the paid police informers. Their continuing income depends on their reliability. Do you have any of these?'

'A few, sir, but they are, so to speak, only recent recruits.'

'Then you need to reserve your opinion of them. However, bear in mind that being new to your employ they will want to impress. I advise you to put them at the top of your list.'

'That I will do, sir. And who do you suggest I put at the bottom?'

'Most of them, but especially any who demand payment before they have provided information, or before the information they have provided has been thoroughly checked out and found to be of value. Such people are either petty criminals or time wasters. I really don't know which are worse. The time wasters have nothing better to do than try to inveigle themselves into your investigation in the hope that they may hear something of interest they can gossip about. And among these troublesome souls are those whose main objective is to indulge in the satisfying emotion of self-importance. Devil take them. They are the bane of a barrister's life.'

'That does not seem to leave many worth considering,' James said.

'Only too true, my boy. But it can be worth paying attention to anyone who demonstrates some actual knowledge of the event or situation in question. In the case of the missing baronet, if an informant can give a reasonably accurate description of him or the circumstances in which he has been encountered, it could be worth devoting a little time to following up the information.'

'Mr Kedron took care to inform the engraver not to provide too much detail of Sir Charles's appearance.'

'Quite. I would have expected no less of him.' Mr Fielding signalled to the pot boy to bring another bottle of the same. 'There is one other category I should mention,' he continued, 'and these are people who, in one way or another, have some connection with the missing person. They may be genuinely concerned for his safety or have a reason for wanting to do him harm. This may, of course, even be an attempt to lay a false trail.'

'This is all rather depressing, sir,' James said.

'Indeed, and the last thing you should do, my boy, is to waste your own time on these people. Do you have assistants?'

James explained that he had clerks sorting the letters and taking down details from the people queuing, and a young reporter ferreting out specific information.

'Good,' Mr Fielding said, 'then you and Miss Kedron can concentrate on the most promising line of inquiry.'

The new bottle of claret arrived and, taking it from the pot boy, the barrister refilled their glasses.

James took the opportunity to say, 'You haven't mentioned altruism, sir, as a motive for providing information.'

'Yes, well, I suppose you may hear something of interest from someone who has nothing to gain except the satisfaction of having done a good deed.' The older man smiled. 'But believe me, my boy, such informants are extremely rare. I, for one, cannot remember encountering one.' He raised his full glass. 'To the success of your investigation, James.'

'Thank you, sir.'

They drank deeply, and then Mr Fielding said, 'Sir Charles's parliamentary ambitions interest me. From what you have told me, he is likely to support the Whig faction. They have been out of Government for some time and this has enabled the Tories to stifle reform. If this government calls an election, do you think he will win the seat?'

James shrugged. 'I have no idea. I think Miss Kedron may be making inquiries about this even as we speak. She is visiting the local vicar in Langley.'

His companion topped up James's almost-full glass, then his own, and then set the bottle down hard. James nodded in thanks. The background festivities, which seemed to be gathering participants as more of the barristers downed tools for the day, did an excellent job of drowning out the clunk as the bottle hit the table.

'In any case,' James continued, 'Miss Kedron is a most intelligent woman, and I am confident she will ask him all the right questions.'

'Excellent.' Mr Fielding nodded. 'The other element in your account that interests me is the possible involvement of the younger brother.'

'Edward, the sugar planter.'

'Exactly. He would seem to have by far the most to gain from Sir Charles's demise. Not only will he inherit the Browning estate, but he will protect his interests in the slave labour on his plantation if his brother is out of the way. When the Whigs do return to Government, total abolition will be high on their reform agenda, as will electoral and other social reforms. Most of the Tories are seriously out of touch with the economic and social changes of the past thirty years, James. We have the loss of the American colonies and the horrors of the revolution in France as a warning to what can happen when the common people rise up. And the British, God help us, have a tendency to riot, given the smallest opportunity.'

Mr Fielding raised his glass and took a long sip. 'No, unless there are major reforms, riots are inevitable in my opinion.'

James took several slow sips to give himself time to consider Mr Fielding's observations. The case of the missing baronet was becoming increasingly complex, and, if only for the political ramifications, well worth investigating thoroughly.

'You think Sir Charles is dead, sir,' he said, putting down his glass.

'Without a doubt. My experience tells me that as there has been no ransom note, we must put aside the possibility that he has been kidnapped. For both political and domestic reasons, he has, I'm sure, been murdered.'

'It will be interesting to learn what Miss Kedron discovers.'

'Indeed it will, my boy. Indeed it will.'

Having exhausted his inquiries concerning the investigation, Mr Fielding devoted the rest of the evening to heavy drinking and the ponderous delivery of anecdotes of the Bar. His favourite topic was the utter incompetence of this or that judge, and the various ways in which he planned to repurpose their judgments. James had heard the barrister revise his opinion on more than one occasion when the judge in question had come around to his line of argument.

Thirty-three

Elizabeth had written a carefully worded letter to the Reverend Mr Somersby, vicar of St Andrews, Langley. In it, she explained that she planned to visit Langley to sketch the beautiful Norman church, accompanied by a companion, and as the accommodation at the local inn would be inappropriate for two unmarried and unchaperoned ladies, she would be most obliged if Mr Somersby could permit them to occupy, for one night only, a room or rooms at the vicarage. A generous donation to a church fund would, of course, be forthcoming.

Mr Somersby had responded promptly in the affirmative, and at midday they arrived at Langley. They immediately sent the coachman to have the horses stabled for the night in the village and walked up the short path by the side of the church to the vicarage.

The women cast their gaze over the forbidding-looking building constructed of local stone—much of it flint—surprised to see that it was in a poor state of repair. Tiles were missing from the roof, and the woodwork desperately needed attention. However, Mr Somersby made up for the depressing appearance of his residence by the comfort and good taste of the interior. He had presumably decided that he could safely leave the maintenance of the building to others as long as he gave careful attention to the interior decoration.

A studious-looking man of about Sarah's age, who wore a cassock with a stiff white dog collar, he was clean-shaven but with sideburns. A black ribbon tied his shoulder-length, straight brown hair at the back.

'My housekeeper will show you to your rooms,' he informed them. 'They are so rarely used that they are rather bare, I fear, and none too warm, but there are linen sheets, thick blankets and so on. Perhaps you will join me for dinner. I usually dine at four so that I have the evening free for my writing.'

'You are a writer, Mr Somersby,' Sarah said. 'Novels? Poetry?'

'Sermons, madam. I am preparing a collection of sermons on various subjects suitable for use on the appropriate Sundays. The clergy are expected to preach twice every Sunday, and many of them lack the time, ability or inclination to prepare their own admonitions. Sales of my collection should, therefore, be adequate but not, I fear,' and he smiled disarmingly, 'anywhere near approaching those of the latest romances.'

'You never know, Mr Somersby,' Sarah said, her dark eyes glinting. 'The life of a novel is brief, but in my experience, sermons go on forever.'

Mr Somersby roared with laughter. 'Oh, very droll, madam,' he exclaimed when he'd recovered his breath. 'I look forward to conversation with you.'

The two women followed the housekeeper up the stairs to their rooms. As Mr Somersby had said, they were spartan and cold, but much cleaner than any country inn would provide.

'It's nearly four now, Elizabeth,' Sarah said, 'so shall we meet in the dining room in a few minutes? I'm so glad your letter achieved the desired result. I have a good feeling about our young ecclesiastic.'

'And I'm so looking forward to sketching the church,' Elizabeth said. 'It's a charming building. I just hope the good weather will hold.'

She opened the door of her room and looked in. It held the minimum of furniture—a bed, a commode, a high-backed wooden chair, and a table with a bowl and a jug of water in which to wash.

'The parish must be fairly poor,' she said. 'If Mr Somersby does not have an independence, he has to live simply. The living itself cannot be worth much, and I doubt if the church will hold a congregation of a hundred. The plate will hardly be laden with gold every Sunday.'

'If he is helpful, I will be as generous as I can afford,' Sarah said. 'No doubt most of what I donate will be spent on the roof.'

'More likely on books,' Elizabeth said.

***

At dinner, they partook of a simple roast with an abundance of fresh vegetables, which Mr Somersby proudly informed them he had grown in his garden. The apple in the dessert pie also came from his orchard, though the cream, he regretted, had been purchased from the village as he did not keep a house cow. Sarah felt grateful that he spared her and Elizabeth the family history of the elderly pig that had provided the roast.

While Mr Somersby carved the meat, Sarah revealed her friendship with Celia and her concern over Sir Charles's disappearance.

'Yes,' Mr Somersby said, 'it is both mystifying and, I fear, tragic. He was, as I'm sure Lady Browning has informed you, a dear friend. We were at Oxford together. Though in different colleges, we spent a great deal of our time in one another's company. We share many of the same interests.'

'May I inquire as to the nature of your interests?' Sarah asked, adopting the clergyman's manner of speaking. Although she tried to avoid mimicry, she sometimes found it difficult to do so, partly because of her need as a playwright to be able to express ideas in the voices of the characters in her creations, but also because her gifts as an actress refused to remain hidden for long.

'Philosophy. History. Politics. Social reform,' Mr Somersby said. 'The role of the church. Where the latter is concerned, I'm afraid, Charles was very critical of the Anglican persuasion. Indeed, he is seriously considering going over to either the Methodists or the Quakers.'

'But not to Rome,' Elizabeth contributed.

'Most definitely not to Rome.'

Mr Somersby sighed. 'It is the Dissenters that are on the march. There is even a chapel in the village.'

'You are losing your congregation,' Sarah said, wondering if Mr Somersby's sermons had anything to do with the decrease in numbers. 'Why is that?'

'The Church of England's appeal, madam, is mostly to the Tories, to which the middling and upper classes are inclined. Such people are few and far between in the village of Langley. The Whiggery of the Dissenters of all kinds is more to the liking of the poor and underprivileged.'

'So, to some people,' Sarah said, 'Sir Charles would be considered a traitor to his class.'

'I fear that is so. He is, of course, no such thing. It is simply his earnest desire to convince the nobility and merchant class that the time has come to change their ways. I would be a happier man if I believed the Church of England would be at the forefront of reform, but I fear the bishops are not that way inclined and, unfortunately, they have influence in the House of Lords.'

'I have been told,' Sarah said, between mouthfuls of pork roast, 'that Sir Charles is a passionate man who becomes quite emotional when speaking in public about the causes he supports.'

'I will confess, madam,' Mr Somersby said, 'that his outbursts sometimes troubled me. He allows himself to be carried away and can become sadly incoherent at times.'

'Are you implying a degree of mental instability?' Sarah said, as gently as she could so that there was no detectable tone of criticism in her voice.

'I fear that I am. He becomes over-excited and emotional. Extreme sincerity is all very well, madam, but it can be self-defeating. Rational argument, delivered in a clear and measured manner, is far more effective.'

'Was Sir Charles the same at Oxford?'

'He established a reputation for being vociferously critical of the authorities.'

'He was a rebel!' Elizabeth exclaimed. 'How splendid. It is how I found him.' She explained that she had been commissioned to paint his portrait, and then asked, 'Did he graduate?'

'No, madam, he left without taking his degree.' Mr Somersby smiled. 'There is nothing unusual about that. Many of the nobility do not want to sit exams which they know they will fail. Only the few scholars do the required work. Other undergraduates attend university for the social life and contacts it provides.'

'That will not be the situation when women are admitted,' Sarah said.

'I doubt if that will ever happen, madam. There is a limit to the benefits of reform.'

Sarah did not appreciate this observation. She thought that, had she been an elderly lady, she would have rapped his hand with her fan. She thought fondly of her spinster's disguise, again hanging in the overstuffed closets of the costume room at the Sans Pareil. Instead, she said acidly, 'I will overlook the absurdity of that remark, Mr Somersby, if you will forgive the impertinence of my next question. It concerns Lady Augusta.'

'Dear me. Poor woman. She is dying, you know. Her doctor gives her a month more at the most. A tumour. And the consumption, I believe. They are causing her to waste away and to suffer much pain.'

'In our brief conversation,' Sarah said, 'she accused Lady Browning of being responsible for Sir Charles's disappearance. She gives the impression of being an exceedingly bitter woman, uncaring of the damage her accusations can cause. Can you explain this?'

Mr Somersby moved his head sadly from side to side. 'Apart from her illness, which must surely be affecting her mental state, I know only what Sir Charles has told me and what I have observed. Apparently, her marriage to Sir Robert was profoundly unhappy. Like so many marriages among the gentry, it was at the behest of their parents. Her father, an iron master who made a fortune manufacturing artillery for the army and navy, had wealth but lacked the social position he desired for his eldest daughter. Sir Robert's father had an inherited baronetcy and estate but insufficient means to maintain the necessary way of life. It was a marriage of considerable convenience.'

'How did the boys get on with their parents?' Sarah asked.

'I understand that Lady Augusta was, again not unusually, a distant mother. I do not think Charles received a great deal of affection from her. As for his father, he was determined to turn Charles into a replica of himself. By attempting to do so, he created a rebellious and unhappy child who was always in trouble with his elders. I did not know Edward, except by hearsay—he left for the West Indies while Charles and I were still at university, but sometimes I think that if he'd been more like Sir Robert, then Charles would have been disinherited in Edward's favour. But Edward was, and I expect still is, not only physically weak but also of an artistic nature and an effeminate disposition. He was an even greater disappointment to Sir Robert than Charles.'

He turned to Elizabeth and smiled wryly. 'Sir Robert had no interest in intellectual or artistic pursuits of any kind. I met him only once. He was a brusque, uncouth, belligerent bully of a man. With parents like Sir Robert and his wife, it is perhaps not surprising that Charles is a little, shall we say, unbalanced?'

'What can you tell me about Sir Charles as a landlord?' Sarah asked.

'He is probably one of the most progressive in the nation, and certainly well-regarded by his tenants and the villagers.'

'Unlike his father.'

'His father was detested. He cared nothing for the well-being of his tenants. He allowed their cottages to fall into disrepair and did nothing to assist the poor and needy. He was positively feudal in his attitudes.'

'Apparently Sir Robert was responsible for having a local poacher transported for seven years. Do you think the man's relatives might be responsible in any way for Sir Charles's disappearance?'

'An act of revenge on the son for the sin of the father?'

'Yes.'

'No, I believe that to be wholly out of the question. I know that Charles is deeply embarrassed by his father's action and has attempted to make amends for it by paying for the education of the young man's brothers and sisters. His family are good people, regular church-goers. Indeed, the father is a church warden. I don't think for one minute that any of them, even the transported young man, would want to harm Charles.'

'That is very good news,' Sarah said. 'It eliminates one of the possible suspects.'

Sarah decided that to continue her questioning would make the conversation too much of an interrogation to be courteous to their host. Accordingly, she turned the conversation to general questions about the village. Elizabeth assisted her by showing interest in the history of the church.

The all-important question about Celia and the horseman riding by would have to wait for the next day.

Thirty-four

After the meal, the clergyman retired immediately to his study to prepare, Sarah assumed, yet another sermon. She suggested to Elizabeth that they should walk to Browning Hall and pay a visit to Celia, and then, if she would receive them, pay their respects to the dowager Lady Augusta.

They arrived at the hall shortly before six after a pleasant leisurely stroll through the balmy evening. Mrs Williams, the housekeeper, seemed pleased to see them.

'My lady will be delighted to see you, Miss Kedron, I know. She is desperately lonely and has no one to talk to except me. Please wait in the library. I'm sure she'll be with you shortly.' She hurried out to fetch her mistress.

Elizabeth scanned the titles of the books on the shelves. 'Sir Charles's father must be turning in his grave. This is the library of a revolutionary.'

Sarah nodded. 'It is certainly beginning to look as if his disappearance could have a political explanation.'

Elizabeth grinned. 'How boring.'

Celia's arrival prevented further conversation.

She ran into the room with her arms outstretched. 'Oh, Sarah, how lovely to see you. I think of you so often. How are you?'

The two women embraced.

'I am very well,' Sarah said, 'which is more than I think you can say about yourself. You are so pale. Are you sleeping badly?'

'Yes. I rarely sleep well. And when I do, I have the most frightening dreams. I don't know what they all mean. But I'm always lost and alone in a large city. Like London, but it's not London. It seems to be a city of my imagination.' She looked at Elizabeth and smiled, waiting to be introduced.

'And this is Miss Stockton,' Sarah said. 'The artist who has been painting your husband's portrait. She has kindly given us permission to have prints of it circulated. We are hoping they will produce a response from someone with information about Sir Charles's whereabouts.'

Elizabeth and Celia shook hands. Elizabeth said, 'I admire Sir Charles greatly, Lady Browning. He cares passionately about many important political matters. I hope you will like his portrait when it's finished. I'm sure he commissioned it as a present for you.'

This statement produced a flood of tears from the girl as if to confirm her immaturity. Between sobs, remembering her manners, she said, 'May I offer you refreshment?'

'Thank you, but no. We have recently dined. We are staying with Mr Somersby at the vicarage,' Sarah informed her.

Celia frowned, seeming both puzzled and hurt. 'But why not here?'

Sarah explained that they wanted to be near the church, so Elizabeth could paint it in different lights. She thought it would be tactless to refer to the shortage of servants to look after the needs of guests at Browning Hall.

Celia nodded, the explanation seeming to satisfy her.

Sarah quickly informed her of the progress, such as it was, of the investigation and then came to the point of the visit. 'I understand, Celia, that Sir Charles has expressed interest in standing for Parliament if the government calls an election. Can you tell me anything about the present member for Langley?'

Celia thought for a moment or two, and then said, 'His name is Alfred Ramsbottom.' She giggled. 'Ramsbottom. Isn't that a silly name?'

'It is quite common in the north of England,' Sarah told her, a little primly. 'I know it sounds funny, but it has nothing to do with rams' bottoms. It's Old English for land at the bottom of a valley.'

'Yes, of course. I'm sorry. Anyway, his wife called and left a card while we were in London. I have not returned the call. I have not really felt like calling on a stranger and having to make the usual social chit-chat. Her husband has a textile mill, or several mills, I think, in Lancashire. He is very rich. He has a house there, one in London, and his wife lives near here at Langley Manor. The house is already huge, and I'm told he is adding to it all the time.'

'How long has he been a member of Parliament?'

'Oh, not long. Mrs Williams has told me a little about him. She says he is very ambitious. She says he wants to become a minister or something and then be made a lord.'

'Given a peerage,' Elizabeth said, 'with a seat in the House of Lords.'

'Something like that. Then his wife will be a real lady—much more important than me. Mrs Williams says that apparently Mrs Ramsbottom doesn't like it that I'm a lady and she isn't. Of course, Charlie is only a baronet. He isn't a lord or anything like that.'

'Is Mr Ramsbottom popular in Langley?' Sarah asked.

'I don't think so. But Charlie says he doesn't have to be popular because he buys up all the properties and fills them with tenants who will vote for him.'

'I see,' Sarah replied, 'So Langley is a Pocket Borough where only the burgage tenements can vote.'

'I think that is what Charlie said,' Celia replied. 'All I know is that Charlie said he would need to work hard to win the seat. And probably spend quite a lot of money.'

Changing the subject, Sarah said, 'My dear, forgive my impertinence, but would you mind telling me how well you knew Sir Charles when he asked you to marry him?'

'I don't mind telling you,' Celia said shyly. 'It was hardly at all. We had spoken a few times after church. I mean, as I was the vicar's daughter that was natural.'

'Of course.'

'Then he asked me to go for walks with him, and my father encouraged that, and then one day he said I was just the kind of girl he needed for a wife.'

'Do you know what he might have meant by that?' Sarah asked.

'Perhaps because I wasn't rich or from a higher class? I don't know really. Anyway, he asked me if he could approach my father. I told him I needed to talk to my father first.'

'Did you want to marry him?' Elizabeth asked, unable to control her curiosity.

'I'd never thought about it.'

'So you weren't in love with him.'

'No, but I liked him. He was kind and respectful.'

Sarah now had to ask the all-important question. 'Were you in love with anyone else?'

Celia clearly didn't know how she should answer this question. She bit her lip, hoping for inspiration.

Sarah pressed her for an answer. 'Was there someone else, Celia? A childhood sweetheart perhaps?'

Celia looked down at the floor.

Sarah thought she was the kind of girl who probably found it difficult to lie. Perhaps she always blushed or unwittingly gave herself away by stuttering or some other mannerism or speech difficulty. 'Perhaps there was a man in the village who was in love with you,' she prompted.

Celia took a deep breath and burst out, 'My father wanted me to marry Sir Charles. You have seen the vicarage. We were very poor. My mother died when I was a baby, and my father brought me up. I did not have a governess or anything like that. The St Andrew's living was barely enough for food and fuel. If it hadn't been for the generosity of the people in the village, we would not have had enough to eat. And father was not well. There was no money for a curate.'

Sarah turned towards the girl and took her hand. 'I understand, my dear. What was your lover's name?'

'Tom. Tom Bridge. He works for the blacksmith. He's the apprentice.'

'And he rides a black horse and has visited you since you returned from London.'

Celia nodded. 'There's nothing wrong with his visits, Sarah. We don't ...' She left the sentence unfinished.

'If Sir Charles is never found and is declared deceased, do you think you will marry Tom?'

'Oh, how could you!' Celia howled, running from the room.

'Oh, dear,' Elizabeth said. 'I think you have your answer.'

'Yes, I rather think I have. Come, Elizabeth, it's time for us to leave. It is getting late. If we hurry, we could call on Lady Augusta on our way back to the vicarage.'

Thirty-five

Miss Simmons did not want to admit Sarah and Elizabeth to the dowager's presence.

'Her ladyship is resting, madam,' she told Sarah. 'She is weak and tires easily.'

'I appreciate that,' Sarah said, 'but we have come from London in connection with Sir Charles's disappearance. I think her ladyship would appreciate having a few words with us. We will not detain her long or overtire her.'

'If you insist. Wait in the parlour. I'll see if she is awake.' With ill grace, the woman showed Sarah and Elizabeth into the parlour.

Elizabeth said, 'She gives the impression of being a gatekeeper.'

Sarah nodded. 'That and more, I think. She has been with Lady Augusta since she was a child, as a nurse, governess, and then maid or companion when her mistress married Sir Robert. I'm not sure which.'

When Miss Simmons returned, she ushered the visitors into Lady Augusta's day room. The dowager lay on a chaise longue, covered with a blanket. Her health had clearly deteriorated further since Sarah's first visit. She took shallow, rapid breaths, and the pain lines on her face had deepened.

'Your ladyship is most courteous and obliging to see us,' Sarah said. 'May I introduce Miss Elizabeth Stockton? She is the artist Sir Charles commissioned to paint his portrait.'

Elizabeth bowed.

Lady Augusta almost growled her response. 'What did he want that for?'

'As a present for his wife, your ladyship,' Elizabeth said.

'Huh! And why should he think she'd want that? I know you've found out nothing because there's nothing to find out. His wife murdered him. Or that blackguard smith in the village has done it. You mark my words.' The effort of speaking exhausted the sick woman. She closed her eyes and breathed heavily.

'There are several other possibilities, your ladyship,' Sarah said.

'Nonsense. You are wasting your time. Who is paying you to pry into our affairs? The girl has no money. Her father is a pauper.'

Miss Simmons, from her position standing in the doorway, said, 'I think you should leave now. Her ladyship has nothing further to say to you.'

Sarah realized this was true. Any further attempt to engage the dying woman in conversation would be pointless. 'Thank you for your time, your ladyship.' She turned and, followed by Elizabeth, left the room.

After closing the day-room door, Miss Simmons said, 'The doctor gives her a month at the most. The tumour has spread throughout her body. I'm keeping her alive with a thin gruel. It is all she can eat.' Tears formed in the woman's eyes.

'I know you have been close to her for most of her life, madam,' Sarah said. 'Please accept our sympathy. She is indeed fortunate to have such a devoted friend as yourself.'

They left the house and made their way back to the vicarage. Sarah did not feel like talking for some time, and they were halfway to their destination when she said, 'I think we have a terrible tragedy unfolding before us, Elizabeth.'

'I'm afraid so. You believe Lady Augusta to be correct. Her daughter-in-law is responsible for Sir Charles's disappearance?'

'I believe Celia's behaviour needs careful interpretation. Her refusal to answer my questions earlier and then the manner in which she left the room could be interpreted as guilt. Then again, she is so childlike that her indecision and hesitancy could simply be a part of her character. I think I should discuss it all with James and my father.'

'You don't think the evidence is strong enough to take to a magistrate?' Elizabeth asked. 'From everything you have told me and from what we have witnessed this evening, I'm sure a competent prosecutor could make a compelling case against the girl.'

Sarah agreed. Celia had married for the benefit of her father's comfort in his final years. She'd had to abandon the man she loved and had expected to marry, and who now, presumably, visited her secretly. Her marriage to Sir Charles had been a disappointment. She hadn't been able to cope with London social life and dreaded having to live the kind of life her husband's social position demanded of her and would do increasingly if he entered Parliament. She had been left to her own limited devices while her husband pursued his political interests, and there was a strong possibility that he had taken a mistress as he had returned home smelling of another woman. Significantly, her mother-in-law, the woman who could be expected to know her as well as anyone, was convinced of her guilt. The only item in her favour was that she had instigated the investigation, but even this, Sarah realized, could have been a deliberate attempt to muddy the waters by pointing her in the wrong direction.

'Elizabeth, I would like to return to London no later than midday tomorrow. Do you mind? If you spend the morning sketching, we shall have carried out the ostensible purpose of our visit. We can always express the hope to Mr Somersby that we may visit again in the future.'

Elizabeth took hold of her arm, gently squeezed it and said with a warm and gentle smile, 'Dearest, of course I don't mind. I'm sure you realize that, as interesting as it may be, ecclesiastical architecture was not the greatest drawcard of this trip.'

They continued walking to the vicarage, now arm in arm. The evening had turned cloudy, and the driveway was dark, blustery and cold. When they reached the vicarage, only one light shone. It came from Mr Somersby's study. However, once inside they found a spluttering candle lamp alight for them on the hallstand. Sarah took hold of it to light their way to their rooms.

'What a gloomy house this is,' Elizabeth said. 'Do you think it is haunted?'

'Not for one moment,' Sarah declared, having no belief in anything supernatural.

'But how can you be so sure?' Elizabeth took Sarah's free hand to boost her confidence. 'There are stories about haunted houses everywhere.'

'You are a silly goose.' Sarah giggled. 'You mustn't believe everything you read. A lot of it is invented by people like me, trying to earn a living. All the Gothic novels that are so popular in the circulating libraries are just nonsense for poorly educated women to read. You are certainly not one of those.'

When they reached the landing, Elizabeth looked towards their rooms, which were located at the far end, and said shyly, 'I'm sorry, Sarah, but I'm frightened to be on my own. Could we stay together tonight?'

'I'd like that, my dear.' Sarah squeezed Elizabeth's arm. 'We can be like two girls in a boarding school dormitory, giggling and talking all night. But I brought nothing to eat, so we shan't have a midnight feast.'

Later, once comfortably settled with the covers pulled right up and the candle doused, Elizabeth asked, 'Do you have a lover? Have you ever made love, you know, properly?'

'Yes. I have made love with several men. Mostly actors. Beautiful to look at but, oh dear, so full of themselves.'

'Are you in love with James Brewster, the man who works for your father?'

'In love with him?' Sarah exclaimed. 'I should say not. Oh, he is good-looking, without quite seeming to realize it— which is a change and a relief. He's clever and the kind of man who would be a good and loyal friend, but no more.'

'And you have not made love yet.'

'No. Oh, I would enjoy him, I expect, but he is the kind of man who would want to marry a woman he loved. Having an affair with him would make our situation tense. You see, I think it likely that my father will take him into partnership if he continues to impress. I don't want to do anything that could damage that. My father is the dearest person in the world to me and always will be.'

Elizabeth lay quietly, trying to digest everything she had just heard. Her art was important to her but only in as much as it provided her with a living and a certain independence. She knew her talent was far, far below that of the most famous portrait painters of the day; she would never be another Sir Thomas Lawrence or Samuel Drummond. She would be happy to sacrifice her independence for a fulfilling relationship.

'Will you never get married, then?' she asked.

'I'm sure I will not. At the most, I might live with someone I love. I don't need marriage, my dear. I'm financially independent, and I have no interest in social position. And I have absolutely no intention of allowing any man to dictate to me how I lead my life and spend my money. I need sexual love and friendship, of course I do, but I don't see why I should tie myself to one person.'

'And you don't want children?'

'No, they don't seem to be important to me. Does that surprise you?'

'Dearest, everything about you surprises me. I want to be able to accept you as you are, but I'm far from sure that I can.' She gently brushed Sarah's long, dark hair from the pillow so she could move a little closer. A few moments later she said, almost in a whisper, 'But for the moment, I'll accept anything you have to offer.'

Thirty-six

When James arrived at his office the morning after his evening with Mr Fielding, a queue of employees, headed by Jack Godwin, waited to see him. Jack appeared poised to deliver his findings and race away on his next assignment. Behind him, the senior clerk grasped in both hands the results of the previous day's culling of correspondence and notes on the interviews with the more than a hundred hopeful men and women. A young man sat on a chair at the end of the queue.

James ushered the young apprentice into his room and closed the door behind him. 'Well, Jack, what have you got for me?'

Referring to his notes, Jack delivered the results of his inquiries: 'It is all negative, sir. There are no records of Mr Edward Browning arriving from the West Indies, nor could I discover anything of much interest about the convict Harness. According to the records of the Hertfordshire Assizes, he was convicted for poaching and sentenced to seven years' transportation to Australia. He was transferred to the hulks, where he remained for three months awaiting a ship. He then sailed from Portsmouth for Sydney on the second of July on the *Admiral Gambier*—Master, Ed Harrison—with two hundred other convicts, assorted settlers and military personnel. The journey took one hundred and seventy-seven days, three lives were lost at sea, and one hundred and ninety-seven passengers and crew disembarked.'

'He was not one of the lives lost?' James asked.

'No, sir. The records of his life in New South Wales are kept there. He should have completed his sentence this year. However, he may have been granted a ticket of leave for good behaviour or because he had skills that were in short supply. The Hertfordshire court records list him as being a carpenter.'

'You have done well, Jack. In this matter, a negative result can be as useful as a positive one.'

'Thank you, sir. There is one more matter I should report on. One of the shipping clerks told me that it would not be unusual for a ship from the West Indies to disembark passengers at a European port, and then arrange for them to be trans-shipped across the Channel.'

'A good point. I shall bear that in mind.'

'Do you have anything for me to do today, sir?' As eager as a puppy hoping for a walk, Jack Godwin quivered with anticipation.

Not wanting to disappoint him, James said, 'I'm sure I shall have something shortly. But first I must deal with all these people. Send in the chief clerk, will you?'

'Sir!' Jack turned smartly on his heel and left the office.

Within seconds the chief clerk entered. He put the pile of documents on James's desk. 'Good morning, sir. We have annotated all the correspondence. Of the men and women queuing to be interviewed, only one seemed to be of interest. We requested him to call early this morning. He is waiting outside. His name is Arthur Wetherby. He may be one of the last persons to have seen Sir Charles before he disappeared.'

James nodded. 'Send him in.'

Arthur Wetherby, a smartly dressed young man with the appearance of a civil servant, had a certain obsequiousness in his manner that suggested an occupation requiring some servility.

'Do sit down, Mr Wetherby,' James said. 'I believe you have information to communicate concerning Sir Charles Browning.'

Wetherby sat and rested his hands on his knees, moving his fingers nervously. 'I wish to make it clear, sir, that neither I nor my good wife are interested in the offered reward, whatever it is. We simply wish to be of service.'

'Thank you. I appreciate that. So?'

'My wife, Fanny, sir, and I frequent Almack's. We are both fond of dancing and the facilities there are to our liking.'

James smiled. 'And to the liking of many thousands of others. Please continue.'

'We were taking a rest and having refreshment in one of the tea rooms, sir. Sir Charles and his wife, Lady Browning, were seated at the table next to ours. We had no idea at the time that they were nobility. Had we even suspected that they were, we would never have been so presumptuous as to attempt to engage them in conversation.'

'But you did.'

'Yes, sir. The lady was most friendly towards my wife and they chatted away, sir, as if they were old friends.'

James imagined the scene without difficulty. Celia, having met someone more like herself, would have wanted to develop a friendship if possible. 'And Sir Charles?'

'He, too, sir, was most accommodating. He asked my occupation, and when I told him that until recently I was a Constable at Shadwell, and that I shall shortly transfer to the new Police Office at Marylebone, he plied me with questions about my work and experiences.'

'He made no attempt to inform you of his title?'

'None, sir. I knew nothing of his social position until I informed your clerk that I believed I knew the man whose likeness is on the print. It was your clerk who informed me that he was a baronet.'

'Why do you think he kept his title, and that of his wife's, a secret from you?'

'I must assume, sir, that he believed that if we knew his social position, we would feel constrained to maintain the appropriate distance and respect.'

'So you believe he wanted your friendship.'

'Actually, sir, he wanted me to tell him about the London underworld and take him to places of ill repute.'

'For the purpose of pleasure?'

'Oh, no, sir. Nothing like that. He is a most respectable gentleman. No, he explained that he belonged to an organization of men, mostly tradesmen and merchants in a small way of business, who wished to reform many aspects of life in the city. He told me that living in the country, as he did, he knew little about such things as gambling dens, brothels and so on. He wished me to escort him to such places.'

'And you had no objection to doing this?' James asked.

'To be truthful, sir, I had little interest in spending my limited free time in such places, but Fanny and Celia—Lady Browning, that is—seemed to be enjoying one another's company so much that I felt obliged to assist in developing the friendship.'

'When was the last time you saw Sir Charles?'

'On the evening of May the fourth.'

'And did Lady Browning have the company of Fanny before then?'

'Yes, sir. On several occasions. They went shopping together, sir. Well, not shopping exactly; just looking, sir. My wife became fond of the lady, sir, and regretted that she didn't have the leisure to spend more time with her.'

'Your wife is employed?'

'Yes, sir. Fanny is a seamstress in the employment of Nathan's, the theatrical costumiers.'

'Have you or has your wife spoken to Lady Browning or Sir Charles since May the fourth?'

'No, sir. We've had no further contact with either of them. We assumed they had returned to the country. I got the impression they had a small farm in Hertfordshire.'

James smiled to himself. The 'small farm' was a two-thousand-acre estate. 'Mr Wetherby, this is most interesting. I am deeply obliged to you for coming forward, as I know Lady Browning will be. You will oblige us exceedingly if you'll provide my assistant with details of all the places to which you escorted Sir Charles. Would that be possible?'

'I shall be pleased to provide whatever information is in my possession, sir.'

'I'm sure my employer, Mr Matthew Kedron, will be able to arrange for you to have a free day if necessary in which to assist us further. He is acquainted with a magistrate at your police office.'

'I'm aware of Mr Kedron's reputation, sir. He is most highly regarded by the constabulary and judiciary, as are you, sir, as the editor of *The Weekly Police News*.'

'Thank you.' James stood and offered Wetherby his hand. 'I wish you good day, sir. If you will be kind enough to take a seat in the outside office for a few moments my assistant will join you.'

The two men shook hands, and Wetherby left the office. James sent for Jack Godwin and explained who Wetherby was.

'Take him to a coffee house or tavern, Jack. Buy him a meal. Get him to tell you the name and address and proprietor—if he knows it—of every establishment, no matter how vile, to which he took Sir Charles. I must know as much about these places and the people the two men met as you can discover. Do you understand?'

Jack grinned, almost beside himself with excitement. 'I won't let you down, sir.'

'I know you won't. Collect five shillings for expenses from the cashier on your way out.'

Jack disappeared from the room as if he'd turned into a mist. James sat back in his chair and looked at the pile of letters on the desk in front of him. He supposed he'd better spend the morning looking through them, just in case one or more revealed something of interest.

Thirty-seven

Sarah and Elizabeth didn't meet Mr Somersby again until breakfast the next day. The clergyman, not a man skilled in small talk, preferred to restrict himself to observations of a philosophical and theological nature, generously larded, however, with items of parish gossip.

After the necessary inquiries as to how comfortable the ladies had been during the night, he said, 'Speaking for myself, I had a sleepless night, concerned as I am by Sir Charles's disappearance and the possibility, no matter how remote, that I may have information that could be of relevance.'

'Such as?' Sarah asked through a mouthful of toast. 'A problem with his inheritance perhaps?'

'No, no. There is no question of a problem with his father's will,' the clergyman replied. 'The estate is entailed to the eldest son and thereafter to the eldest male heirs, so there is no problem pertaining to Sir Charles inheriting. Lady Augusta received an annuity and the right to reside in the dowager house during her lifetime. And there were a number of very small bequests to servants and other employees. Sir Robert was not known for his generosity.'

'There were no other substantial bequests?' Sarah asked. 'Nothing for Edward?'

'Nothing for Edward.' He smiled, knowingly. 'You are wondering if perhaps Sir Robert had a mistress. There is nothing in his will to suggest this. That does not mean, of course, that he didn't have a liaison of some kind. He may simply have not been desirous of accepting financial responsibility for the lady in question after his death.'

Elizabeth said quietly, 'I suppose if he'd made a substantial bequest to a lady who was not a family member, this would have revealed the existence of a mistress to his wife.'

'Oh!' exclaimed the clergyman. 'That would not have worried Sir Robert in the slightest. From what Sir Charles told me, it is my understanding that his father's relationship with his mother was far from close. Indeed, in a word they were estranged. And, of course, it is a common practice among the upper classes for the men to keep courtesans under their protection. In the case of Sir Robert and his wife, it would have been surprising if Sir Robert had not sought comfort elsewhere.'

'But they continued to live together,' Elizabeth said.

'Of course. Divorce was out of the question. A Private Act of Parliament would have been necessary. And the social stigma would have been unacceptable to Lady Augusta. She'd married Sir Robert wholly for social position. There was no possibility that she would agree to losing this. No, according to Sir Charles, they disliked one another intensely, and resided in separate parts of the hall. If and when a need to communicate arose, they would do so by note, carried from one end of the building to the other by a footman.'

The vicar smiled, preparing his face for a small joke. 'I expressed the view to Sir Charles that the use of carrier pigeons might have been a sensible alternative method of conveyance.'

Sarah acknowledged with only the smallest of smiles the attempt at wit. 'It must have been a miserable household. I'm not surprised that Sir Charles was in total revolt against that way of life and everything it entailed. I suppose he married Celia believing that he could enjoy an affectionate marriage based on mutual love.'

'I would like to think so, but I fear it is more likely that he married her as part of his rejection of the kind of family he'd been born into—one concerned mainly with wealth and position. He is a troubled man, Miss Kedron. He means so well but creates the most unfortunate situations for himself.'

Sarah remembered Mrs Bradshaw's observations concerning his behaviour at the meeting of The Abolition Society. 'He was quick to offend, I understand, because of his beliefs and passionate nature.'

'Precisely, and it was these that resulted in Viscount Stroud demanding satisfaction.'

'A duel!' Sarah exclaimed, eyes flashing.

'Indeed. I don't know all the details, but Sir Charles met the viscount at a social function of some kind, and they had an unpleasant altercation on the subject of slavery. Apparently, Sir Charles called the viscount a heartless blackguard for supporting and benefitting from the practice.

The viscount, who has a reputation for duelling in defence of what he maintains is his honour, challenged Sir Charles.'

'And they fought?' Elizabeth demanded to know, wide-eyed with horror.

'I don't know. In the light of the following day, when the effects of alcohol had worn off and Charles had recovered his temper, he realized that, having never fired a pistol in his life, he was likely to be mortally wounded in a duel. He wrote to me, requesting that I should be his second, asking me to intercede with the viscount's second, and if negotiations for an apology failed, to attend the duel on his behalf.'

'And you agreed?' Sarah said.

Mr Somersby prevaricated slightly. 'I wrote to the viscount's second, as instructed, and made a copy of my letter, but I didn't receive a reply.'

'So there was a duel,' Sarah said.

'If there was, my services were not required. I know only that about ten days later I was informed that Sir Charles had disappeared.'

'So if there has been a duel, he could have been killed.'

'Yes. Not only that, but steps would have been taken to protect the viscount from prosecution. As you know, duelling is illegal, and to kill a man in a duel is now considered an act of murder. Had there been a duel, and had Viscount Stroud been charged, tried and found guilty, he would almost certainly have been hanged. Unless, of course, he had friends in very high places.'

'You mean royalty,' Elizabeth said. 'The Prince Regent perhaps.'

'Certainly at that level of royalty. But it's my understanding that the viscount is greatly disliked in society. He is a ruthless brute of a man, quick to anger with a reputation as a duellist, and for the unpleasant treatment of women. I think that if Charles has been killed by him, everything possible will have been done by the viscount's cronies to protect him from the consequences of his action.'

Sarah sighed. 'A secret burial by a few thugs in a forest somewhere. Sir Charles's body may never be found. Have you reported this possibility to the magistrate?'

'It is a matter that exercises my mind without relief,' Mr Somersby said. 'On the one hand I believe I ought to make my suspicions known, but what evidence have I? Any inquiries of the viscount will meet with a denial. Unless the few men who actually attended a duel are prepared to give evidence, no steps can be taken against him. And, as I have intimated, if he has killed Sir Charles, then this will not be his first murder. He will undoubtedly have made the necessary arrangements in advance.'

'How long did you say it was after you wrote to Viscount Stroud's second that you heard that Sir Charles had disappeared?' Sarah asked.

'About ten days.' The vicar rose to his feet. 'I must now ask you to excuse me. I have a sick parishioner to visit.' And with these words, he bowed and left the room.

As soon as they were alone, Elizabeth said, visibly distraught, 'What can you possibly do about this?'

'I have no idea. Probably nothing. My father will advise me. But come, my dear. I think Mr Somersby will understand our early departure after hearing this news. I shall leave a note. I want to return to London as soon as possible.'

'Yes, of course.'

'We can come here again, dearest, and sketch when this matter is concluded.'

Elizabeth smiled, reached out and took Sarah's hands in her own. 'I would like that very much, Sarah.'

Thirty-eight

Late that afternoon, James, Sarah and her father met to discuss developments.

'I'm becoming convinced,' Sarah began, 'that the solution to this mystery will be found at Browning Hall.'

'You think that Lady Browning could be responsible?' her father asked.

'If she is not directly responsible, I suspect that someone has either acted on her behalf or for her benefit. I think it very likely that she has or had a lover in the village by the name of Tom Bridge, an apprentice blacksmith. The worst possible situation is that Celia has either encouraged or instructed him to remove Sir Charles so that she may, at an appropriate later date, marry him.'

Sarah continued to explain her suspicion. 'Consider this: she broke off her arrangement with Bridge in order to obey her father and marry Sir Charles. Bridge was jilted. He would have no liking for the baronet, who, from his point of view, stole his intended wife. Although it will be likely that Bridge will be suspected of foul play if Sir Charles is never found, the possibility of his ever being formally charged, let alone convicted, of murder is remote. He would only have had to ride to London, stake out Sir Charles's house, and accost him at an appropriate time, with or without the assistance of a paid accomplice. He wouldn't have needed to look far to find a scoundrel desirous of a well-paid hour's work. So you see, even if we could prove that Bridge spent a night in London around the time of Sir Charles's disappearance, that would not be sufficient evidence that he has been responsible for it.'

'That is all very feasible,' Matthew Kedron said, 'provided that Lady Browning was unhappy in her marriage and wanted her freedom from her husband.'

James interjected: 'We may have some evidence of that.' He described his meeting with Wetherby and concluded by saying, 'It is quite possible that Lady Browning confided in Wetherby's wife, Fanny, that she was unhappy in her marriage. Apparently, they spent a great deal of time together.'

Sarah's eyes lit with excitement. 'That's very likely, James. She would have been desperate to have a friend of her own age and class. Fanny's evidence could be vital. Do you have an address for her?'

'Not a home address, but she has work as a seamstress with Nathan's.'

'Nathan's! I know it well. I have ordered many costumes from there. It will be a simple matter to ask for Fanny to be spared from her work for an hour or so.'

'You may be right in your intuition, my dear,' Matthew said, 'but we should not overlook other possibilities.' He turned to James. 'I believe you have been inquiring about the possible return to Britain of Edward Browning and that young poacher.'

'There is no record, sir, of either of them having arrived during the past six months. That does not mean, of course, that neither of them has returned. They could have disembarked on the continent, at Boulogne, for example, and trans-shipped from there. I doubt there is any record of their arrival if they did so.'

'Quite,' Matthew said. 'So that means they must both remain on our list of suspects. Who else is there?'

'Viscount Stroud,' Sarah said.

'That ruffian!' her father exclaimed. 'How is he involved?'

Sarah explained about the probable duel.

Matthew shook his head sadly. 'The man prospers on evil. He is a member of that group of reprobates who meet at Medmenham Abbey for heaven knows what debauched practices. If he has killed Sir Charles, obtaining evidence will not be easy. He will inevitably deny any connection with the baronet's disappearance, and his seconds will have been adequately bribed to maintain silence on the affair.'

'The only other suspect I can think of,' James said, 'is Albert Ramsbottom, the MP for Langley. With all this talk of an election, if Sir Charles stands, that could be the end of Ramsbottom's parliamentary career, especially if the Whigs win enough seats to form a government. The man has a strong motive for removing his rival and more than enough wealth to pay for its execution.'

'This is all very interesting,' Matthew said. 'You are making excellent progress. Now what we have to do is investigate as much as we can those possibilities you have listed. I suggest you ignore at this stage the possible return of

Edward Browning. He will surface eventually to claim his inheritance.'

'Mr Somersby, the vicar of Langley,' Sarah interjected, 'thinks it most unlikely that the family of the transported poacher is involved. They are God-fearing and well-disposed to Sir Charles.'

'Some of the worst criminals on earth are God-fearing, my dear,' Matthew said. 'Never be misled by protestations of godliness. But I think he must be considered the least likely suspect. I believe you should you talk to Fanny Wetherby first. And you, James, could visit Mr Ramsbottom in the person of a feature writer for *The Informer*. Tell him you have been commissioned to write a series of profiles of members of Parliament whose seats depend on the burgage tenements. Speak as though you see his service as essential to the government. He is the kind of man who will feel flattered.'

'Should I approach Viscount Stroud?' James asked, 'and discreetly raise the subject of Sir Charles's intemperate behaviour and how he manages to insult people? That might produce at least an indication of the viscount's attitude towards him.'

Matthew shook his head vigorously. 'No, James. Keep away from that man. He is notorious for picking fights with people. The slightest suggestion that you suspect him of improper behaviour, and he will interpret it as an imputation against his honour. Within twenty-four hours you could find yourself flat on your back with a bullet in your chest.'

James turned a little pale.

'James, for goodness' sake, take my father's advice,' Sarah exclaimed. 'Nothing good can possibly come from risking your life. In any case, it is more than likely that the viscount accepted the apology in Mr Somersby's letter in his capacity as Sir Charles's second. Isn't that so, Father?'

Matthew agreed. 'The man would have to accept a suitable apology. It is the done thing if honour has been satisfied. In any case, I shall put it about among my nefarious collection of informers that I am interested in the outcome of yet another of Viscount Stroud's degraded and possibly murderous activities. Let us leave it at that.'

He sat back and smiled. 'You're both doing well. I hope to hear of a conclusion to your efforts soon. On Monday, James, I have a meeting with the investors in the new daily newspaper I propose to call *The London Monitor*. I would like you to attend.'

'If you wish it, sir, but—'

'But you have no desire to become the editor of a daily newspaper?'

James wasn't sure he'd heard his employer correctly. 'You wish me to edit your newspaper?'

'You are not interested in such a position?'

'Sir, I … I know not what to say.'

'"Yes, I am," will be sufficient.'

Without thinking, Sarah touched James's arm. 'James, I'm so pleased for you.'

Matthew smiled. 'I'm pleased to hear you say that, and as for your future, my dear, I'm sure you have a novel or play awaiting your attention. Your interest in Lady Browning's plight, if that is what it is, should not be allowed to continue indefinitely.'

He stood up and brought the meeting to an end by saying, 'If you have no engagement for this evening, James, I would be obliged if you would dine with me. We have much to discuss.'

Thirty-nine

The next morning, Sarah and James breakfasted together at the Chapter House Coffee Shop before setting off on their respective missions: Sarah to the premises of Nathan's couturier, and James to the London address of Alfred Ramsbottom. Parliament was sitting so James expected him to be in residence there.

He sent in his card and waited on the doorstep of the splendid residence in Manchester Square while a footman inquired of his master whether the journalist should be admitted. He didn't have to wait long. Matthew Kedron had not been wrong in assuming that the opportunity to be written about in *The Informer* would not be rejected, and James was admitted to the library without further delay. While he awaited the arrival of the MP, he glanced at the shelves of, he guessed, unread books, for it was a library designed to impress rather than to educate.

Alfred Ramsbottom was, as his name suggested, a bluff Yorkshireman. Self-made, he had seized the opportunity in his twenties to risk establishing a spinning mill at the beginning of the textile boom. The availability of cheap labour, water and, later, steam power had made his fortune. His remaining ambitions were to stay in Parliament, be given a ministry, and then a peerage. This would appease his equally ambitious wife, who would then be known as Lady Ramsbottom, as well as his three plain spinster daughters, all long past the usual marriageable age, who would suddenly become attractive to impecunious fortune-hunting bachelor members of the nobility.

As he entered the library, he offered James his hand. 'Good day to you, Mr Brewster. You are fortunate to find me at home. I'm usually attending a committee at the House at this time.'

Having immediately established his importance, he indicated that James should sit down. 'What can I do for you, sir?'

James explained the purpose of his visit and concluded with, 'So I will be greatly obliged, sir, if you will allow me to ask you a few questions about your political beliefs and policies.'

'I shall do my best to answer your questions, but I am a blunt and busy man, sir, and do not have time for fancy talk.'

'Thank you, sir. I am obliged.' His pencil poised, James said, 'Reform of Parliament is much discussed at present, sir. What are your views on enlarging the franchise?'

'Parliament functions perfectly well as it is,' Ramsbottom replied. 'The reformers are not concerned with what is to the benefit of the nation, but only with their own self-serving ambitions. Give any man who wants it the vote, and there will be chaos in the country. The rabble will take over. There will be so many unnecessary regulations and interferences with business and industry that profits will fall, and the economic power of this great nation will be a thing of the past. Already the millworkers are trying to form organizations that, if allowed to exist, will endanger the future of the industry.'

James nodded. His place was not to argue with the subject of his profile, but to listen and report accurately what he said. It would be for others, such as Matthew Kedron in his editorials, or correspondents to the letters page, to express opinions. 'There is a movement to abolish slavery in the colonies,' he said. 'Are you opposed to this movement?'

'Most definitely. There is already legislation prohibiting our ships from carrying slaves. This has seriously affected the income of the slavers. If slavery is abolished in the plantations, the price of sugar will take it beyond the reach of the general population. The interests of the ordinary people must be protected. The blacks are incapable of any kind of skilled employment. As things are, they are fed and provided with shelter. They are no worse off than many agricultural workers in Ireland.'

'And what are your personal ambitions, sir?'

'To serve my country to the best of my ability. And to support my party. I seek no other reward.'

'But you would not refuse a ministry?'

'If the Prime Minister, Jenkinson, Earl of Liverpool sees fit to make use of my experience in such a position, I would not, of course, decline. It would be my patriotic duty to accept such a burden.'

James controlled his disgust at all this hypocrisy by studiously writing the man's responses in his notebook. In an even tone, he asked, 'There is some speculation that the Earl of Liverpool might call a general election, and if he does, Sir Charles Browning will oppose you as a Whig. As lord of the manor, will he not have a substantial following?'

Ramsbottom showed no surprise or concern at this statement. James assumed that he'd been expecting it and was prepared for it. Certainly, James thought, he would have been a less than competent journalist if he'd not raised the matter, and the MP would have known this.

'The man is little short of an agitator,' Ramsbottom growled. 'God damn, it! Does he want a revolution like the French with the terror that followed? Views of men like him encouraged the rebellion in America and lost us the most valuable of all the colonies. They are a rabble, sir. You are no doubt aware that, towards the end of the last century, members of The London Corresponding Society planned to overthrow the Government and even more recently, they sent one of their number to France to encourage that monster Napoleon to invade. They believed they could take London with fifteen-hundred men and hold it until the French arrived. Madmen, sir, madmen. It was only by the swift action of the government that the ringleaders were arrested and sent to the Tower. Two of them were hanged. Damned traitors!'

James ignored the outburst. 'I understand that Sir Charles Browning has disappeared. It is feared that he has been murdered.'

'If he has been, then I am not surprised. There are many patriotic gentlemen for whom he is a danger. I do not, of course,' he added quickly, 'countenance acts of violence of any kind, but his disappearance does not surprise me.'

'Surely it would concern you if you were believed to be responsible for it.'

'Responsible? Absurd opinions and rumours do not worry me, sir. As a Member of Parliament, and as an industrialist, I am familiar with the lies of my opponents and of my disgruntled employees. It takes a certain constitution to build a career in business and politics.'

And so the interview continued. James detested Ramsbottom's extreme conservative views, but he said nothing that was in any way a criticism of them. And the man gave no impression of being concerned by the possibility of being held responsible for Sir Charles's disappearance. Nevertheless, James felt sure that a man of such extreme views and convictions would stop at nothing to protect his interests. Whatever he did he would consider it to be no more than his 'patriotic' duty.

Satisfied that he'd heard enough of Ramsbottom's philosophy, James moved away from politics to the domestic aspects of his subject's life. It soon became obvious that the politician was a devoted family man for whom the happiness and well-being of his wife and daughters were paramount.

James brought the interview to an end by saying, 'We would like to have a print of your likeness, sir, to be published alongside the article. Would you happen to have a portrait we can borrow for a few days?'

Ramsbottom smiled broadly. 'I do indeed. Only recently completed.' He rang a bell for a footman. 'Bring my portrait.'

The footman bowed and did as he was bid. When he returned, accompanied by another footman to assist him, he carried a full-length portrait of Alfred Ramsbottom, MP for Langley. James took in the man's ruddy face, softened somewhat but still an excellent likeness. His eyes fell on the artist's signature, and he drew a sharp breath. In the bottom right-hand corner of the painting was the neat signature of Elizabeth Stockton.

Forty

Sarah had no difficulty obtaining an interview with Fanny Wetherby. Her immediate employer, the cutting-floor supervisor at Nathan's, knew Sarah by name and happily gave Fanny an hour in which to meet the highly regarded assistant manager of the Sans Pareil Theatre. He thought it likely that Sarah planned the purchase of her next costume and wished to consult an expert. Fanny herself felt less enthusiastic, having been forewarned by her husband to expect a visit from the well-known publisher's daughter.

Sarah greeted Fanny with the words, 'Mrs Wetherby, it is so good of you to spare time to talk to me. I'm greatly obliged to you.'

'I don't want to make no trouble for no one, Miss Kedron,' Fanny replied.

Sarah tried to put the young seamstress's mind at rest. 'I'm sure you won't make trouble for anyone who hasn't done anything really bad. Now, shall we visit a pleasant tea room and talk there?'

'I don't know how we can help. Yesterday, my Arthur, Mr Wetherby that is, told me the couple we met at Almack's were titled people and the man is missing, but it is weeks since we saw them.'

'Ah, yes, but it is the events leading up to the disappearance of Sir Charles that I'm interested in. Please, let us postpone serious conversation until we have ordered our tea and cakes.'

As they strolled to the nearest tea room, Sarah questioned Fanny lightly about her work at Nathan's and learned that she had ambitions to be a costume designer. Sarah thought she seemed an intelligent and quietly confident young woman for whom achieving her ambition was a real possibility, especially if given just a little assistance. Although she knew she could easily borrow a costume from the theatre for her portrait sitting, Sarah thought it would help Fanny considerably if she asked Nathan's not only to make a costume but also for Fanny to design it.

Once seated and after Sarah had ordered, she asked, 'How often did you meet Lady Browning?'

'Oh, about three times. I get little free time from work, except for occasional days. Then she liked me to go shopping with her. She loved Bond Street.'

Sarah laughed. 'Don't we all! But what is your opinion of her? Please be totally honest with me. It is important that I should have the opinion of someone who has spent time with her socially.'

'She is very kind. Very considerate. Not like a society lady at all. To be honest, Miss Kedron, when I found out her standing I was so embarrassed. You see, she spoke to me as if I was her equal.'

'But, Mrs Wetherby, you are. Celia is at heart a delightful country girl.'

Fanny nodded. 'Yes. Yes, I discovered that. And she is so unhappy and tells me she is lonely with no one to talk to. When she said her husband, Charlie, as we called him, was really a baronet, she made me promise not to tell my Arthur, that is, Mr Wetherby. "And don't call me my lady," she said. "We are Fanny and Celia. Good friends, and don't forget that."'

'Is she unhappy in her marriage?'

'Very. Oh, not because Charlie is unkind to her. She says he is the kindest of men. But ...' and here Fanny tittered, 'but she says she can't understand most of what he says. It all goes over her head. And she is very uncomfortable in society. She says she just doesn't know how to behave or know what to say to the women she meets at dinners and dances and that kind of thing.'

'Did she ever tell you about her life before she married Sir Charles? A childhood sweetheart, perhaps?'

Fanny nodded, though reluctant to break the confidence of her friend. 'She did. She told me about him at our last meeting. I think his name was Tom Bridge. He was a blacksmith in the village. She told me they'd planned to marry as soon as he finished his apprenticeship, but then she had had to marry Sir Charles for her father's sake. She said it broke her heart, but she had to do what was best for her father. He's old and ill and was very poor. Now she pays for him to live comfortably.'

'And what about her suitor?' Sarah asked.

'She told me he was very angry. Apparently, he was a big problem for her. He called at Browning Hall whenever Sir Charles was away. Which was often 'cos he attended many meetings in London. She told me she had begged Tom Bridge to stay away, to leave her alone and accept that she could never marry him, but he wouldn't listen. She was worried that he might do something, you know … rash.'

She leant forward across the little table, and whispered, 'She told me he swore that he would never give up hope of marrying her and making her happy. She said he is a good man, but he has very strong feelings. And he has lots of friends in the village—men who don't care for the gentry.'

'Oh, dear,' Sarah said. 'That is rather alarming. You know, of course, that Sir Charles has disappeared, and no one has any idea where he is or what has happened to him.'

'Yes. Mr Wetherby told me. He also told me to tell you everything I know. But please, Miss Kedron, don't pay too much heed to what I have told you. People often say things they don't really mean when they are angry or upset, don't they?'

'Only too often,' Sarah said sadly. 'Only too often. I sometimes think it's easier to say what one doesn't really mean than what one does.' She reached across the table and touched Fanny's hand. 'Thank you for your honesty. And don't worry about anything you've said. You have done no more than report a conversation you had.'

She sat back and smiled. 'Now, let me tell you about a costume I would like you to design and make. I'm sure I can persuade Nathan's to give you the work.'

Fanny's face lit up, shining with enthusiasm. 'You mean I am to do everything—not just the sewing?'

'Everything, my dear. We will choose the different materials together. You shall rough out a design, and when we are both agreed, you shall make the costume. Do you know Dr Goldsmith's play *She Stoops to Conquer?*'

'Oh, yes. Mr Wetherby and me, we love the theatre. When we have a little money to spare, we go to Drury Lane and Covent Garden. Only in the pit or in the top gallery, of course. I have seen that play. It's very funny. And I love the character of Kate Hardcastle.' Fanny cast down her eyes. 'But it can be a bit vulgar; don't you think?'

'No more vulgar than many real-life society ladies of my acquaintance,' Sarah said with a laugh, 'and a great deal less than some.'

At this point the tea and cakes arrived, and for the next half an hour or so, the conversation continued in a desultory way on the subject of Fanny's work at Nathan's.

Forty-one

James took a sedan chair from Manchester Square back to his office. He wanted time to think about what he had discovered. Elizabeth Stockton was not just acquainted with Albert Ramsbottom, she must have spent many hours in his company. And yet, as far as James knew, she had never revealed this to Sarah. This troubled James. Why had Elizabeth been so secretive?

She would have known—for surely Sarah would have mentioned it—that the MP was a person of interest in their investigation. Therefore, her secrecy was intentional, and had to be considered suspicious. As the chairmen jogged along on their journey through the busy streets, the only acceptable explanation that occurred to James was that she'd been embarrassed by having taken money from a man who held such reactionary and anti-reformist views. But surely, he thought, if the two women were as friendly as he believed them to be, Elizabeth Stockton would have wanted to confide in Sarah her concerns about the man and what he stood for.

Various possible reasons for Elizabeth Stockton's secrecy went round and round in his head, the most likely explanation being that the artist had put herself under the MP's protection. In short, she was his mistress. Most MPs had mistresses because the majority were men of wealth and could afford one, or even two. Yet his interview with the man a short time earlier had revealed his devotion to, or at least fear of, his ambitious wife. James wondered if Ramsbottom had managed to resist the abundant opportunities for dalliance that the city provided to men of means.

As for Elizabeth Stockton's reasons for accepting the life of a courtesan, he knew her income from portraiture would be meagre. She was young, little known, not a member of the Royal Academy of Arts or an artist being promoted by a gallery owner, so she would be reliant for her income on commissions from middle-ranking merchants and politicians. Though worth a hundred pounds or so for a portrait, she would obtain perhaps half a dozen of these a year if she were fortunate. Invariably, she would be kept waiting months, even years for payment as the wealthy often disliked paying their bills on time. Her clients would treat her the way most men of means treated their tailors and other tradesmen. Gifts from a man such as Ramsbottom, and, even more importantly, introductions to his acquaintances in the cloth trade and parliament would be worth a great deal to her. James knew only too well that, in order to succeed, connections were often more important than talent, especially in the arts.

Assuming this was the case, James's next problem was whether to say anything to Sarah before he had conclusive proof of the reason for Miss Stockton's secrecy. His decision on this matter was to be the most serious mistake of his life so far, a mistake that had the potential to create ruinous consequences for him. In short, he decided not to confide in Sarah yet, but first to find out as much as he could about Elizabeth Stockton, even if this involved spying on her movements.

He meant well in his reasoning for taking this course of action: he didn't want to worry Sarah unless there was something important for her to worry about, and he knew she was becoming increasingly fond of her new friend. Unless it was absolutely necessary, he didn't want to do or say anything that might damage that friendship. If he discovered that Elizabeth Stockton no longer maintained contact with the MP, then, until a more appropriate time arrived—such as evidence that Ramsbottom was in no way responsible for Sir Charles's disappearance—there would be no need for him to mention the connection. If, on the other hand, it became obvious that she met frequently with the MP, then Sarah would have to be told, due to the implications for their investigation.

James determined to take action immediately on his arrival at the office. He expected that Jack would be awaiting his next assignment, as indeed was the case.

'Here is a list, sir, of all the gambling houses, brothels, bagnios and so on that I could discover from printed sources as well as from asking around. There are hundreds of them, sir. It will take days to visit them all with the likeness of Sir Charles and ask if anyone has seen the gentleman. And that, sir, assumes that the owners or employees of such establishments do not throw me out on my neck for being inquisitive. Many of these places are outside of the law. And they employ some most frightening-looking individuals. I don't think they would hesitate to behave in a violent manner to any constable or journalist they considered to be a threat to their continued livelihood.' He paused, breathing heavily from the effort of his exposition.

'Quite,' James said. 'Give me your list. I will look at it later. In the meantime, I have a safer task for you.' He smiled. 'That is to say, I hope that it will prove to be safer. However, it is of a most confidential nature, Jack, and the kind of task that every journalist finds himself having to perform in the pursuit of a good story.' He beckoned. 'Come closer.'

All ears and agog, Jack moved nearer to the desk, and on tiptoe, almost over-balancing in his eagerness, leaned towards James.

'I want to know, Jack, where a particular lady goes and who visits her. This will entail keeping a daily watch on her residence. There are often hackneys waiting for custom in the nearby streets. Hire one by the hour. Sit in it. Watch. Note and follow the lady whenever she leaves her residence. Do you understand?'

'Yes, sir!' Jack could hardly control his excitement at being asked to do what he believed, quite correctly, a certain class of gossip-mongering journalist was required to do. The weekly journals were full of their discoveries concerning who was conducting a liaison and with whom. Their readers could not, it seemed, have enough information—or, more accurately, innuendo—about the activities of the current batch of celebrity courtesans and their lovers. Names were disguised, so that it was usually, 'Miss A or B has been seen departing late from the residence of Lord C or D,' but everyone who followed the course of such liaisons knew exactly to whom such statements referred.

'Pay the cabbie by the hour, Jack. Keep out of sight. The lady does not know you, but I do not want her to suspect that she is being watched. Do you understand?'

'Completely, sir.'

'Good. The lady's name is Miss Elizabeth Stockton. She lives at number 2A Cheyne Walk, Chelsea. She is an artist and looks like one. She is blonde-haired, a bit plump but otherwise attractive, even beautiful.'

James gave the boy five shillings and brought the interview to an end.

Forty-two

As soon as Jack had left, eager to begin his mission, James tried to take his mind off the problem of Elizabeth Stockton by going through the list of places, mostly of dubious reputation, where young bloods were wont to spend their time and waste their fathers' money.

From what he knew of Sir Charles's character, James thought it unlikely that the baronet would have visited such places in search of pleasure and excitement. It was likely, however, that he would have done so as part of his inquiry into the seamier aspects of London life. As a social reformer he would have been concerned by the curse of gambling and by the tragic lives of so many of the prostitutes and their fatherless children. He would have been deeply ashamed by the vast gap between the way of life of the wealthy and of the desperately poor, and he would have discovered that the lives of so many women were blighted through no real fault of their own.

Seduced for the fun and challenge of it by the young master, for whom female servants were an easy target for their lust, many servant girls, as often as not still in their teens and fearful of losing their places, succumbed to unwanted attentions that frequently resulted in pregnancy. Discharged then for immorality, without a reference, with no money and only basic domestic skills to offer, they resorted to prostitution to live. Many thousands of them worked on the streets of London or in the brothels and bawdy houses. Then, as often as not, they died of the pox or consumption before they reached thirty.

The more attractive, better educated and sexually proficient of the women worked from rented rooms in the Covent Garden area and attracted regular customers. Higher still in the sexual social and economic hierarchy were the courtesans—often actresses and other theatrical performers—who became mistresses of the wealthy and, if fortunate, eventually married their protectors on the death of the man's wife. So many women died comparatively young that a patient mistress had a good chance of eventually marrying her protector.

James felt sure Sir Charles would have wanted to investigate this side of London life. He would probably have visited several of the establishments on Jack's list. Apart from dalliance, they offered everything from card games to bear baiting and dog fighting. One of them, *The Lamb and Flag*, known as 'the Blood Bucket', specialized in bare-knuckle pugilism. The problem was going to be finding the time to visit even a small selection of these places in the hope that, at one of them, someone would remember having seen Sir Charles. And even if such a person existed and was prepared to admit to having met or spoken to him, there was no guarantee that he or she would have any information of value.

A knock on his door interrupted these somewhat despairing thoughts, and the chief clerk half-entered and put his head round. 'An urchin brought this note for you, sir. I thought perhaps you should look at it.' He carried the note to James's desk and proffered it uncomfortably as if it were heavily contaminated by germs and other filth—which it probably was.

'Thank you.'

The clerk left the room and James considered the cryptic contents of the badly written note: 'Ask Millie. Joe's place.'

He consulted Jack's list and found Joe's Place listed as a gambling den in a room above a low tavern in Cheapside.

James rang the bell on his desk for the chief clerk. When he returned, James asked, 'Did you ask the urchin who gave him this note to deliver?'

'He said a woman, sir. She stopped him in the street and gave him a penny to bring it to our address.'

'He didn't describe the woman? Was she well-dressed? A servant girl?'

'I regret that I failed to ask the lad for further information, sir. He was in a great hurry—just thrust the note into my hand and ran off.'

'Of course. He probably would not have been able to tell you much anyway. But thank you.'

'It is interesting, sir?'

'Who knows? But no reward is asked for. Unlike our visitors this week, whoever sent this note does not want anything for herself. It is either an altruistic gesture or perhaps an attempt to get a rival into trouble. I shall have to follow it up.'

'Very good, sir.'

The hour was now four o'clock and time for James to leave for Portman Place. Matthew Kedron liked to dine early, and he had arranged that during the meal they would discuss developments so far. James had to report on his meeting with Mr Alfred Ramsbottom MP, and Sarah would, no doubt, report on her meeting with Mrs Fanny Wetherby.

James wondered whether, if he had the opportunity, he should raise the problem of Elizabeth Stockton with his employer. He didn't like the idea of keeping anything important from him. On the other hand, he found something distasteful about talking to Sarah's father about her behind her back.

Forty-three

Matthew Kedron waited until Sarah and James had finished their meal and were relaxing over the remains of their claret before coming to the purpose of the small dinner party.

'I have acquired premises for *The London Monitor* next to the Kings Arms in Fleet Street,' he said. 'Printing will be undertaken here in Paternoster Row. Distribution is arranged. All that is needed is a strong editorial team.' He beamed paternally at James. 'I'm assuming, my boy, that you will have no objection to moving immediately from the editorial chair of the *Police News* to that of *The London Monitor?*'

'None at all, sir. There is no move I would rather make. But you do me so much honour, I feel that I am undeserving of such a position at my age and with no experience of a daily newspaper.'

'Very few journalists have such experience,' Matthew said. 'Most daily newspapers flounder within a few years of being established, mainly because their proprietors and editors have no clear vision of what kind of publication they want theirs to be. Most of them are interchangeable gossip sheets. I intend *The London Monitor* to concentrate on financial, political and foreign affairs in as much as they affect business and industry. This great nation is on the verge of amazing developments of all kinds, especially political, scientific and industrial. It needs a newspaper of quality to cover all such developments.'

James's employer's enthusiasm infected his own feelings about his work. 'It will be a great challenge, sir. When do you expect to publish the first edition?'

'In two months. We shall need to devote all our energies to the preparations. There are many prospective reporters and production people to be interviewed and appointed. All that kind of thing I must leave to you.'

'Of course, sir. It will have my full attention.'

'But we are still a long way from solving the mystery of Sir Charles's disappearance,' Sarah exclaimed.

'Ah, yes, "the Case of the Missing Baronet" as I have come to think of it,' her father replied. 'I appreciate that it could be difficult for you to continue without James's assistance, but we are in the publishing business, my dear, and it is this to which James must attend from now on. I suggest that by Sunday night, you prepare an account of your investigation, which I will take to a magistrate. It will be for him to decide how to proceed.'

For a moment it seemed that Sarah might object strongly to her father's decision. At first, she considered arguing that she was capable of continuing the investigation without James's involvement, but a moment's thought convinced her that this was not possible. The deeper they probed, the more at risk their own lives became. It seemed probable that they were investigating a calculated and brutal murder. This was not a theft of 'my lady's' favourite brooch.

'But tell me, how far have you reached in your inquiries?' Matthew asked.

'We have identified three major suspects, sir,' James replied. 'There is Tom Bridge, a local blacksmith and Celia's childhood sweetheart. There is Albert Ramsbottom, the Langley MP, and there is Edward Browning, the heir presumptive, although he is probably not even in the country. And we must still follow up the hundreds of responses to the print of Sir Charles's likeness that has been widely distributed. I have one lead I should like to attend to later this evening.'

'Which of the three do you favour, Sarah?'

'Unfortunately, Father, I'm now inclined to the young blacksmith. He has everything to gain from the baronet's death. He would gain Celia as a wife and may even think that she will inherit the Browning estate.'

'Do you think Lady Browning herself is involved?' her father queried.

'I don't want to think that she is, but it is a real possibility. I prefer to think that she came to me because she fears that Tom Bridge may have killed her husband but hopes to be able to clear his name so that she will not find herself marrying a murderer.'

'An interesting insight.' Matthew turned to James. 'Who do you favour?'

James was all but convinced that the MP was responsible. He believed the man to be ruthless, callous and wholly self-serving. With the government in such turmoil, if the Prime Minister was forced to call for an early election, it would be vital to his political and social future that he should be re-elected. If he had found out that the Browning Estate owned as many or more burgage tenements, then Sir Charles stood an equal, if not better, chance of being returned as the MP. Ramsbottom could either spend more money buying up the tenements or arrange the removal of his opponent. However, James suspected that whatever he said about Ramsbottom, Sarah would, quite innocently no doubt, pass on to Elizabeth Stockton, who, in turn, probably not so innocently, would warn the MP. He didn't want the man to be made aware that he was a murder suspect. If he knew this, he would inevitably take further steps to protect himself from discovery.

Noting his hesitation, Matthew said, 'You do not have a favourite, James?'

'Frankly, sir, we do not have enough evidence to kill a cockroach, let alone hang a murderer. I suppose, though, that Edward Browning is the obvious suspect.' Wanting to sound convincing, he enlarged on the possibility. 'He is dependent on the income from his plantation, which in turn is dependent on slave labour. The abolitionist movement is active again, and I'm confident that, when we have a Whig government, further legislation will be passed making it illegal to own slaves in the colonies. That will be the end of Edward Browning's financial independence.'

'Very interesting, James. And this means that he may not want to wait until his brother dies a natural death before he inherits the title and estate.'

'Precisely, sir. And, of course, he does not have to be in England to have arranged the murder of his brother. He has ample means to hire assassins.'

'You mentioned a new lead,' Matthew said. 'One of the respondents.'

'I have received a simple note stating nothing more than, "Ask Millie. Joe's Place"' James quoted. 'I have identified the place. It is a low gambling den. I plan to visit it later this evening and ask a few discreet questions.'

'You be careful, my boy. I don't want to lose my new editor.' Matthew turned to Sarah. 'Do we, my dear?'

Sarah smiled. 'Most definitely not. He becomes more valuable as each day passes.'

James blushed, but not with humility or embarrassment. He turned red from guilt and anxiety. He had set Jack Godwin to spy on the close friend of a woman who trusted him completely and admired him for his integrity. He feared not only that he was in danger of losing her friendship and respect, but also that if she complained about him to her father, he could lose the kind of position that every journalist in London dreamed of being offered. He began, somewhat selfishly, to regret ever having offered to help.

He could only pray that Elizabeth Stockton had an acceptable explanation for keeping silent about her acquaintance with Albert Ramsbottom.

Forty-four

After deliberating for some time, James decided that the most appropriate persona, manner and dress for a visit to Joe's Place would be that of an impoverished clerk, desperate to win a little at the tables to buy food for his family. Accordingly, James dressed as dowdily as his limited wardrobe allowed and assumed an expression that he hoped would convey quiet desperation.

Joe's Place was in a room above a small tavern down a mean side street near the St Giles Rookery, the most violent and dangerous district in London. The doorkeeper, a burly thug, admitted him without question, recognizing him for yet another fool ripe for picking. Thick smoke from the cheapest tobacco, the stench of sweat from the unwashed men and women packed around the tables, the pungent, acrid aroma of the scent and powder that the whores drenched themselves in, and the foul odour rising from the raw sewage flowing along the open gutter in the filthy street outside made the air in the room barely breathable.

The only game available, faro, the most popular card game and wholly a game of luck, required no skill. An inexperienced gambler, therefore, had as much chance of beating the banker—assuming the banker was honest, which was an unwise assumption—as any experienced member of the aristocracy for whom gambling away many thousands of pounds a night was but a daily routine. Fortune or destitution could depend on the turn of a card.

Within seconds of entering the room, one of the whores approached James. Summing him up with a glance, she realized that a little careful attention would reward her with at least a few shillings. 'New here are you, dearie?' she wheezed. The foul breath from her consumptive lungs and decayed teeth almost made him retch. 'I can bring you luck, you know. I know all the tricks of the trade.'

Linking an arm in his, as if protectively, she led him to one of the tables where a gap opened up among the players just large enough for them to squeeze in. 'You'll share any winnings I get for you, won't you, dearie?' she whispered. 'I can always tell a generous gentleman when I meet one.'

James wanted to shake her off, but he knew this would be the worst thing he could do. Obviously an habitué of the place, she would probably know who Millie was and where he might find her. She might even be Millie.

'I have only a few shillings,' he said. 'I owe too much to a moneylender. I must win something.'

'Of course you must, dearie. Trust me. I can read the table the way others read a book.' She coughed and wiped phlegm from her mouth with the sleeve of her cotton dress— a cheap but showy gown cut so low that her heavily powdered and exposed breasts were in danger of falling out. Not that she would find this a problem. Had they done so, she would have calmly restored them to their proper place with a sly wink to hint that, for a shilling or two, there were more delights to come.

Although James had never been to a gambling hell before, he assumed that the bawd's role was to encourage him to continue to gamble until he had lost everything. In league with the banker, she would advise him what to bet on, and at first, he would win sufficiently to keep him playing. But his luck would be short-lived, and he would soon hit a losing streak. By this time, the woman would have disappeared, having collected her commission on her way out.

James, who had never played faro or any card game except whist with family and friends at home, was wondering how soon it would be appropriate to ask the woman if she knew Millie, when someone tapped him on the shoulder. He turned to see a neatly and cleanly dressed be-wigged middle-aged man standing behind him.

'Forgive me, sir,' the man said, 'but I have reason to suspect that you have little or no experience at the tables.'

James sighed inwardly, assuming that the man had to be some kind of card sharp, even more capable of parting him from his money than the now ill-tempered looking bawd by his side.

'I understand that skill is not necessary,' he said.

The bawd hissed at him, 'Don't pay any attention to 'im, dearie. 'E's just a troublemaker. Let me get you a tipple.' With a sneering look at the man, she detached herself from James's arm and hurried away.

'She will fetch a beverage, my friend, that you will drink at your peril,' the man said.

'May I ask who you are, sir?' James inquired.

'Henry Arkwright from the Methodist Mission. I'm allowed here under sufferance, as you will appreciate. You are clearly a stranger to such places.'

James felt a little miffed that he had not played his part more convincingly. Overcoming this, he decided that the preacher was probably well-informed about the women who frequented the gambling dens, presumably attempting to 'save' them from the appalling lives they led. He took a folded print of Sir Charles's likeness from his pocket and handed it to the preacher.

'Have you ever seen this man?' he asked.

Henry Arkwright studied the print carefully. 'I have seen this posted about the city,' he said. 'Who is it?'

'Sir Charles Browning. He has been missing for a month or more. I have reason to believe that he may have visited here and even come to some harm here. Do you know a woman named Millie?'

The preacher smiled ruefully. 'Ah, Millie,' he said. 'Is there a connection?'

'I don't know. Where can I find her?'

'If she is still alive she will be in the Magdalene Hospital in Marylebone. She was admitted a few weeks ago very near her time.'

'Pregnant?'

'Pregnant.'

'What kind of woman is she?'

'Years ago, it was called the Magdalene Hospital for the Reception of Penitent Prostitutes. They have changed the name but not the character. Millie is similar to the poor creature doing her best to seduce you.'

'The tipple she is fetching,' James said. 'Will it be drugged?'

'Sufficient to make a man drowsy and not in control of himself. But why would a man such as Sir Charles Browning visit a place such as this? Surely a club such as White's or Boodle's would be more to his taste and class.'

'Sir Charles is a radical, sir, a dedicated social reformer, hoping to enter Parliament. He would want to have first-hand experience of places such as this.'

'I see. And your connection?'

James handed the preacher his name card. 'I am attempting to find the whereabouts of the baronet.'

'Then it is possible that Millie may have the information you need, though whether she will be prepared to part with it is another matter.' He smiled, then added, 'And I doubt if the nuns will admit you to the Magdalene. Do you have a female acquaintance who could visit Millie on your behalf?'

'I do indeed, sir.'

He handed the preacher his purse. 'A small sum that I intended to lose at the table, sir. Perhaps you will accept it for your mission.'

Henry Arkwright bowed and took the purse.

James offered him his hand. 'I am truly obliged to you,' he said. 'You have saved me from a most unpleasant evening. And a meeting with Millie may provide the answer to the mystery of Sir Charles's disappearance.'

The men shook hands and James left the tavern. Sarah would follow up what looked like the most promising lead they had so far.

Forty-five

When James joined Sarah and her father for breakfast the next morning, he reported on his experience at Joe's Place. Matthew's response explained what had been puzzling him a little.

'It is interesting that Joe,' Matthew said, 'or whoever owns the enterprise, allows the Methodist minister a free run of the place. It is probably some kind of insurance.'

Sarah frowned. 'I don't understand, Father.'

'Well, my dear, these places are all illegal, and from time to time the Runners raid them and close them down. It is a complete waste of time, of course. They simply open up in another low tavern. I think it likely that some kind of arrangement has been come to by which the presence of a minister of religion prevents the worst abuses, and even provides the prostitutes with some kind of spiritual and practical assistance.'

'Such as arranging for a pregnant woman to have her child in a hospital instead of on the streets,' James said.

'Precisely. We need to bear in mind that most of those women are not plying their trade by choice. They have no other means of survival. Tragically, as often as not, many of them were either seduced or raped by their employers and then, especially if they became pregnant, dismissed for immorality without a reference.'

'It's disgraceful,' Sarah exclaimed. 'And nothing, nothing is being done about it.' She turned to James. 'Do you think that Sir Charles was there on some kind of mission?'

'I'm sure of it. Everything we have found out about the man confirms that he is, or was, a radical social reformer. And an important one. Most of the radicals can do little more than agitate and make a noise. For there to be any changes made they must come from Parliament. This means that the power to effect change is wholly in the hands of the MPs.'

'Wilberforce and Wilkes are perfect examples,' Matthew added. 'Without men like Wilberforce in Parliament, those with the ways and means to introduce private members' bills, nothing will change. Most of the Tories are happy to keep things as they are.' He took off and folded his napkin. 'I must go. I have a morning full of appointments.' He bent to kiss his daughter's head. 'I hope you have a useful visit to the Magdalene Hospital, my dear.'

After Mathew had left the room, leaving Sarah and James alone, she said, 'What did you think of the prostitute who befriended you, James?'

James considered her question for a moment.

'Did you find her attractive?' she pressed.

Eventually, he made a reply. 'Sarah, I found her repulsive, and I cannot understand how any man could possibly want to go with … I was going to say "with such a creature" but I'm trying not to think about her in such a cruel and dismissive way. I know she isn't what she is by choice, and that she and the thousands like her in this city are forced by poverty into selling themselves for a few pennies.'

'Do you think,' Sarah said, speaking deliberately, 'that they are any less moral than the women who, as courtesans, sell themselves for an annuity of twenty thousand pounds a year? Or any less moral than the many women who marry wholly for social position? There is a hierarchy in the sex trade, James. At the top are the courtesans and ambitious wives. At the bottom is the kind of whore you encountered last night. It is an economic, a financial hierarchy, not a moral one.'

James nodded. 'I know what you mean. It is the same with criminal behaviour. I ask myself what is the moral difference between the slaver whose way of life depends on the brutal exploitation of enslaved negroes, and the street robber who holds one up for the few coins in one's purse? It is, as you say, an economic hierarchy. Not a moral one.'

'My dear,' Sarah said softly in an affectionate tone, 'I'm so relieved we agree on these matters. You are about to become the editor of a daily newspaper, one that my father will ensure is as influential as *The Times*. You will be able to do much good by promoting reform. The politicians are desperately concerned that if unrest is allowed to develop we could face a terrible equivalent to the French Revolution. Thousands of men and women would die or, at best, be imprisoned. As you and my father know, the people on their own can do little. It is the politicians who must be forced to act. They, and only they, can effect change.'

'I know. I shall do whatever I can, Sarah. And I hope I am not being presumptuous when I say how greatly I value your friendship and the confidence you and your father place in me.'

The shadow of Elizabeth Stockton's possible deceit and duplicity lurked at the edge of his mind. Come what may, somehow, he had to protect Sarah from the possible consequences of her friendship with the artist.

He stood. 'But now I must go to Paternoster Row and spend a day in the office of *The Weekly Police News*. I have to hand over the reins to my assistant. Will you go to the Magdalene Hospital and ask to speak to Millie?'

'This morning,' Sarah replied. 'And then I shall have lunch with Elizabeth.'

Forty-six

The Magdalen Hospital was located in St George's Fields in Southwark, a district south of the river. It provided accommodation and a kind of sanctuary for girls and women of the streets, many as young as fifteen. Nearly all had been betrayed by men. The 'penitents' were given training in laundering and needlework. Also, they were required to attend two religious services each day. Most of them stayed for about three years. Any babies born in the institution were usually put out for adoption.

At the time of Sarah's visit about a hundred and thirty women and girls resided at the institution. They all wore greyish-brown stuff gowns, broad handkerchiefs and flat straw hats with ribands pulled over their faces. Except for those too ill or too near their time to work, they spent long days labouring in the laundry.

Sarah thought the place little like a hospital; it was more like a cross between a workhouse and a nunnery.

She explained to the matron the purpose of her visit, and one of the younger girls escorted her to the sick room. Here the women gave birth, or a visiting apothecary treated their diseases, mainly consumption and venereal infections.

Millie, her face deathly white, sat up in bed partly covered by a thick blanket. Of her infant, Sarah saw no sign. Neither could she gauge her age, but clearly the woman was very ill. Her face was flushed and deeply lined, her dark-brown hair lank and thin on her scalp, and coughing fits seized her frequently.

The smells of unhealthy women, steam from the large and profitable laundry, and the institutional odours of boiled cabbage and cheap, fatty cuts of stale meat permeated the air, making Sarah anxious to leave the place as soon as possible.

She kept her distance from Millie and held a scented handkerchief to her nose and mouth. 'My name is Sarah Kedron, Millie. I have come from Joe's Place. You must answer truthfully the questions I shall put to you. If you lie to me, I shall know it. Tell me the truth, and I promise that no harm will come to you. Do you understand?'

Millie nodded. She didn't feel well enough to care what happened to her. Her child had been taken from her; she was dying of consumption, and what life was left to her had nothing to offer. Only the church services, especially the singing of the girls in the choir, gave her any succour. If there had ever been any fight in her, it was now wholly dissipated.

Sarah showed her the print of Sir Charles's likeness. 'Have you seen this man?'

Millie nodded slowly, as though the movements of her head were too much to bear. 'I didn't mean 'im no 'arm.'

'Did you give him a drink?'

Again, she slowly nodded. "Yeah, a hot toddy."

'Then what happened?'

'He played a few 'ands and lost a bit. Then 'e was took ill.'

'Because of the hot toddy.'

'There's no real 'arm in it. Just makes the punters drowsy.'

'Is there laudanum in it?'

'Just a little. No more than lots of people takes to 'elp 'em sleep. Sometimes there's just enough to make 'em careless in their gambling.' She attempted a smile. 'Then they lose more.'

'And I suppose,' Sarah said, 'you get a commission on the amount they lose?'

Millie just shrugged, and then coughed up a lot of blood which she spat into a small bowl.

When she had recovered sufficiently to speak, Sarah said, 'Then what happened?'

'I 'elped 'im down the stairs. 'Is coach was waitin' for 'im. And there was 'is servants to 'elp 'im.'

'How do you know they were his servants?'

'They was in livery. Red and black.'

'Did the coach have a crest on the door?'

'Couldn't see. It was dark.'

'What happened then?'

'One of the men gave me two shillings for the 'ot toddy, and the coach drove off. That was the end of it, my lady, I swear. I didn't mean no 'arm. I thought I was being paid to give 'im the drink to stop 'im from gambling and losin' too much.'

'When did they approach you? What did they say to you?'

'One of 'em—not one wearin' the livery—came in just after the gentleman …'

'Sir Charles.'

''E said that's who 'e was. 'E said 'e was workin' for Lady Brownin' and every night with the others they waited round the corner from 'is 'ouse for 'im to come out an' then followed 'im to wherever 'e was goin'. It was their job to stop 'im from comin' to any 'arm.'

'And he gave you the drug to put into a hot toddy.'

Millie just nodded, the effort of speaking now almost too much for her.

'Is there anything you want, Millie?'

Millie slowly shook her head, as if to say, 'What can I possibly want? I've only a short time to live.'

Sarah took the girl's hand, put a half crown in it, and then, turning away from the bed, she hurried out of the room. She would have liked to have found out more about the poor woman, even to discover what had happened to bring her to such a sorry state, but she had nothing to gain from delaying her departure. Obviously, Sir Charles had been the victim of a carefully planned abduction.

The coach and attendants would have been hired and would now be untraceable. The kidnappers' task would have been to deliver the drugged baronet to whoever had hired them. Whether Sir Charles had then been murdered and his body disposed of or he had been kept in captivity somewhere and was still alive was going to be difficult, if not impossible, to establish. What had seemed to be the most promising lead so far had now taken their investigation to another dead end.

Celia and her lover, Tom Bridge, could have organized the abduction, Sarah thought, as could Albert Ramsbottom or Edward Browning, even if the latter had not been in the country to do so. As little as twenty pounds would have paid for the services of the kidnappers, who had almost certainly not known the identity of their employer. And, of course, Sarah had to admit to herself, her list of suspects could be missing the most important one. It was just as likely that the culprit was someone unknown to them as it was one of the small number of people on their list.

Feeling depressed by the tragedy of Millie's life and that of the other inmates of the hospital and beginning to despair of ever solving the mystery of Sir Charles's disappearance, Sarah hailed a hackney and gave the cabbie Elizabeth's address. Her friend's lively company and affectionate nature was, she thought, just what she needed. Perhaps they would go to Vauxhall together, wander the gardens, listen to the music and take tea in the new Chinese tea house, which was currently very fashionable. All kinds of chinoiserie fascinated Elizabeth.

Forty-seven

While Sarah visited the Magdalen Hospital, Jack Godwin sat in a hackney in a position in Cheyne Walk that provided a clear view of Elizabeth Stockton's front entrance. Though only a few houses up from number 2A, Jack felt confident that as long as he remained out of sight inside the cab, its stationary presence in the street would not arouse suspicions among the residents. Hiring cabs in this way was a common practice for some people who had various appointments during the day, social or business. It was cheaper than maintaining one's own equipage and all that involved, and if they chose the driver carefully, it was a great deal safer than hiring the first cab that came along when one needed one. And there were real advantages to having one's own hackney standing by in inclement weather.

He had taken up his position at eight o'clock, but no movement had come from Elizabeth Stockton's residence until an hour later. Then she emerged, elegantly dressed as for a social visit, and walked to the main road where she soon waved down a cab. Jack was relieved that she'd not decided to take a chair, as to follow one without being noticed would have been difficult. As it was, he was able to follow her easily, keeping only a short distance behind.

After a comparatively short journey, she stopped outside a fine early Georgian residence at 15 Manchester Square. She paid off the driver and rang the doorbell of the house. Within moments she was admitted and, Jack thought, clearly expected. She remained at this address for about half an hour, then a carriage arrived at the house, the front door opened, and Miss Stockton emerged accompanied by a man whom Jack later discovered was Ramsbottom, the MP. He handed Miss Stockton into the carriage, gave the coachman an order, and it drove off. Jack followed at a distance. It stopped at the Burlington Arcade. Miss Stockton accompanied the man into the arcade, where they remained for about an hour, after which they returned to the carriage, which had arrived from where it had been parked. It drove to Cheyne Walk, where it deposited Miss Stockton, and then, with the man inside, continued on its way.

Jack resumed his previous position in the street and decided to make a report to James. He wrote a note stating only Miss Elizabeth Stockton's destinations and the times. He gave it to his cabbie, instructing him to run to the nearest main road, hail a cab and tell the driver to take the note to the offices of *The Weekly Police News* in Paternoster Row. There, on delivery of the note, he would receive his fare. Then, assuming that it was unlikely that Miss Stockton would leave her residence immediately, Jack took the opportunity to relieve himself. He had enjoyed several ales with friends the previous evening, and the remains of these now demanded release. Jack knew that if he didn't act soon, he would have an embarrassing and uncomfortable accident. Fortunately, a convenient tree stood a few yards away, and he took the necessary action against it.

As he did so, Sarah approached in a hackney and could hardly avoid noticing the young man facing away from the road as if talking to a tree. When he turned away from the tree, she saw his face and recognised him instantly as Jack Godwin, one of her father's apprentice reporters.

She alighted from her cab and walked up the steps to the front door of Elizabeth's residence. Then, before ringing the bell, she turned and saw Godwin return to his transport and climb into it. The cab remained stationary. Of the driver she saw no sign.

Though not a naturally suspicious woman, Sarah could not avoid thinking it strange that a member of her father's staff had, she assumed, hired an empty hackney cab from which to watch Elizabeth's house. She found it difficult to avoid thinking that for some reason her father ... no, not her father! James! The Godwin boy worked for James! It was James, not her father, who had sent the boy around the clubs and other unsavoury haunts to establish the whereabouts of Joe's Place. It must be James who had instructed him to watch Elizabeth's residence, and yet James had said nothing to her about this decision. For some reason he had decided to spy on her friend without telling her.

But this interpretation of the situation made no sense. Sarah saw no possible reason for James to suspect Elizabeth of any involvement in the disappearance of Sir Charles just because she had painted his portrait, and he had sat for her. So why had he set the Godwin boy to spy upon her? And without telling her.

Now an even more disturbing thought occurred to Sarah. Was it possible, she asked herself, that the Godwin boy was not spying on Elizabeth, but that it was her own movements James was interested in? She prayed that this was not so. Several aspects of male conduct disgusted Sarah, and one of them was the male propensity to be jealous and overly possessive. It produced all kinds of disgraceful behaviour.

Sarah felt profoundly uncomfortable. She didn't know what to think or how to deal with the situation. For a brief moment, she thought she should confide in Elizabeth, but at the back of her mind resided the thought that if it were, in fact, Elizabeth in whom James was interested, then he must have a reason. Until she ascertained the reason for James's extraordinary behaviour, it could be unwise to alert Elizabeth to the possibility that she was being spied upon.

Of one thing Sarah was certain: the next few hours with Elizabeth, the woman with whom she was developing a close and affectionate friendship, promised to be strained. She instantly resented James for tainting her visit in this way.

She decided there was only one thing to do. She had not yet rung the bell, and Elizabeth was not expecting her. They had made no arrangement to meet on this particular morning. Accordingly, she would postpone a meeting with her until she knew what was going on in James's mind.

Having so decided, she turned from the door and quickly walked across the road to Jack's cab. She rapped on the door. A nervous hand pulled down the window and Jack's head appeared.

'May I ask, Godwin,' Sarah demanded, 'what you think you are doing keeping watch on Miss Stockton's house?'

Jack's mouth dropped open, speechless for perhaps the first time in his life. He had obeyed instructions, and now his employer's daughter was obviously furious with him.

At last he found his voice. 'I ... I,' he stammered, 'I have been sworn to secrecy.' This seemed to be the safest thing to say.

'Who by?'

Jack said nothing, but just looked downcast.

'Oh, very well, Godwin,' Sarah said, realizing that the boy was in an impossible situation and that whatever he said would almost certainly turn out to be wrong. 'I shall speak to Mr Brewster. No doubt he will enlighten me. I just hope for your sake that you are not spying upon Miss Stockton on your own account. Now get out of this cab. I need it to take me to Paternoster Row. I assume there is a driver somewhere or have you taken up the profession of cabbie?'

Forty-eight

During the journey to Paternoster Row, Sarah let her temper get the better of her judgement. She felt betrayed. James Brewster, who had her to thank for his position, had set his spy on her. Or, if not that, he had demonstrated that he had no faith in her closest female friend or in her judgement of Elizabeth's character.

Sarah not only felt angry but also profoundly hurt and disappointed. She was also furious with herself for allowing her feelings to overcome her usual caution where her relationships with men were involved. Too many feckless, unreliable, self-obsessed actors and writers had let her down too many times, and, like one of the weaker women in a romantic novel, she had not had the sense to realize what a man's true feelings and ambitions were.

And James was ambitious. Of that she had no doubt. From the moment they had met on the Norwich coach, he had revealed that his real interest was in meeting her father. She had been blind not to see this. And he had later used her interest in him to ingratiate himself with her father and obtain a position in the company. The growing friendship between them had pleased her father, and James, with his barrister's cunning, had sensed that Matthew was beginning to look on him in more than a professional manner.

James had not, of course, really cared for her, she told herself. Having made himself indispensable to her father and achieved his ambition as editor of a daily newspaper, he was now turning against her, showing his true colours, perhaps even attempting to come between her and her father. He had been using her. Once again, she had allowed a man to use her for his own selfish purpose. Sarah's writer's imagination told her that James now intended to undermine her influence with her father.

When she arrived at Paternoster Row, therefore, her outraged feelings were wholly in charge of her behaviour. Brooking no delay in obtaining an explanation from James, she stormed into his office, where he was holding an editorial meeting.

'Leave us,' she instructed his staff.

The four men, two of them senior and respected clerks, looked to James for guidance, amazed that their employer's daughter should behave in this way to the editor. Barely controlling his irritation, James nodded curtly to them, and within seconds he was alone with Sarah.

Before she could launch into her own attack, he stood up and, glaring at her, exclaimed, 'How dare you! You may not be aware of basic business etiquette, Sarah, but I can assure you that your father will not support such ill manners.'

Beginning to realize that she was in the wrong to have dismissed his staff, Sarah became even more aggressive. Placing both hands on his desk, she leant forward and snarled, 'By what right did you set the Godwin boy to spy on me?'

With a heavy sigh, James sat down. *Damn! She's seen the stupid boy. Well, that's the end of his employment.* There was only one thing to do now: he picked up the note that Jack had sent and thrust it towards Sarah.

'Read this, then try to control yourself.' He could not have been blunter or more assertive—as if he knew they had reached a crisis in their contest of wills. Unless he took control of the situation, he had no future in Kedron & Co.

Sarah grabbed the note and stared at it. Her anger caused her eyes to swim over the page. It meant nothing to her. 'What rubbish is this?'

'15 Manchester Square is the London residence of Alfred Ramsbottom, MP. He is our most likely suspect as he has a great deal to gain from Sir Charles's disappearance. When I visited him to research the profile I'm writing on him for *The Informer*, I saw his portrait in his library signed Elizabeth Stockton. This morning your friend visited him, then left with him on what was clearly a shopping expedition. I wonder what he purchased for her? Diamonds, perhaps. They are a courtesan's best friend.'

Sarah could only bluster: 'How dare you! You have no evidence she has such a relationship with him.'

'If that is so, then why has Miss Stockton kept it from you that she is acquainted with the man? I'm sure you have told her that he is one of our suspects. Or perhaps she didn't need you to tell her. She had only to sit in on your meeting with the Reverend Somersby to learn of our interest in him.'

Sarah's anger slowly evaporated, but there was still fight left in her. 'Why didn't you tell me she had painted his portrait?' she demanded.

'I thought it sensible to wait until she had a plentiful opportunity to tell you herself. I did not wish to say or do anything that might damage your friendship with her. I am aware that it means a great deal to you, and I respected your feelings for her.'

'Then why put your spy—'

'Before broaching the subject with you, I needed to be sure of my facts. It was one thing for her to have painted his portrait. It was something far more significant for her to have continued to visit him, in secret from you, knowing what she undoubtedly does about our investigation.'

Sarah stood. 'I shall go to her immediately and demand an explanation.'

'If he is our man,' James said, calmer now, 'that is the last thing you should do. Although we still have no evidence who was responsible for the abduction, Ramsbottom is by far the most likely culprit. If you want to warn him of our suspicions, then telling Miss Stockton of them may be the most effective way of doing so.'

Sarah remained silent for a moment. Then, unable to think of anything else to say, she said, 'I suppose you think you're extremely clever. You are not in court now, you know.'

'Go home, Sarah,' James said bitterly. 'Write your serial story or a new play. I have work to do.'

Sarah stood and, with as much dignity as she could muster, turned and walked to the door.

As she put her hand on the doorknob, James said, 'If you still feel aggrieved that I have behaved badly, I suggest you ask your father what he would have done if he were in my position. I'm sorry that I have hurt you, but I acted for the best. I hoped to be able to save you from even greater pain.'

Sarah left his office without saying another word. She had no intention of raising the matter with her father. To do so, she believed, would achieve nothing, and it would be unfair to put him in a position in which he felt he should take sides. She also realized that she had made a fool of herself, not by being hurt and angry but by behaving before his staff as if James were little more than an office boy. She had shown no respect for him and had undoubtedly damaged him in the eyes of his subordinates. Whereas, she told herself, there was an excuse for what he had done, she could say nothing in justification of her own behaviour.

As for James, he tried to resume his work but felt as near to tears as he had ever been. Without warning, the friendship he valued most had been shattered. To ease the despair, he told himself that Sarah was far too emotionally volatile for him to cope with. He had misjudged her. She was not the strong, rational and sensible woman he had thought she was. Her imagination and emotions influenced her far too much. He even wondered if he should resign his editorial position. He still had a career at the Bar to pursue. But common sense prevailed. Taking a deep breath, he managed to force himself to accept that now was not the time to even consider such a possibility. He needed to do so only when he felt completely calm and the pounding of his heart had subsided.

He decided to resume the editorial meeting and arrange for one of the clerks to take a hackney to Cheyne Walk and recall the incompetent Jack Godwin. At the very least, he would give the boy a severe dressing-down for allowing himself to be seen.

Forty-nine

Before Sarah left the offices at Paternoster Row, a letter arrived for her, forwarded by the housekeeper at Portman Place. Sarah quickly broke the seal. The contents, wholly unexpected and penned in a childlike hand, read, 'Dearest Sarah, my only true friend, please come quickly. I need you. Celia.'

Sarah decided immediately that she should go to Browning Hall. Clearly something had happened to alarm Celia. There must have been an important development.

She knocked on her father's door.

'Come!'

'Father, I'm sorry to interrupt you.'

Matthew Kedron looked up from his writing and put down his pen. Twenty-seven years of bringing up his daughter from a baby to an impetuous and determined young woman had made him accustomed to her interruptions. 'Of course you are, my dear, but I'm sure it is a matter of some urgency.'

This was not just a fortunate guess. He could see her flushed face and that she had been recently crying. He hoped this didn't indicate another problem with James.

Sarah handed him Celia's note. 'What do you think of this, Father?'

Matthew took it from her and peered at it closely. 'It is very uninformative.'

'Celia has had little education and was distressed when she wrote it, I'm sure.'

'Is the handwriting hers?'

'I don't know. I have never seen her handwriting. But it looks like the kind of writing she would have learned at the village dame school.'

'Have you any idea why she needs to see you so urgently?'

'None, Father. I can assume only that something has occurred to distress her.'

Matthew handed back the note. 'Do you intend to go to Browning Hall?'

'I think I should. I don't think she would have written in this way unless something was really worrying her.'

'Then you must take someone with you. I'm afraid James cannot be spared at present. He has important appointments for most of the week.'

'I am perfectly capable of going on my own with our coachman.'

'That is as may be. What you don't know is who other than Lady Browning may have sent that note and the reason for it. Take the carriage and I will ask for two strong men from the print room to accompany you.'

At another time, Sarah would probably have argued with her father and insisted that James be spared, if only for one afternoon and night. But she found her father's decision more than a little welcome. She had been concerned about going to Browning Hall without James, without even asking him to accompany her. She knew he would have interpreted this as further evidence of her displeasure and made her seem petty and vindictive. Her father had at least temporarily solved part of the problem with James. He had removed him from the investigation.

Knowing his daughter as well as he did, Matthew said, 'Is there a problem with James?' He was tempted to add, 'What has he done wrong now?' but decided such a question, with what Sarah would probably infer from it, would not help matters if there were a problem.

Sarah sat down, and as calmly as she could, she explained the situation with James.

When she had finished, Matthew said, 'You both have my sympathy. I can well understand why you feel hurt, Sarah. I can also understand why James acted as he did. He is certainly correct to suspect Miss Stockton of involvement with Ramsbottom. I believe James to be justified in assuming that she has to have a reason, not necessarily innocent, for keeping her acquaintance with him a secret from you. It may be a harmless reason. It could equally have a bearing on your investigation. Where James was wrong was in keeping his suspicion from you and in setting young Godwin to spy on the woman. I do not accept for a single moment that he was spying on you.'

Matthew stood and, after walking around his desk, stopped at Sarah's chair and put a hand on her shoulder. 'My dearest girl,' he said gently, 'please try to understand that James means no harm. My heart tells me that he cares greatly for you and respects you. I am sure he would never do anything to harm you or hurt you in any way. The simple truth is that although he is a very clever young man, full of good character and the best intentions, he is wholly inexperienced with women. He has no sisters and, as far as I know, has never been in any kind of romantic situation. He does what his head tells him, not his heart.'

Matthew knew, but did not add, that most men would have behaved in the same way as James, but for less acceptable reasons. Believing that women are essentially frail, lacking in common sense, requiring protection from all unpleasantness, capable of little more than giving birth, issuing instructions to servants, passing the time in idle gossip and a little light novel reading, most men would have done what James had done and even been admired for it by a grateful wife or lover. Sarah was not this kind of woman. She believed herself to be the equal of any man in every respect. She expected, no, she demanded to be treated as an equal, and when she was not, she responded first with anger and then with disappointment.

Matthew also knew that if his daughter and James were to manage their confused feelings for one another, they would both have to make serious allowances for their different approaches to life.

He didn't know whether to be optimistic about their future or not. He knew only that it was a problem he would prefer to be without.

'Go home, my dear, and prepare yourself for the journey. I will instruct one of the clerks to organize the carriage.'

Sarah stood up and embraced her father. 'Thank you, Father. I expect it is just a storm in a teacup. Celia is such a sad little thing.'

Fifty

Sarah knew that she should get to Browning Hall as soon as possible, but after agonizing more about the situation with James, she felt that rightly or wrongly, she had to give Elizabeth an opportunity to explain her relationship with Mr Ramsbottom. She had begun to care deeply for her new friend, her only woman friend outside of the theatre. If Elizabeth were in a close relationship with the MP and had told him about their suspicions, confronting her would not damage their investigation, she told herself. The man was not a fool. He would already know that he was a suspect in Sir Charles's disappearance.

As the coach rumbled along, she brooded on her relationship with James. She'd had several lovers, and although she had no serious regrets about her liaisons, she had never felt for them the warmth and respect she had come to feel for James. They had been attractive men physically, often amusing and, occasionally, sexually satisfying, no more. Her feelings for James were of an emotionally much deeper nature, and this knowledge made his behaviour all the more painful. She asked herself if the quarrel really meant the end of their friendship; would he become no more than one of her father's employees, someone to be bid 'Good day' to and otherwise ignore?

If her father were correct in his judgement of James, Sarah told herself, then although his behaviour had been misguided, perhaps he deserved to be given the benefit of the doubt. It was certainly true that Elizabeth's secrecy had been suspicious. She had been present at the meeting with Mr Somersby when the possibility of Mr Ramsbottom's involvement in the baronet's disappearance had been raised.

Why had Elizabeth not simply said, 'I know the man. He engaged me to paint his portrait.' She could then have given her opinion of his character. To have said nothing was inexplicable unless she was his mistress or had some other personal connection with him of which she, for some reason, felt ashamed. There had to be a reason why, after the portrait had been painted, delivered and, presumably, paid for, that she had considered it necessary to visit Ramsbottom at his home and then accompany him on a shopping expedition to the Burlington Arcade. Godwin had not mentioned that she or Ramsbottom had left the arcade with parcels, but this meant nothing. People of the *ton* did not carry their own shopping. They either had it delivered to their residence or carried by a servant.

Aware of Elizabeth's unexpected behaviour, James had felt it necessary to at least attempt to establish the truth, not only for Celia's sake but for hers. If she were being used, betrayed even by Elizabeth, whom she believed to be a close friend, then it was essential that she should be told the truth about the woman's motives. It was just such a pity, Sarah felt, that James had not had sufficient faith in her judgement to tell her what he suspected and trust her to do what was appropriate.

To have set a junior reporter to spy on her friend had been a disgraceful thing to do. This, Sarah decided, was what she had found unforgivable. At the same time, she was prepared to accept her father's belief that James would never have set the boy to spy on her personally.

She sighed as the coach jolted over the pot-holed road. This was all so difficult, especially as she had no acceptable excuse for bursting into his room and dismissing his staff the way she had. It was not at all surprising, or even unreasonable, that he had lost his temper the way he had. She had been in the wrong.

All these thoughts went around her mind as if in some kind of endless loop. Finally, she decided that whatever the nature of Elizabeth's relationship with Mr Ramsbottom, she had to confront her with her suspicion that she was the man's mistress. She could not leave London, perhaps for days, without finding out the truth.

Leaning forward, she ordered the coachman to turn around and drive to Cheyne Walk.

Elizabeth was at home. Her maid stood back to allow Sarah to run up the stairs as fast as her travelling dress would allow. She burst into the studio.

Elizabeth turned, her face lighting up at Sarah's unexpected appearance. 'Dearest!' she exclaimed. 'How lovely to—'

'What is your relationship with Mr Ramsbottom?' Sarah demanded. 'Are you his mistress? Why didn't you tell me you were still in contact with him?'

This outburst so startled Elizabeth that for several moments she could do nothing but stand still with her mouth open. Then, controlling her anger as she realized that Sarah's affection for her caused her distress, she walked forward and said, 'My dear, it is not what you think. Come, sit down and I will explain. I didn't tell you before because I was uncertain of the outcome.'

Breathing heavily, Sarah sat, and awaited an explanation.

Fifty-one

When, much later, Sarah arrived in Langley, the Reverend Somersby welcomed her warmly, almost as though expecting her, and offered her accommodation as before.

'Thank you. I will gladly accept as I don't know what the situation is at the hall.'

'I also know very little,' the clergyman said, as he poured them both a warming glass of claret. 'I have been away from the village at a diocesan meeting in Hertford.' He smiled modestly. 'I have been appointed rural dean.'

Sarah wasn't sure what a rural dean was or did, but the expression of the clergyman's face was such that she felt confident he had received some kind of ecclesiastical promotion. 'My congratulations,' she said. 'I am happy for you.'

'I can tell you,' he continued, 'that I have received a message from the hall requesting my immediate attendance. Lady Augusta is near death, and I should prepare to administer the last rites.'

This was not surprising news. The dowager had been moving steadily and irrevocably towards the end for some months. Sarah thought it unlikely that Celia had sent for her because of this. She had no love for the woman, and the dowager's life or death was of little consequence to her own situation.

'Perhaps, Vicar, I can make room for you in my carriage,' Sarah said, 'and you will permit me to bring you up to date with our investigation.'

'I shall be most obliged.'

As soon as they were seated in the carriage, Sarah continued, "We are nowhere near obtaining evidence of who is responsible for Sir Charles's disappearance. We know only that he was abducted, almost certainly by hired criminals, and that he is either dead—murdered—or being kept in captivity. We have two main suspects, Alfred Ramsbottom, the MP, and Tom Bridge, the blacksmith and Celia's possible lover. If Bridge is the culprit, then it is likely that Sir Charles is dead. If it is the MP, then he may be in captivity while there is still the possibility of an election.'

The vicar said, 'I fear a general election will encourage minor riots on the hustings and endless speeches promising benefits that, no matter who is elected, will not materialize.'

'How large is the electorate for Langley?'

'As you may already be aware, Langley is a Pocket Borough having a relatively small electorate in a few burgage tenements. These tenements are split almost equally between the two larger estates. No doubt, Mr Ramsbottom has persuaded his tenants that their tenancy is dependent upon their continued support. However, now that Sir Charles has shown an interest in politics, he may well perceive him as a threat. Ramsbottom will need to increase his estate to guarantee a majority.'

'It's all rather a farce,' Sarah said.

'Not for Ramsbottom. He has a great deal to gain, and it is not just his return to Parliament, but with a Tory majority, he is almost certain to receive his promotion to ministerial office, and then who knows? A peerage perhaps? If Sir Charles wins the seat, Ramsbottom loses everything. As for your other suspect, Tom Bridge, his involvement would seem to be the more likely reason for Lady Browning's distress.'

'Do you think she has discovered it and does not know what to do?'

'That is one possibility. Her correct course of action in this event would be to inform the magistrate. Bridge would then be arrested, tried, found guilty and, most likely, hanged.'

'By informing on a man who loves her, who was her lover perhaps, she will be condemning him to death.'

'Precisely.' The clergyman took some snuff, more to give him time to prepare his next remark than for any comfort it might provide. When his sniffing was complete he said, 'We should perhaps bear in mind that the cost of hiring the kidnappers, their female accomplice and an appropriate equipage would be considerably more than a village blacksmith could afford.'

Sarah nodded. 'That is true. Ramsbottom could have paid for it.'

'And laid himself open to blackmail? No doubt if he is responsible, he would have to hire somebody, but the necessary negotiations would have been carried out by a third party, someone who would benefit from the MP's continued position in Parliament. No, Miss Kedron, perhaps we need to take into account Lady Augusta's allegations.'

Sarah had tried not to consider this possibility, but she knew it now had to be faced. 'You are suggesting that Celia paid for her lover to kill her husband.'

'It is a possibility.'

'Perhaps she has evidence that another person is responsible and that is why she has sent for me.'

'That is certainly yet another possibility. It may well be, of course, that there is a person, someone for you still to discover, who will benefit from Sir Charles's death. We can hope only that Lady Browning is not in any way responsible.'

'Well,' Sarah said, as the carriage came to a halt outside the Dowager House. 'I shall soon know the worst.'

Fifty-two

Shortly before Hedron and Co closed for business that day, a note arrived at the office for a much-chastened Jack Godwin. Fearful of James's further wrath but suspecting that the information the note contained could be important, he knocked timidly on his employer's door.

'Come.'

He opened the door a little way and put his head round.

'I don't need another apology, Godwin,' James snapped. 'I've said all I have to say and so have you. We shall all do our best to put your incompetence behind us.'

'Begging your pardon, sir, but I think you should see this note. It arrived but a few minutes ago.'

'Very well. Give it here.'

Jack handed James the note. It was from the West Indies Shipping Company and bore the information that a Mr Edward Browning had disembarked from the West Indiaman, *Thetis* that had arrived from Antigua at eight of the clock the previous evening.

'You arranged for the shipping company to keep us informed should Mr Browning arrive?'

'Yes, sir. It seemed the sensible thing to do.'

'It was, Jack. It was. You have almost redeemed yourself.'

'Thank you, sir.' He turned and left the office.

Alarmed, James knew he had to inform Sarah of this development without delay. If Edward had left the West Indies docks on the Isle of Dogs and ridden through the night, he might already be at Browning Hall. He stood and prepared to leave the office immediately for Browning Hall.

Before he could do so, Matthew Kedron put his head round the door. 'Did Sarah tell you she had a note from Lady Browning?'

'No, sir.'

'It's all rather strange. The girl wants Sarah to go to her so she has gone. I sent a couple of men to accompany her, just in case there is any kind of trouble at the hall. I told her that I could not spare you.' Matthew saw worry lines on James's brow. He smiled encouragingly. 'Do not worry, James. She will come round in time.'

'It is not that, sir. I have just received information that Edward Browning arrived back in England late last night. This could be the explanation for Lady Browning's note.'

Matthew entered the room and sat down. 'To claim his inheritance?'

'I think that would be premature, sir. The fastest ship to the West Indies takes three weeks, a little longer for the return journey, depending on the winds. He cannot have received news of his brother's disappearance and taken passage home in such a short time.'

'Unless,' Matthew said quietly, 'he knew in advance that his brother was going to disappear.'

'Because he had arranged it. Good God! If he is a murderer ...'

'And Sarah confronts him!'

'With your permission, sir, I will hasten to Browning Hall without delay.'

'Yes, my boy. Go to her. I will attend your appointments. If you ride throughout the night, you will be with her in the early hours.'

Within an hour, James was galloping out of the city towards Hertfordshire. As he rode, he could not help wondering how Sarah would react to his arrival. It was possible, he thought, that she would take offence at what could be interpreted as a lack of confidence in her ability to take care of herself. On the other hand, if she were in any kind of danger, she would almost certainly welcome his concern and assistance.

He had to get to Browning Hall as fast as possible and hope for the best.

Fifty-three

The massive oak doors of Browning Hall creaked open even before Sarah reached the top of the short flight of stone steps. Mrs Williams stood there, her face drained of its usual high colour.

'Oh, madam!' she exclaimed. 'Thank the Lord you've come!'

'What has happened?' Sarah demanded, assuming that some tragedy had occurred involving Celia.

'She's gone, madam.'

'Gone? Who? Where?'

'My lady, ma'am. In the middle of the night.'

Sarah moved into the house. 'We'll talk in the library. I need to know everything about what has occurred.'

She walked quickly across the baronial hall to the library, followed by Mrs Williams, who found it difficult to keep up with her. Once in the library, she sat and indicated that the housekeeper should do the same. 'Now take your time, Mrs Williams, and tell me exactly what has happened.'

'Yes, ma'am.' Bringing her heavy breathing under control, the housekeeper said, 'When I took up her hot water this morning, her bedroom was empty. There was no sign of her. She had left some time during the night.'

'Do you know what she took with her?'

'No, ma'am. I've never been her maid and since her abigail left she's looked after herself. It was no hardship for her. Being a village girl.'

'Were there any signs of a struggle?'

'No, ma'am.'

'Had the bed been slept in?'

'It looked as if it had. But that could have been from the night before.'

Sarah was attempting to establish whether Celia had left of her own accord and, if so, whether it had been a planned departure, or one decided on the spur of the moment. Something had to be seriously wrong. She would not have been summoned otherwise.

'Did you hear her departure? The slam of a door? Horses?'

'No, ma'am. I go home at night. I live with my husband in one of the farm cottages close by. But her favourite mare has gone. She must have harnessed the gig herself and took off as soon as it was light enough to travel.'

This suggested that Celia had left of her own accord. If she had been abducted, she would almost certainly have been bundled into a coach of some kind.

'Do you know that she sent me a note asking me to come as soon as I could?'

'Yes, ma'am. I took it to the village to be posted. She told me what was in it.'

'Were you surprised?'

'I didn't give it much thought.'

Sarah felt sure this was a lie, but she let it pass for the moment. 'It is strange that she suddenly decided to leave even though she must have known I was on my way. This suggests that she was suddenly frightened of something. Can you think of anything?'

Mrs Williams shook her head. 'She never confided in me, ma'am. We were never close.'

Sarah sat silently for several moments, considering various possibilities.

The housekeeper interrupted her thoughts: 'P'raps she's eloped, ma'am.'

'She can't have eloped, Mrs Williams. She's already married. But you think she might have run off with Tom Bridge?'

'She's very fond of him. Everyone knows.'

'Has he called recently?'

'Nearly every day. It's a scandal.'

'I shall go to the village and inquire after Bridge. If he, too, has left, we shall have our answer. If he is still there, then there must be another explanation. Do you have any ideas where she could have gone? If she were afraid and wanted somewhere safe?'

'I believe she 'as an aunt married to the lock-keeper at Stockers Lock near Rickmansworth. He has a public house there and a family that lives on the canal.'

Sarah could imagine the scene. A long narrowboat, manned by Celia's cousins, tied up at the lock, ready to leave. Horses on the towpath would pull the boat along the canal branch until they reached the Grand Union Junction, when the cousins would decide whether to go south to London or north to Manchester. No one need know there was a girl stowed away. She would be safe from whoever wanted to harm her.

'Mrs Williams,' Sarah said, 'think carefully. Do you know of anyone who would want to harm Lady Browning?'

The housekeeper fought within herself as to whether to tell Sarah what she suspected. She decided to state only the bare fact and leave it for Sarah to infer what it implied. 'Lady Browning is pregnant, ma'am.'

Sarah let out a long 'Aaaaah'. Then, 'Well, that raises all kinds of possibilities. How do you know, Mrs Williams? Did Lady Browning tell you?'

'No ma'am. But I heard her every morning. Poor thing. She's been very sick.'

Morning sickness was as good an indication of pregnancy as anything. It meant that Celia had probably conceived between six and ten weeks ago, not long before her husband's disappearance. She would be aware that she could be carrying an heir.

On the other hand, it could be Tom Bridge's child. This would be even more worrying. Either way, Celia would feel afraid for herself and for her unborn child. It explained her urgent summons of the only woman she believed she could trust.

It did not explain, however, why she had decided to leave Browning Hall secretly in the middle of the night.

'Who else knew Lady Browning was pregnant? Did you tell anyone?'

'Me? Oh no, ma'am. I never said a word to anyone.'

This, Sarah was sure, was another lie. The news would have been all around the neighbourhood within an hour of the housekeeper diagnosing her employer's condition.

Sarah stood up. 'I shall go to the village,' she said. 'What I do next will depend on what I discover there.'

Fifty-four

Sarah returned to Langley village and, despite the late hour, was relieved to see Tom Bridge working at the blacksmith's forge. Clearly, he had not taken Celia away somewhere with him. Although she thought it more likely that Celia had gone to her aunt's place, where she had cousins who would protect her, Sarah instructed one of her two guards to remain in the village in case Celia turned up to meet Tom Bridge. The carriage driver insisted the horses should rest, and travelling on unfamiliar roads in darkness might not be wise. With the Reverend Somersby at the Dowager House, Sarah had no choice but to accept the hospitality of the inn for the night.

When Sarah arrived in the carriage at Stockers Lock early on the following morning, the elderly lock-keeper was busily opening the gates to allow a narrowboat to pass. Sarah waited until he had completed his task before approaching him.

She had given much thought to what she would say, and as she left the carriage, she decided to come straight to the point. 'Good day to you. I am Sarah Kedron, Lady Browning's friend. She has sent for me.' She handed the lock-keeper Celia's note.

Reading was clearly not one of the lock-keeper's strongest points as he turned the note upside down and around several times and then stared at it from all angles before deciding that the young woman was probably telling the truth.

'I'll tell 'er you're 'ere, ma'am,' he said.

'Thank you.'

While her driver moved the carriage towards a horse trough, Sarah sat on a bench seat at a wooden table set outside for drinkers. She didn't have to wait long. Celia ran out and embraced her, bursting into tears.

Sarah held her closely and stroked her back. 'It's all right, Celia. It's all right. No one will harm you,' she murmured, not really knowing what to say. 'I'll help you, whatever your problem is.'

Gradually, the girl recovered and wiped her eyes on the sleeve of her simple dress. She also wore an apron, so Sarah guessed she had been helping her aunt prepare breakfasts in the kitchen of the inn.

'Now sit down and tell me what this is all about. Why have you run away from Browning Hall?'

Celia sat on the bench next to Sarah and pulled a crumpled piece of paper out of the pocket of her apron. She handed it to Sarah.

The note, written in capital letters, said 'YOU ARE IN DANGER. YOU ARE NOT WANTED AT BROWNING HALL.'

'Have you any idea who could have written that?'

Celia shook her head.

'When was it delivered?

'Just before I wrote to you.'

'Did anything happen to make you decide to run away before I could get to you?'

'I was just so frightened. I woke up in the middle of the night, and I just knew I had to get away before something terrible happened.' She turned to Sarah, took both her hands in her own and looked up at her. 'Sarah, I'm going to have a baby. I couldn't risk anything happening to it.'

'Is it Charlie's child?'

Celia nodded vigorously. 'Tom and I have never ... you know. He wanted to, but I knew it would be wrong.'

'So you are carrying the heir to Browning Hall.'

'Yes.'

'And you think that's why you are in danger?'

'What other reason could there be?' Celia put her hand to her mouth and began nervously chewing one of her fingernails. 'If Charlie has another woman, a mistress, and ... and she has his child, would that baby be the heir? It would be his seed, yes?'

'I'm not an attorney, Celia, but I think such a child would be illegitimate and have no right to inherit. But I really don't know, dear.'

It occurred to Sarah that if Charles had a mistress and if Celia could be disposed of so that Charles could marry the mistress, then an offspring with him would inherit. Sarah was well aware that some mistresses would stop at nothing to legalize their situation. If someone knew that such a mistress existed, then it could explain the warning note to Celia. She decided to say nothing about such a possibility. Nothing would be gained from making Celia even more afraid than she was already. Celia had been sensible to leave Browning

Hall. To continue to live there alone, night after lonely night, would be inviting disaster.

She said, 'It could be, dear, that someone sent you that note just to frighten you. Some people can be very cruel. If there is a girl in the village who is setting her cap at Tom Bridge, then she would want you out of the way, wouldn't she? I'm not suggesting that is actually the explanation for the note, but it is a possible one.'

In fact, Sarah did think this might be the explanation. A handsome young blacksmith with a business to inherit was a good catch for many a village girl. There might well be one who knew that her own chances with the man would greatly benefit from getting Celia out of the way. With Sir Charles having disappeared and probably dead, Tom Bridge would know that in time, Celia would marry him. He would be a lost cause for the other girls in the village.

'What can I do?' Celia asked, bewildered and desperately fearful.

'I think you should stay here in case you are in danger. You need to be somewhere safe with people who can protect you. Unfortunately, we do not seem to be any nearer to discovering what has happened to Sir Charles other than we have evidence that confirms he was abducted. Although we have no idea why or whether he is alive or dead. With the Earl of Liverpool facing so many rebellious Tories in his own party, he may need to call an election before the end of the month. As everyone in the district knows that Sir Charles intends to put himself forward as a candidate, there could be a political reason for his abduction and we can only hope that he is being kept in captivity to prevent him standing. It is an explanation that makes a great deal of sense and it means that he will soon be released, and you can continue your lives together.' She smiled. 'With your new baby.'

Celia dried her eyes with a corner of her apron and stood up. 'You are so kind, Sarah. And I'm forgetting my manners. Please come inside and have a meal with us. I'll send something out for your coachman and the other man.'

'Thank you. I would like that. It is some hours since I've eaten.'

Fifty-five

James rode throughout the night and arrived at Browning Hall in the early hours of the morning. Edward Browning was already there.

'He's in the library, sir,' Mrs Williams said. 'Writing letters. He's very distressed.'

'His mother?'

'She died during the night. She's at peace now; God rest her poor soul.'

'And Miss Kedron? Is she—'

'With my lady, sir. At her aunt's near Rickmansworth. Her husband's the lock-keeper at Stockers Lock.'

James didn't question the housekeeper further. He would be joining Sarah before long, so his main concern was to meet Edward Browning. 'I don't want to intrude on his grief, madam,' he said, 'but I would appreciate being introduced to Mr Browning.'

'You won't intrude. He wants to meet you and Miss Kedron. He knows about his brother and that you are trying to find him.'

'Good. Then perhaps you will be kind enough to take me to him.'

Mrs Williams led the way to the library. She opened the door and said quietly, 'Mr Brewster is here, sir.'

She nodded to James and he entered the book-lined room.

Edward Browning sat at an escritoire, writing. He turned and looked up at the door. His appearance was not what James expected, having in his mind's eye a caricaturist's image of a slave-owning, whip-cracking planter. Edward, who had clearly been weeping, wore a farm-labourer's smock and baggy trousers. His long blond hair fell to his shoulders, and his ascetic-looking features were those of a well-bred Englishman. Only his mahogany skin, burned by days spent working in the West Indian sun, indicated that he had been living abroad.

He stood and walked forward, offering James his hand. 'It is kind of you to come.'

'It is my pleasure to meet you, sir,' James said. 'Please accept my condolences on your sad bereavement.'

'It was almost as though she waited for me. As soon as I arrived, she held my hand and her life slipped away. Please sit down, Mr Brewster. We have much to discuss.'

At this moment James didn't understand why he took an instant liking to Edward Browning. He knew nothing about the man except that everything about him suggested the poet or the painter. Edward appeared to be a truly sensitive and gentle man.

As James sat in the armchair indicated, Edward said, 'I am most grateful to you and to Miss Kedron for being so good to my sister-in-law. It must have been a terrible time for her.'

'She has been very brave, sir. For one so young.'

'Quite. I have yet to meet her, of course. I left Browning Hall before my brother and Celia became acquainted.'

James wanted to ask Edward Browning many questions but now was not the time to ask them. He had to leave it to the grieving son to ask the questions.

'You are surprised by my appearance, sir.' Edward smiled slightly. 'I am not your typical remittance man.'

'Indeed you are not, sir.' James believed that the typical remittance man was a drink-sodden idler sent to live abroad on an annual remittance by relatives who were ashamed of him and wanted him out of their lives. 'Neither,' he continued, 'do you look like the image of a bullying planter.'

'I thank God daily for that. My first task on arriving in Antigua and moving into the plantation homestead was to free the slaves. I then offered each of them paid work and had their living quarters rebuilt to a proper standard. Several are now shareholders in the plantation.'

'A magnificent gesture, if I may say so, sir. But one hardly likely to endear you to the other planters.'

'I am treated as an outcast, a leper, sir. But I do not need their approval. The times are changing. Before long they will have nothing to feel superior about.'

James risked a question. Edward's manner seemed to invite one. 'Will you be returning to Antigua?'

'Of course. It is my home. There is nothing I want here. To be frank with you, Mr Brewster, this is the last place in the world where I would want to live. It's haunted by the misery of my childhood. But I'm being a bad host. You will have ridden hard to get here. Allow me to order you some refreshment.'

'Cold water will suffice, sir. I am obliged to you.'

Edward stood and walked to the bell rope. After pulling it, he said, 'Miss Simmons, my mother's companion, will be joining us shortly. As will my sister-in-law and Miss Kedron, I understand. Miss Simmons has told me that she has information to impart. She was too distressed to talk to me at any length earlier. As I am sure you know, she was devoted to my mother. Taking care of her has been the sole purpose of her existence.'

The door opened, and Mrs Williams stood there. 'Sir?'

'Water for my guest and bring tea, as well, please. I assume you have sent a message to Rickmansworth.'

'Yes, sir. The groom left as soon as we heard the news. If they set out straightaway, Lady Browning should be arriving during the morning.'

'Excellent.' He smiled at James. 'I should change my clothes and make myself presentable. Please excuse me.' He bowed to James and left the room.

'Not what you expected, sir,' the housekeeper said. 'He was always his mother's favourite.'

'Why did he quarrel with his brother?' James asked. 'Was it anything to do with having slaves?'

'Oh, nothing like that, sir. It was much simpler than that. Sir Charles felt abandoned, you see. The two boys were inseparable. When his father ordered him out of the house, Edward felt he had no choice but to accept his grandfather's support and settle in the West Indies, Sir Charles felt betrayed. He felt that Edward was showing cowardice by deserting him and not standing up to their father. Sir Charles—though he did not yet have the title, of course—loved his brother dearly. He could not understand how he could leave him to bear the pain of Sir Robert's violent temper on his own. Sir Robert had tried to beat the radical out of Charles and failed. As he had tried to beat the artist out of Edward and failed.'

She shook her head sadly, adding, 'Both boys were a deep disappointment to him, in different ways, Edward especially. He's so much more like his mother, and that was a terrible thing for a Browning to be. The worst possible crime. And now, if you'll excuse me, sir, I have a luncheon to prepare.' Mrs Williams left the room.

James stood irresolutely for a few moments and then decided to ride towards Rickmansworth and meet Sarah and Celia on the road. Miss Simmons would presumably postpone whatever it was she had to say until everyone concerned was assembled.

Fifty-six

Before James could depart for Rickmansworth, the housekeeper re-entered the library.

'The vicar has just arrived, sir. Shall I show him in here?'

'I suppose you should,' James said. 'Perhaps he has information of value.'

When Mr Somersby entered he bowed stiffly to James and said, 'I was hoping to see Lady Browning, sir.'

'I expect her here soon, accompanied by Miss Kedron,' James informed him. 'I understand she has been visiting her aunt in Rickmansworth.'

'Ah,' the cleric said. 'Then I must tell you that I am sorry to be the bearer of sad news.'

'Lady Augusta is dead.'

'You have heard.'

'Edward Browning informed me. He is here and will join us soon.'

'Yes, he arrived as she took her last breath, so he was with his mother at the end.' The clergyman could not hide his surprise, but quickly recovering, he said, 'Does his presence complicate matters.'

'I do not think so, sir. Indeed, it may have considerably simplified them.'

'I fail to understand you, sir.'

'He is returning to Antigua. He has no wish to live here or, should his brother be deceased, inherit the title and estate.'

'Ah. Yes, well, I suppose that should have been expected. I gathered from Sir Charles that Edward was never happy here. It seemed his father treated him with contempt from the moment of his birth. The poor boy.' Mr Somersby shook his head sadly at the thought of Edward's childhood, then he said, 'I was summoned to administer the last rites to the dowager. She died peacefully almost as soon as Edward arrived.'

James said, 'The family will be obliged to you, sir. Do you happen to know if Mr Edward Browning had any conversation with his mother?'

The vicar replied, 'I think not, sir. He arrived a little too late.'

'So you don't think he is aware of her accusations concerning his brother's disappearance.'

'I'm sure he is not, unless she has written to him, or Miss Simmons has informed him of them. We must pray that is not the case. I'm convinced the dowager's suspicion of Lady Celia was no more than a tragic fantasy. But how sad that Mr Edward was not with her in those final weeks. I'm sure he would have been a great comfort to her. The cruellest thing Sir Robert did was to send the young man away. His mother doted on him. As did his brother.'

The arrival of Sarah and Celia interrupted further conversation.

Sarah hurried towards James and took both his hands in hers. 'My heart tells me why you are here, James,' she said. 'You were anxious for my safety.'

'As is your father.' He smiled. 'But you are clearly in no danger. And neither, I'm sure, is Celia.' Concisely, he explained Edward's situation and decision, and that any kind of inheritance matter was clearly not the reason for Sir Charles's abduction.

'So you are no nearer to finding out what has happened to Charlie?' Celia exclaimed.

'I fear not. But I am now strongly inclined to the explanation that it will be found to be of a political nature. And this could be a blessing.'

'A blessing! How can you say such a thing, sir?' the clergyman demanded. 'A murder is a murder, whatever the motive.'

'We don't know that Sir Charles has been murdered. If his abduction is solely to prevent him from gaining the seat in Parliament if and when the Prime Minister concedes the need for an election, it is highly likely that he is being held in captivity until it is too late to register as a candidate.' James turned to Sarah. 'I am truly sorry, Sarah, if this means that Miss Stockton could be a party to the conspiracy.'

Sarah said nothing. She turned away, walked to the bow window and looked out. Immediately her mouth dropped open with surprise. 'Well,' she exclaimed, 'we shall soon know the solution to the mystery. Sir Charles and Miss Simmons are walking up the drive.'

'Charlie's here!' Celia cried. Picking up her skirts, she rushed out of the room to meet him.

As soon as Charles saw Celia in the doorway, he lengthened his pace and strode purposefully along the drive, his head back and jaw thrust forward like a man with a mission. Miss Simmons walked slowly behind him, lost in her own thoughts and grief.

Mr Somersby said, 'The death of the dowager seems to have brought matters to a head.'

Fifty-seven

Fifteen minutes later, Sir Charles, with Celia by his side, was standing with his back to the fireplace. Sarah and Mrs Williams sat together on the sofa. James and Edward Browning sat side by side on the window seat, and Miss Simmons and Mr Somersby sat in armchairs on either side of the fireplace.

Dressed from head to foot in black, Miss Simmons was already in deep mourning. Her face was drawn and haggard, and she seemed to be trembling. No one spoke except for Sir Charles, who whispered to his wife. The occasion was not the time for small talk or trivial conversation.

Sir Charles bowed to the assembled persons to indicate that he was about to speak. The room was so silent that it seemed as if the occupants all held their breath.

'I want to begin,' he said, speaking slowly, choosing his words with the utmost care, 'by thanking Miss Simmons for her devotion, courage and determination. Without her participation in the shocking events that she will relate, I would not be here. I would be dead—my corpse either abandoned in some lonely wood or sold to the anatomists for dissection. I will ask her to explain the situation. And I shall be greatly obliged if what she has to tell you can remain within the four walls of this room.' He smiled warmly at Miss Simmons.

Celia hurried to her and put her arms around her. 'Bless you. Bless you!' she exclaimed and then returned to her husband's side.

Miss Simmons, who had clearly been weeping profusely, dabbed at her eyes with an already sodden handkerchief, sniffed back her tears, and began to speak in a small voice, so low that everyone strained to hear what she had to say. Fortunately, as she gained confidence in her narrative, her voice became stronger.

'What I must relate to you has a long history,' she said. 'To understand what has occurred and why, it is necessary to go back twenty-six years to the marriage of Sir Robert and Lady Augusta Browning.

'You must understand that I loved Augusta. Her mother died young, so I was first engaged as her nursemaid, later her governess, and finally her trusted companion. We kept each other's secrets, and, in many ways, we have been as sisters. She was a fine beauty and attracted many a young beau hoping to marry into her father's fortune. However, her father was a wealthy ironmaster who, more than anything, wanted to be accepted by the nobility. When he discovered Sir Robert Browning had a substantial gambling debt and was near bankruptcy, he saw My Lady's marriage as an opportunity to advance his social position. Despite Sir Robert Browning being a repulsive brute, Lady Augusta had a yearning for the life of a lady, so she agreed to the marriage to appease her father, but she made it clear from the outset that the marriage would never be consummated.'

'What? How is that possible?' Celia exclaimed.

'Please, my lady, let me continue. I know that what I have to say will be painful, but the truth must now be told.'

'But if what you say is true—' Celia declared, but Miss Simmons cut her outburst short.

'Sir Robert had a mistress,' she continued. 'A few months after his marriage to My Lady, he announced that his mistress was with child. He embarked with both wife and mistress on a grand tour of the continent for a whole year. After giving birth to a son, his mistress succumbed to fever and died.'

'Oh, my God!' Celia exclaimed.

'I know this only because Lady Augusta confided in me, but she swore me to secrecy. When they returned to England, Sir Robert proudly announced that her ladyship had given birth while they were in Italy. Lady Augusta did not even tell her father the truth.' Miss Simmons closed her eyes. Clearly the woman was exhausted and in great distress.

Sarah realized that she had probably not slept for several days, having kept watch over the dying dowager.

Mr Somersby said, 'You say, Miss Simmons, that the marriage was never consummated; then who is Edward's father?'

Sir Charles put up his hand, indicating that the clergyman should be silent and allow Miss Simmons to continue in her own way and at her own pace.

'You will understand,' she said, 'that Lady Augusta was deeply unhappy in her marriage. She and Sir Robert lived wholly separate lives, even to the extent that they lived in different wings of the house. Almost as soon as they returned to England, Augusta ...' She paused and bit her bottom lip with embarrassment. 'Augusta looked for love elsewhere. She found it and had an affair with a captain in the local militia. The consequence was a son, Edward.'

'Oh, my God!' Celia exclaimed again. 'But I don't understand. Why didn't Sir Robert divorce his wife?'

'Pride. Simple pride, I'm sure,' Mr Somersby said, and by way of further explanation added, 'As I mentioned to Miss ... erm, Miss Kedron the other day, to obtain a divorce Sir Robert would have had to request a private act of Parliament. The disgrace of having been cuckolded was, I'm sure, more than he could bear.'

Miss Simmons nodded. 'But it was more than that. Augusta had no wealth in her own right, so Sir Robert still relied on her father's money for maintaining the estate. To have divorced her would simply lead to his bankruptcy, but Sir Robert was a cruel and vindictive man. As soon as Edward came of age, he cast him out without a penny. Lady Augusta appealed to her father for help, but he thought it better for Edward to leave the country, so he funded a small sugar plantation in Antigua. It broke Augusta's heart, but before she could reveal the truth and bring Edward home, her father passed away. With her father's death, Sir Robert became a wealthy man, and then, almost overnight, everything changed. Lady Augusta realized that when Sir Robert died, Charles would inherit her father's wealth. She quite rightly believed that Edward had more right to inherit her father's money than did Charles, but Sir Robert was determined that Charles would inherit everything, and Edward should again be cut off without a penny.'

'Did he say as much to Lady Augusta?' Sarah asked quietly.

'Yes, and he even gloated. He visited her rooms almost daily and boasted as to how he had swindled her out of her inheritance. He told her that Edward would fester and die in penury. I believe that was what turned her mind. She became obsessed with plotting for her own son to inherit the title and the estate.'

The appalling implication of what Miss Simmons had said hung heavily in the room.

Eventually, she continued. 'However, Sir Robert died before he could squander the inheritance, so the baronetcy, the estate and what remained of her father's wealth passed to Charles. But Augusta was determined that her own son would inherit her father's money, and with it, the title and estate, not only for his sake, but for her own. She wanted revenge against Sir Robert for making her life a misery. To Augusta, the matter became more urgent when Sir Charles married, so she decided he had to die before his new wife could produce an heir.'

As if what she'd told was not serious enough, Miss Simmons gritted her teeth and held onto the armchair to give her body some support. No one in the room dared to speak. Everyone knew she had more to tell.

'I knew,' she continued, 'I knew for certain she was capable of organizing Sir Charles's murder. She assumed that, with Charles out of the way, she would have more than enough money to pay handsomely for an assassination. I decided there was only one thing I could do. I persuaded her that I knew of distant members of my family who would carry out the assassination for her. In that way, I could save Sir Charles's life. I knew she was dying and that within weeks, a few months at most, Charles would be safe.'

Sarah said, 'It was you who arranged the abduction.'

'Yes. I have a nephew in London who …' she managed a thin smile, 'who has some disreputable friends for whom the business was amusing.' She looked up at Sir Charles.

He nodded and said, 'I will continue this tragic saga. My movements were followed, and when it was realized that I was frequenting a disreputable gaming establishment as part of my research into the effect of an addiction to gambling on people of all levels of society, I was drugged to make me an easy prey, then carried off to a secret destination. When I recovered awareness, I realized that I was locked in a comfortable room of a country house. I was looked after as if I were an honoured guest and assured that my incarceration would be for only a limited time, after which I would be freed. No explanation was offered for my sojourn in captivity.' He bowed to Miss Simmons, who continued her narrative.

'I informed Lady Augusta of the situation, and she was deeply grateful. She showed no remorse for what she had instructed me to do and which she believed I had carried out to the letter.'

Edward Browning said, 'The letter I received from her did not refer to Charles at all. It stated only that she was seriously ill and begged me to return to England to be with her during her last days.'

'That letter,' Miss Simmons said, 'was dispatched at least a month before the plan to kidnap Sir Charles was put into effect. You had no idea what your mother was planning. I need to make that clear.'

'Thank you,' Edward said.

'There was, of course, no way by which I could inform Lady Celia of the situation. She had to be kept in ignorance even though I knew that Sir Charles's disappearance was most distressing for her. I told myself that, as what I was doing was for the best, I need not feel too guilty about causing her to suffer. When the news got around the village that she was with child, a possible heir, I decided that she should leave Browning Hall for her own safety. Accordingly, I wrote her an anonymous note.'

Sir Charles said, 'I think that, now, all has been said that needs to be said. Miss Simmons is profoundly exhausted, and I shall be obliged, Mrs Williams, if you will arrange for the carriage and escort her back to the dowager house, which will remain her home for as long as she wishes.'

Mrs Williams stood and moved to take Miss Simmons's arm. As they walked slowly out of the room, Charles left Celia's side, walked quickly towards his stepbrother and embraced him.

'Edward, my dearest brother, stay with us for a while at least. We have much to talk about. And I need your forgiveness if I am to be at ease with myself.'

Edward, perhaps not surprisingly, James thought, burst into tears. 'Oh, Charlie, it is so good to see you. You can't know how much I have missed you.'

'Come, we will go to one of our favourite secret places and talk until there is no talk left in us.'

Arm in arm, the two men left the room.

For several moments no one else spoke. There was so much information to take in. Sarah, aware that their investigation had discovered nothing, looked at James, shrugged and smiled ruefully.

He smiled in return and nodded to indicate that he understood her message.

Mr Somersby stood up. 'Extraordinary. Quite extraordinary,' and, aware that his presence was no longer appropriate, he also departed.

Only Celia, Sarah and James remained in the room.

'Well, Celia,' Sarah said, 'you have your husband back, no thanks to us. I'm afraid that as detectives we have been less than successful. But all is well that ends well, as the great bard tells us.'

Celia rushed towards her and embraced her, her eyes soft with tears of joy and relief. 'I thank you from the bottom of my heart, Sarah.' She looked at James. 'And you, Mr Brewster. The support you have both given has been so important. You believed in me. That mattered so much.'

'All will be well now,' Sarah said, and, releasing herself gently from Celia's embrace, she moved towards James and put a hand lightly on his arm. 'Come along, James. It's time I got back to the theatre and you to *The Weekly Police News*.'

As they left the hall and walked to the stables where their horses were being cared for, James said, 'I was clearly wrong to suspect Elizabeth Stockton of any wrongdoing. I hope you will forgive me.'

'There is nothing to forgive,' Sarah replied. 'Your suspicion was justified, James, though totally unfounded. I called on her before I left London and required from her an explanation of why she had kept from me her acquaintance with Alfred Ramsbottom.'

'She is no doubt ashamed of being his mistress,' James said.

'That,' countered Sarah, 'could not be further from the truth. Why do you men always jump to the wrong conclusions where female behaviour is involved? She was certainly concerned that I would suspect her of having a liaison with the man, hence her secrecy, but in fact, he is a patron of the arts, no more. He wishes to establish a reputation for being interested in painting—it is all part of his attempts to turn himself into a gentleman. Elizabeth has persuaded him to open an art gallery specializing in the works of women artists. As you know, they are badly represented in the Royal Academy. She is advising him on acquiring a collection and displaying it in premises in the Burlington Arcade but didn't want to announce this in case he changed his mind.'

'Ah!' James exclaimed. 'Not an explanation I would have thought of in a hundred years.' He grinned. 'The Ramsbottom Collection. Hmm. It doesn't have quite the right ring to it, but it is a fine idea, and I am relieved by this explanation. I'm especially glad that she is not the man's mistress. He is a master of pomposity.'

They continued their walk to the stables. 'Are you glad it's all over, Sarah? Now that we can concentrate on our respective occupations?'

With a wicked smile, Sarah replied, 'Is there any reason why we can't have a second string to our bows, James? We make a good team.'

A Note from the Author

Did you enjoy my book?

If so, I would be very grateful if you could write a review for
The Missing Baronet and publish it at your point of purchase.

Your review, even a brief one, will help other readers to decide
whether or not they will enjoy my work.

Do you want to be notified of new releases?

If so, please sign up to the AIA Publishing email list. You'll
find the sign-up button on the right-hand side under the
photo at www.aiapublishing.com. Of course, your
information will never be shared, and the publisher won't
inundate you with emails, just let you know of new releases.

By Ken Methold

<u>Television</u>
Jackson's Crew (telemovie)
Animal Park (children's drama series)
Gogo's Adventures in English (educational series)
The Story of Nickel (documentary)
The Room Next Door (drama)

<u>Stage</u>
Any Fool Can (drama)
Murder Upstairs Downstairs at Upton Priory (mystery)
For Services to the Community (Comedy)
Moonlight Over the Estuary (Comedy)
Annie's Awful Aunt (Children's)
Etc.

<u>Radio</u>
An Item on the Agenda (BBC)
Sweet Singing in the Choir (BBC)
Queen's Pawn Gambit (BBC)
All Suspect (BBC)
The Symbol (RTE)
Star Dance (ABC)
The Head Hunters (ABC)
All in the Mind (ABC)
Etc.

<u>Fiction</u>
The Man on His Shoulder
Death by Defamation
The Case of the Kidnapped Kanaka
Turn Up a Stone